The Ransom
of
Istanbul

To Tom,

friends in the
Fellowship (
in stores of memories of
Eddie + Arthur.
Earl Show

Bob Hawken
Feb 13, 2006

The Ransom of Istanbul

An Entertainment

Robert Hanlon

Library of Congress Cataloging-in-Publication Data

Hanlon, Robert, 1932
   The ransom of Istanbul : an entertainment / Robert Hanlon.
     p. cm.
   ISBN 1-58966-101-X
 1. World War, 1939-1945--Turkey--Fiction. 2. Intelligence officers--Fiction.
3. Russians--Turkey--Fiction. 4. Istanbul (Turkey)--Fiction. 5. British--
Turkey--Fiction. 6. Defectors--Fiction. I. Title.
   PS3608.A7155R36 2005
   813'.6--dc22   2005042239

Distribution:

The University of Scranton Press
445 Madison Avenue
Scranton, PA   18510
Phone: 1–800–941–3081
Fax: 1–800–941–8804

PRINTED IN THE UNITED STATES OF AMERICA

Principal Characters

Istanbul

Nicolai Romanovitch Sarkov: Vice Consul in the Russian Embassy in Turkey, but NKVD operator, and defector.

Irina Sarkov: His wife and mother of his two children.

John Reed: Assistant to the British Ambassador to Turkey, and liaison for MI5 operations.

Ambassador Peterson: British ambassador to Turkey.

Race: Peterson's nephew.

Colonel Galip Tor: Chief of Turkish Intelligence.

Yuki: Tor's assistant.

London

Phillip Sloan: Chief of Russian Counter-Intelligence, but traitor to the Crown.

Aileen: Sloan's companion and mother of two children.

Anatoli: Sloan's Russian contact.

Sir Alfred McKenzie: Control of MI5.

Charles Carolyn: Security Chief of MI5.

Moscow

Vladimir Basilevich Bakov: Head cypher clerk of NKVD, and later, agent in Istanbul.

Beria: Head of NKVD, the predecessor of the KGB.

Merkulov: Beria's assistant.

PART I

ISTANBUL

1

Seven minutes after he entered the British embassy in Istanbul, Sergei Mikalovich Sarkov knew he had made a mistake, a blunder so serious it could cost his life. He had assumed that all British staff were spies, as they were in Russian embassies, and that the first person who understood his mission would usher him to the chief of espionage operations. Sarkov realized his mistake as soon as he saw the boy across the foyer. The boy was not a spy. He hadn't the age or the face for it.

Without looking at Sarkov the boy said, "The offices are closed," with the primal finality of one who is sure the intruder will leave without argument.

When Sarkov did not turn and leave, the boy, short but elongated with circular spectacles, eyed Sarkov with disdain and then returned to his papers.

"My name is Sergei Mikalovich Sarkov," the Russian said. "I am first secretary of the Russian legation." As Sarkov moved closer, the boy did not move his head, but studied the approaching feet.

"We haven't spoken to your embassy this morning," the boy said. "It's not like them to send a message without calling first."

"I'm not a courier," Sarkov said. "I came on my own. To defect."

"Defect?" The boy shot up.

"Yes, I want to come over to the West," Sarkov said. "I talked with your chargé Sunday evening. I can't remember his name. I should remember. He said he would help."

"I'm sorry," the boy said. "I don't know any thing about this. How could we possibly help?"

"You could summon that man, the SIS man," Sarkov answered, holding up his hand in supplication. It was another mistake. The SIS had broken away from British Military Intelligence the year before, 1944, and the man he had spoken to belonged to Military Intelligence.

"There's no one attached to the Secret Service here."

"Please," Sarkov answered. He searched his memory for the name, but even the spy's face eluded him. He had met the man at the Markiz and they jokingly debated who would be the head of the new civilian branch of the Secret Service. Sarkov had studied the British system so well and his wife analyzed their procedure so thoroughly that they were convinced McKenzie would be the new head. The Britisher argued for Myles Stewart.

McKenzie was elevated in July. The two men chanced to meet after McKenzie's appointment and the Britisher had continued the irony, saying they should have wagered. Sarkov would have won. Then they talked "shop": troubles they had with transmits, dissatisfaction with policy, and of course, their mutual hatred of Turkey. Just before they broke off Sarkov mentioned that his wife had heart trouble and the Britisher said, casually, "Perhaps we could help with that." It was the last statement which prodded Sarkov over the edge to defection. He said in reply, "Yes, you might, and sooner than you think."

What was the spy's name? If Sarkov could remember, the boy might be persuaded to wait. "He's a tall fellow with light hair and a soft voice. He runs your messages."

"That's Mister Reed. He's Under Secretary."

"He worked in Brussels seven or eight years ago. Was it 1938?"

The boy shook his head "yes" and said, "He's in Ankara arranging our return."

"I'm sure he's the one," Sarkov answered. "May I wait?"

"He said he would be back this afternoon, but I can't allow you to remain in the building without notifying the ambassador."

"May I stay in the garden?"

"I told you. I have to inform the ambassador."

Sarkov knew the geometry of exposure. If Ambassador Peterson was informed, he would talk to Kiktev before noon. Kiktev would issue the ukase to arrest and by one o'clock twenty security guards would be combing the city for him. He couldn't risk Peterson's knowing of his defection before contacting Reed.

There must be no dangling between allegiances, and as little delay as possible. It was talk which brought down spies, talk, more than money, or women. He had the feeling that he had to be brought in by the British today, or he would be dead by nightfall.

The boy positioned his fists on his hips and demanded, "What shall I tell him?"

First, Sarkov had to win this boy over. His fear propelled him to be direct. "My wife has heart disease. She won't survive unless she is treated in the West. If you want other reasons they are the usual ones, but the truth is I am leaving because of my wife."

"So you know where she has to go?"

"Yes. And I believe you people will help when you understand the importance of the information I have."

"Information?"

"Yes. Secrets."

"And that's all you have?"

"It's quite important."

"But we don't deal with secrets here."

Sarkov's desperation turned to pleading. "Please. Your man will be eager to hear what I have to say."

"I have no idea what you're trying to do, or how we could help you."

"Yesterday I tried to contact Major McKenzie in London." He hesitated, waiting for recognition. "Your chief of Intelligence."

The clerk had no answer.

"One of my clerks overheard me."

"You didn't get through?"

"No," he answered. "There was a break in the line. But now my people suspect what I was doing. This morning there was an order from my superior. I had to come. Today."

"We're in an awkward position. What are we supposed to do?"

"All I'm asking is that you contact Mister Reed. Please." Although his English was very good, Sarkov hesitated for the right phrasing. "He will signal London. They will send a man, most likely General Thomas. He's Chief in Cairo, but he's on leave. I will ask for Thomas because he knows me and will know how important my information." He tried to appear confident, something he was not.

Sarkov had spent the last few years trying to appear unassuming because his family was the Dulgoruskys who were bound by blood to the Czars and, consequently, frowned on by the new regime. It was rather easy for him to be inconspicuous because he was that way by nature, and by stature: short legs, crumpled suits, lumpy at the shoulders, and receding hair which he brushed back at the temples. Although brilliant at his work, which was information analysis, he had never played at the dangerous game of espionage. He had risen in the NKVD on brains, not guile.

General Thomas' name seemed to have some authority with the boy. So Sarkov asked, "Do you know General Thomas?"

"I've heard the name."

"I am a Major in the NKVD, and vice consul at the embassy."

The boy was impressed with titles, no doubt, so Sarkov made the connection. "You should know how important the next few minutes will be, for you. Help me, and it will go well for you. It could go very well."

The boy looked as though he had learned a lesson. "My transfer will be the most important event in twenty years. If it goes well your Foreign Office will commend you." He tapped his folder. "I have five pages of documents, all classified, some most secret." He laid his hand on the folder and then handed the folder to the boy.

He picked up the folder as if it were precious.

"Can you tell me the terms? I mean, what do you want?"

"As few should know as possible, and it must be done quickly."

"Money?"

"In time, yes, I'll need money, but right now I must talk to Reed. He will take care of it, I'm sure."

"Why him?"

"Because he knows the procedures. He'll send word to London, by pouch."

"Wouldn't the wire be quicker?"

"It would be, "Sarkov answered, "but we're listening. Your code is broken. We know every word you send. No, no wires. No."

"You've broken our system! How is that possible?"

"Trust me. It's done. We know every message. All negotiations under my name have to go by pouch. That's why we have to act quickly. If the pouch goes tomorrow, London will have it Monday. If all goes well, the contact will be here in ten days."

The boy was trying to remember last week's messages. How could the Russians have broken the code when the operator changed pads every day? But this Russian appeared certain. If it were true than the Russians knew that the English knew about the musical boxes along the Turkish border, the money problems in the embassy, and even the ambassador's gout.

Sarkov could see from the flickering eyes that he was winning over the boy. He would go further and explain what he expected in the transfer. "Would you look at these papers?" He asked. "This is the floor plan of our new building in Dzerzhinsky Square, and this is the alarm system. Here is a list of all our agents working in Turkey. This one, the list of all master spies working in Europe. There is more, much more."

The boy stepped back, as if slapped.

Sarkov knew that his persuasion had worked. He walked to the window. Dust was swirling in the street. It covered an abused Plymouth, closed the eyes of a tethered donkey, and swept around the foundation of an obelisk in the square. The dust was a curse. It caused bronchitis, skin ulcers, and inflammation in the eyes. More than religious practice, the dust was the reason women wore the veil. Istanbul is a city of dust, Sarkov thought, and the dust covered unseemly truth.

He looked back at the boy studying the pages. "Do you recognize any names?"

"No."

"I have three which are the most important. Here," he pointed to his chest. "They work for us. Two of them have been giving us information since the depression. They are very high placed."

The boy did not react.

"One sleeps with members of Parliament, and another has a very highly placed position. If I say more someone will know who they are."

"For this, what do you want?"

"You've asked this. But I'll tell you what I expect. I want a laissez passer to Cyprus." He counted on his fingers. "For my wife and children. Medical help, as I said. Employment, naturalization for the family. A new start. Some money. Yes.'

"This is a big risk."

"I've already begun.'

"I'm not sure."

"I know,' Sarkov said in his exhaustion. "Let me tell you what will happen. There is a prison near Bratsch, Chuma, where they will send me if I am caught. If I am not seen by Mister Reed, today, I will die in Chuma before the month. If not there then in the street here. Maybe even today."

After some silence the boy walked to the main door, behind him. With his hand on the knob he looked back and said, "I'll explain this to the ambassador. Wait here."

If I had a gun, Sarkov thought, I would shoot him.

.

2

"Let's have some tea," Ambassador Peterson said, ringing the buzzer. "I'd like some, but watch what you say," he whispered as the door opened. "I don't trust Ekmal. They caught him pinching jam. God knows what else he takes out."

The longer Peterson stayed on in Turkey, the more he patronized the citizens. It was the effect of isolating from the people. He belonged to that class of men whom Green dubbed, 'children of the sun,' affected gentlemen whose arrogance was inbred. They held to a code that they were superior.

Ekmal rolled in the cart, poured the tea, served it and situated the cart to the right of the door. He bowed and left. The ambassador waited until the door had closed before he drank or spoke. The assistant did not drink.

"No tea?"

"Thank you, uncle. I'll take some later."

"You know," the uncle said without interruption, "There are two valuable rules for advancement: handle the press, and know someone in Whitehall. Mind you, the first is more important. Like this call. Negri had me on the line and he asked me what I thought of . . . " He could not remember what it was Negri had asked him. And just as quickly, he remembered. "The atom bomb. That's it. The bomb." He was delighted with himself for remembering.

"He asked me what I thought of the bomb dropped on Hiroshima, and Japan half a world away!"

He sipped his tea and then asked the assistant, "Aren't you taking any tea? What is it? Too much Raki last night? It's the only liquor in this Godforsaken country which maintains the water. That's important. Where were you last night? Down at the Cinar? I cannot understand why they allow that fat pimp to loll around outside. In my time they always had a substantial madam."

"I was not at the Cinar, nor was I drinking. I stayed here last night. Remember?" The curtness caused a pall, a momentary stillness. As new as the assistant was he had learned that the direct method was the only method in dealing with the ambassador's distractions. He also knew that the ambassador would neither take offense nor would he respond curtly. He simply asked, "What is it you want?"

"There's a man in the outer office, a Russian. He's the vice counsel at their embassy."

"Well, what does he want?"

"He wants to defect." The assistant cleared his throat.

"What? Why would he want that? We're friends with the Russians. I was talking with Nicolai yesterday."

"Do you want to speak with him?"

"What on earth for? He can't come here. Do you realize how much this kind of underhandedness would disrupt our relations with the Russians? We're getting along fine. I don't want them upset. You'll have to tell him to go away." He pointed to the door. "Tell him there are other ways to settle his problems. He's not to come here." He was shouting. "Whatever would Nicolai think?"

He began pacing in front of his desk as if the obligation had already fallen on him, like a man recently diagnosed terminally ill. The tips of mouth sagged and the moustache exaggerated the slump.

"He's a frightful looking fellow," the assistant said. "Looks like a sikert model, all trousers and collar."

"He does?"

It was another fluff, a distraction which the ambassador would follow until another came along. To get the conversation back before it left, the assistant said, "He is important. We may take some criticism from London if we mishandle a master spy. He may even go to the Americans."

"Let him. Why not?"

"Suppose he's a big fish and Whitehall wants to hear what he has to say."

"No," the ambassador said gravely, "it's too dangerous. Let him go. Tell him to go back to where he came from."

"He can't go back. He tells me his people will imprison him."

"Really? Why does he want to leave? Did he tell you?"

"He said his wife is ill. I don't believe him. I think he has financial problems. All embassy personnel have financial problems."

"Must we be bothered by his problems? God, how did we get into this? The intrigue of this city astounds me. 'The capital of deceit,' Kiktev calls it. I won't allow treason in my embassy. Treason, it's all treason."

"What shall I tell him? He's brought along information he says the SIS will be interested in."

"They may, but I'm not. All this cloak and dagger rot disturbs me. I won't have espionage in my embassy." He was pleading. "I want him out of here. My embassy will not be a nest of spies. Who else is part of this web, do you know?" He was mixing his metaphors, but the assistant was not confused.

"There's no one else, but he did say he would like to talk with John."

"Of course, Reed. He's the man to handle this."

"He won't be back until evening."

"No, he's back. I sent him down to Beyazial for some Dijon mustard. Madam will not serve ham without it."

"Will he know what to do?"

"Certainly. He always knows where to find things."

"I mean, with the Russian."

"Oh, I admire Reed's methods. He's absolutely first rate. Here's another rule in diplomacy: find a good man and delegate." He was pointing as if he were a teacher. "To succeed one must delegate." He paused for a moment and then continued, "Of course he is everything you and I were taught to abhor: red brick, council estates, new towns, the antithesis of your upbringing, but he is a master at planning and execution. He'll never prosper, but he makes an excellent aide."

"I'll tell the Russian to wait."

"Yes, do. Make sure they talk in the common rooms. We can't allow anyone to see the Russian here."

The assistant bowed.

"And Race," the ambassador said, "when you see Reed, tell him to bring the mustard to the scullery before he does anything else."

3

Sarkov waited in the ante room which resembled an English study: Dutch tiles, small pieces of Renaissance sculpture, china dogs, and elongated vases. The English civil servants who built the embassy had made no attempt to furnish the room, the building, or the grounds, with anything Turkish. The compound might just as easily have been set in the West End.

The building suffered from the same indifference to place, even though it was built on the street which is the center of Turkish intrigue. The architect was Sir Charles Barry who was better known for constructing the Houses of Parliament. There was little to indicate that both buildings were designed by the same man except that both were clearly British. There was nothing complex about the embassy, nothing distinctive, except that it was built near Turkish structures and stood out, like a patch. The address was the Grand Rue de Pera which juts off from Isteklal Caddesi at Galatasary square. The Grand Rue is as narrow as the comprehension of its denizens and as serpentine as their deceits. Plots were hatched there, and spies squirm out from there, but never from the British embassy. The embassy was like an innocent in the midst of guile; the same could be said for the ambassador.

Sarkov rubbed his finger across the desk top. There was no dust, even though the large patio window was open. For distraction he turned from the desk to the portrait of

William White, a former ambassador. Of course Sarkov had no idea who the man in the portrait was. But he did reflect that he had seen hundreds of such portraits. They are so common in government buildings, studies of men, severe but poised, sitting to an angle and facing front, with no other thought than sternness, if sternness is a thought. Sarkov looked away thinking, why is it that every British diplomat looks like the penurious Dickens?

He was about to pace when the assistant returned. A crumb hung from his cheek; it distracted Sarkov. He remembered his own hunger.

"You weren't long," he said.

"I didn't have much to report," the assistant snapped.

"No, I'm happy you're back. A short meeting means good news."

"It didn't go well."

"He refused?"

"No, but he washed his hands of the whole affair," the assistant said, making a gesture of washing.

"I asked you not to tell him."

"He's put Mister Reed in charge."

"He did? Wonderful. Where is Reed?"

"He's in the building. I asked that he be sent here directly," the assistant said as if Reed were a servant. Without warning, he walked over to the dining room door, opened it, and spoke in a low voice to one of the servants. From his place near the door he asked Sarkov, "May I ask," and then he hesitated and put his finger to his lips, as if he were unsure how to frame the question. Sarkov watched the morsel on his cheek dangle like a mountain climber hanging from a precipice. "What we should do about the wireless?"

"You're current Triple X cipher is DL 38T 63. Change the combination tomorrow morning and we will know the numbers by night, before you've sent your first message."

"What should we do? Keep changing?"

"Nothing. Your information is not worth much. What went through last week? You dismissed your archivist for drinking. The same day you discovered one of our radios in Urgup. I told you about the codes to tease you," Sarkov said rubbing the tip of his forefinger against his thumb as if enticing a pet, "so that you would speed my transfer. I'm certain London knows you have a leak. It's difficult, the security. It won't be the first time we've broken your wires, from the inside."

"From the inside? Do you have a spy here?"

"Not a, what do you say, *razvedchick*, but a man who is in need of extra money. It's always the easiest way to break a code."

"Will you tell us who it is?"

"It wouldn't be in my best interest. If the negotiations go well, I might tell you what I know."

"Do you always do what suits you?"

"I don't think you appreciate my position," Sarkov said. "Did you ever hear of the *Otdyel*? It is a secret force of *Istrebitelli*, how do you say, 'mobile executioners', like the Mafia. They kill people. Not in Siberia but in Paris, in Mayfair, Ottawa, in the face of the police. They search for years so there is little chance of escaping. They are already after me. I am sure they are nearby right now."

"Will you be less safe if you tell me?" There was an attitude of distaste in his voice, as if he had found himself in the presence of a man with a physical malfunction.

"My dear fellow," Sarkov began, but he became weak as if he had been breathing a noxious gas. He sat and put his head back. "I'm sorry. I have to rest."

Sarkov had altered his course irretrievably. He had turned his ship toward the West and there was no going back. Like Odysseus at Messina, Sarkov would have to pass the test of the Western Scylla or turn back and be crushed by the rocks of Charybdis. The *otdyel* had already been awakened. Like Odysseus Sarkov had no alternative but to suffer the yapping of this Western dog.

"I'll compromise," he said. "I'll tell you the name on the day that London approves of the negotiations."

Without being noticed, a tall man in a beige summer suit had entered the room. When Sarkov turned his head he saw the man. He recognized Reed. The tall man bowed in greeting, but said nothing and waited for the conversation to end.

He has an air of strength, Sarkov thought. He would be good at court games and attractive to demure women, although faithful to one. I already trust him, Sarkov thought.

The assistant became aware of Reed and made the introductions, awkwardly. He forgot Sarkov's name and Sarkov had to spell his name for Reed. The two men shook hands. Reed saw the morsel on the assistant's cheek and brushed it off without embarrassment. The assistant picked up a letter from the desk and left.

"First thing: coffee," Reed said. Without waiting for an answer, he opened a sliding door to the dining room and bent over a cart. Sarkov watched him pour. There were two cakes on the saucer Reed handed to him.

"I haven't eaten since yesterday," Sarkov said. The two men sat.

"We'll do something about that," Reed commented after Sarkov had eaten a cake. "Last Sunday I thought to myself 'how good his English is.' Where did you learn?" "School mostly," Sarkov answered. "I worked in London for two and a half years and in Washington I headed the information desk in thirty-eight and thirty-nine."

"Did you know Dick Donaldson?" Reed asked. Like clergymen, spies enjoy a world-wide collegiality.

"Yes, surely," Sarkov said. "Nice fellow. He was related to someone in Transportation."

"Ministry of Education," Reed corrected.

"Yes. Dick was a gifted fellow. Your people were high on him."

"That's right," Reed said. "He's second in Brussels, doing very well."

"Was he an operator? It seems to me he was, but your system confuses me."

"It does me too."

"This boy, just now, treated me like an unwanted salesman. I think he was uneasy in the circumstances. He frightened me. I've had a bad hour."

"He's not part of the network."

"I thought not," Sarkov said. "I'd forgotten how your diplomats look down on intelligence people. It's the opposite with us."

"Race has been in Turkey less than a month," Reed said. "He's nephew to the ambassador."

"I'm not angry," Sarkov said. "Just frightened and tired. I'm in a bad position. I want to come over and I'm desperate that you make the exchange as quickly as you can."

Reed had the serious look of a man who is about to make the most lucrative contract of his career.

"I don't expect sanctuary today. I'll hide until London sends someone, but I expect you to do everything possible to make this happen quickly."

Reed nodded.

"Before today I had planned to come here and then go back to work as if nothing was out of the way, but I know my people are suspicious. And you and I know that the word has gone out. I have been here without authorization."

"The boy won't talk," Reed said, "and the ambassador was careful not to hear your name." Reed smiled like a conspirator who knew about weak links.

"Are you saying that I should go back to work?"

"Certainly not," Reed said clasping the chair. "That would be unwise."

"I couldn't go back. I'm almost certain Kiktev knows. But I'm thinking about time."

"Will you be alright for ten days, two weeks?"

"It will be ten days anyway, won't it? That would be the fifteenth."

"We can't send a wire. Race told me that you have broken our cipher."

"Yes," Sarkov said. "We have your book."

"I thought you were listening in."

"When the messages slowed, we thought you knew we were listening. You sent two last Saturday."

"How did you break the code, if you don't mind?"

"The usual thing. We stopped your radio man at a party, got him drunk and found out he needed money. As easy as that."

"So you know all our business."

"It's not very important, but you and I can't send anything over the wires about this. Everything by pouch and that means I'll have to hide." He said, and then added, "But you'll have to care for my boys and my wife."

"Where are they?"

"Babek. Our dacha. Do you know the area?"

"Some."

"Tell your people to be gentle with my wife. She has heart disease."

"I'll fly them out tomorrow."

"Yes, do."

"Will you tell her to be ready?"

"Yes."

"What's the place? Babek?"

"You write it down so your agents won't make a mistake."

"What else?"

"There are two children, nine and seven. Do you think this will be a problem?"

Reed smiled. "Let's say it is not impossible. If I can't do it, I have a friend in the *Ikinci Buro* who could stage a coup if I needed it."

"A coup might be easier than this."

"You think so because it is your family, but I don't see any problems getting them out. We've done this before. This man has a plane and we have the means of getting your family to the airport." Reed stood and walked to the desk and opened the folder Sarkov had brought. He looked at the contents quickly and reached into the second drawer for stationary.

"What should I tell the chief in the covering letter?"

"Tell him I was transferred from the second directorate. No," Sarkov said, "he'll know that. Just spell my name correctly."

"Never mind," Reed said. "How should this information go?"

"We've had good luck photographing. The *seyazuyie*, how do you say?"

"The courier."

"The courier carries the film in the bag. If anything goes wrong, he opens the bag and the film is exposed, useless."

"That's all right, but full of risks," Reed said.

"I know. Many things can go wrong, but I want you to do it that way. Whom do you think London will send?"

"I have no idea."

"I was hoping it might be Thomas. He's in London."

"You know a great deal. Have you met Birdie?"

"I knew him when he didn't talk about golf," Sarkov said.

"That was before he took up the game. He does talk interminably about it, doesn't he?"

The Russian smiled; the two were getting along well. Reed said, "He speaks Russian, which would influence McKenzie, although there is no language problem here. He would get quick clearance from the FO. But you can never be sure who they will send, holidays and all."

"Will the Foreign Office delay this?"

"There's been a change in government, but you know that."

"Who's head at the Foreign Office?"

"Bevin," Reed answered. "They say he wanted Treasury, but Attlee needed him at the F O."

"Bevin did a creditable job filling in for Eden at Potsdam."

"Yes, but the boys in the trenches wanted Dalton at the FO."

"Do you think Bevin might hold up my papers?"

"They won't pass over his desk. Don't worry. I'll see to it."

"Then you think the arrangements for the fifteenth are satisfactory?"

"Yes."

"When the contact arrives here, then what?"

"You will be brought out the same day, most likely to Cyprus, as you have indicated here."

"Will Morrow be questioning me?"

"Perhaps," Reed said. "It may be Skardon."

"Your best man," Sarkov said. "Are they using sodium pentothal, do you know?"

"I don't know," Reed said. "The subject is supposed to be incapable of lying."

"You don't believe that, do you?"

"The Russians have been using pentothal for years, at least I've been told they do."

"Yes," Sarkov said. "The effects are easy to disguise. One becomes immune quickly."

"Then why did you ask?"

"To tell the truth, I have a feeling that my information is not worth much. Your man out there didn't think much of it, and I'm afraid that London might be a little suspicious that my defection is just another Russian trick."

Reed stood. "How could Race know anything about these papers? I know how important you are."

"I know you do," Sarkov said. "But when you are afraid any idea looks weak." He sat. "When will you send the pouch?"

"Tomorrow morning," Reed answered. "The earthquakes and the floods have delayed the airplanes, but this will go first priority. How do I contact you when our man arrives?"

"I'll expect nothing for ten days," Sarkov answered. "On the fifteenth I'll knock on that door at ten thirty. I don't like the phone, the tref, or the drop, nothing's safe; but the phones the best. If the contact comes before we expect him, call this number." He wrote the numbers on the back of an envelope. "Tell the girl where you want me to meet you, and when. Don't use any names." He stood and took a few steps toward the door.

"Before you go, may I ask two questions?" Reed was pleading.

Sarkov looked down, solemnly. He did not want to relent on his principle not to reveal; but like a merchant in business, he was prepared to compromise.

"How extensive are the Russian operations here?"

"For Checka?"

"Yes."

"We have triple what you have, expert coders, technicians, boxes, contact people, five transmitters in this area and two in Ankara."

"What are they after? Is it true that Molotov wants Kars-Ardahan?"

"Certainly," Sarkov answered. "But that's not all. Right now we're watching Athens since the fall of the EAM. We have an invasion route all mapped out. We're studying the NATO bases, how to strike them, and the American installations."

"Would they risk war for Greece?"

"Maybe yes, maybe no," Sarkov answered. "But you can be sure that Stalin would give his soul for a port on the Bosporus. He wants Istanbul. He'll try negotiations. Next week at Potsdam could be crucial. If he doesn't get what he wants, who can tell what he will do?"

"What's the name of the man in charge of espionage here?"

"Me," Sarkov said. "Do you see how important I am? I came in February."

"What about 'day-to-day' operations?"

"Moscow prefers to keep agents separate. We learned that from the West. We only know what we need to know."

"It produces all kinds of reduplication and expenditures."

"The NKVD does not meet a budget, like MI 5 nor are we interested in efficiency. Ultimately we get what we want. Last week the Americans dropped the atom bomb on Nagasaki, and this week we have Uranium 235. It cost money, but it was worth it." He swung his left hand out, and then his right, as if he were on stage. He smiled for the third time.

"Who are the names you mention in this file?"

"You mean our agents in Europe?"

"I was thinking of the leaks in Europe."

"I don't know every one, but Maria Knuth, the German actress, is one of your people, but she works for us, too. Do you know her?"

"No."

"She has been helpful with military information," Sarkov said. "It's the other names which will interest Control, the most important are the three penetration agents in London. One of them is a homosexual who sleeps with cabinet ministers." Sarkov stopped for a few moments, and then said, "Our most important man has a high desk, not at Bletchley, but at Broadway. He has access to all top secret documents.

"We've known every high level move the Allies have made in the last three years. This man will be even more helpful now that the war is over. His name is my treasure. If nothing else, he insures a quick reply."

"That highly placed?"

"I'll tell you this," Sarkov said. "Our man is so important to your operation that McKenzie will not believe it at first. He can't. You see, when the truth is known, McKenzie will have to dismantle the whole service."

They were silent and then Sarkov said, "That's all, Mister Reed. Don't forget my wife."

"I'll take care of her, as if she were my own," Reed said picking up the mustard.

"What's that?"

"Lady Peterson's mustard," Reed answered. "She won't serve ham without it. Do you like ham?"

"I do," Sarkov said. "I got to like it when I was in Washington, but I won't be eating ham today."

"No, I expect you won't."

They shook hands. "Well, comrade," Reed said. "I'm going to do everything I can to see that in the near future you have the opportunity to eat some ham."

4

Sarkov opened the door and tried to leave the room, but Race blocked the passage. Like a horse in repose, the assistant stood on one leg, in the frame of the door. He would not move. Sarkov had no recourse but to stand and wait until the assistant let him pass.

"Are you satisfied with Mister Reed's plan?"

Sarkov held his ground and nodded. He did not want to answer any more questions, but he realized that he would not pass until the assistant finished. Sarkov decided to endure, but as silently as possible.

"What are the arrangements?" The assistant asked.

"Mr. Reed has taken care of it. I didn't see the other man."

"The ambassador?"

"He didn't come in."

"He knows you're here, and why," the assistant said. "But now you're leaving. I asked you, 'what are the arrangements?'"

If I had plans, you would be the last to know, Sarkov thought. He threw up a hand. "If you mean 'where shall I go from here,' I haven't thought about it."

"There's a story going around about a Greek whom the Turks were looking for. He murdered a local, but he was also on the run from his own people. The Greeks and the Turks were both after him. The Turks were so mad they assigned a platoon. They knew the Greek was here, and they searched and searched, but never found him. He was murdered in his own bed by a woman. He had been living next to Central Police all the time," Race said. "And listen to this: For over a year, he scrubbed the jail cells."

"What's the lesson? Stay nearby?"

"Russians are far sighted. If I were you, yes, I would stay close."

Sarkov resented the generalization about Russians, but he had resolved to endure the conversation and he did. Like the assistant, Sarkov could have generalized about the assistant's type: he had achieved his medium level position through nepotism. He wore a school tie, played tennis at the Colony, and stayed out of trouble. It was the same in any embassy. Embassies were overrun with people who had little to do, and did less.

"Do you know the city?" Sarkov asked.

"No, not very well."

"You've just come, haven't you?"

"Yes, I was in Lands."

"How long have you been in Istanbul?"

"Six weeks."

"I've been here two months," Sarkov explained. He wanted to leave, to disappear among the crowds at the Long Market. He took a step, but the assistant did not move. The assistant took Sarkov's sleeve like a policeman exercising authority.

"Just a minute," the assistant said. Sarkov almost lost his temper, but he understood the enormous trouble a scene would cause, and he allowed himself to be held. "Did you ever hear anything about Bayar?"

"What do you mean?"

"What is he looking for? In the negotiations?"

"I'll tell you this. He was right about Kars and Ardahan, but that is only a section of the new policy. We want to renegotiate the whole Montreux."

"So the fears are justified?"

"If that's what he's afraid of, yes."

"Does Moscow understand Saka's resolve?"

"Maybe they do; maybe they don't. The question is did Saka see the cruiser steam bye this morning, the Hemlick? If he didn't, he was the only one in Istanbul who didn't. The reason the admiralty sent the cruiser was to let the Turks know the Russian resolve. Do you think they got the message?"

Sarkov winked menacingly, but the assistant had turned away as if to reflect on the threat to Turkey, and he missed Sarkov's gesture.

The time was right and Sarkov said, "I have to go."

Without looking at him, the assistant asked, "Then it's true about the Kurds in East Anatolia?"

Like a teacher about to inform a student that the moon was several million miles away, Sarkov smiled pedantically and nodded 'yes'.

"By the way, are you going back to your chancery?"

"No."

"Do you have a place to stay?"

Sarkov shook his head 'no.'

"I know a chap who owns a *han*. His name is Behcit Casim. The place is just run-down enough to hide in."

Is it possible, Sarkov asked himself, that this man could help him? The eagle must now and again descend and learn stealth from the crow. The assistant handed Sarkov a slip of paper with the hotel's name. Sarkov slipped it into his breast pocket, knowing full well that he would at least inspect the *han*, if not hide there.

5

Reed heard the conversation between Sarkov and Race, but he walked beyond earshot not only because protocol, but good judgment, dictated that he not interfere.

He did, however, violate protocol when he walked into Ambassador Peterson's study without knocking.

The ambassador was waiting, his head bowed, weight resting on his knuckles like the accused about to be sentenced. "I'd prefer not to hear what went on, but I know I have to," the ambassador said waving a hand, but not looking up. "By the way," he asked, suddenly changing his mind and looking up, "did you find the mustard?" When he saw the jar in Reed's hand, said, "I see you have."

"It's dry," Reed said. "You'll have to mix in wine or vinegar."

"I prefer raisin sauce to mustard," the ambassador said. "Isabel mixes her own concoction. Mind you, it's very good."

"I don't care for ham," Reed said. "Too salty." He placed the jar on the desk. "We've enticed a bear into a cage," he said. "What do you propose we do?"

"It's more in your line. I'd like to keep it that way."

"I'll take full responsibility," Reed said, "but his 'coming over' will cause a stir in your circles. Have you thought about that?"

"I'm trying to imagine how Kiktev will react," Peterson said. "He's elusive as a snake, but very smart. Most likely he won't say a word."

"Or he may raise the devil. That's why I want you to know every move I make. We have to keep Kiktev in mind at all times. It's like the mustard."

"Like the what?"

"Like the mustard. You have to depend on me."

"Yes, of course," the ambassador said. "I'll stay out of it completely, unless there is a flap. What are you going to tell London?"

"That the Russian will bring a windfall of information. He knows the full range of Russian intentions here. He hinted that they are ready to invade Greece if the elections fail. He knows operators in Europe which we didn't know existed. If it were up to me, I would bring him in today and get on with the questioning, but I can't do that. I have to have orders from Broadway." He stopped talking for a moment and then continued. "I'm certain McKenzie will send someone as quickly as possible, but I don't like this fellow wandering around this city for ten days with a dozen Russian killers looking for him. I'd like to fly him off to Cyprus, today."

"Why don't you? It sounds like a good idea. It would spare us the publicity. It would protect him from his own people. Surely, as you say, they will be hunting him. What's the point of letting him wander about? Just wire London that you've flown him out and go from there?"

"To begin with, I have no authority to transport a non-English resident. The Turks would be furious. And if I did whisk him out, the Russians would know before the plane left the runway. And, I have no airplane."

"I'd forgotten that the Ruskies are listening to our radio. Did he say anything about that?"

"Just that it's true. They've had our pads for some time, just as we suspected."

"I suppose we shouldn't take chances, sending messages, I mean."

"He and I decided that we would do business with London by pouch. He wanted to send the information on ripe film, which is all right, but very dangerous. Last year an agent brought aircraft markings back from France to England on ripe film. He was stopped at Victoria and forced to open his bag for inspection and the film was exposed. All sorts of things can happen with ripe film, although I suspect Sarkov is not worried. His best secrets are in his head." Reed looked back to see if anyone was in the room. "If I'm not mistaken, he is the highest ranking operator we have ever brought in from the East," He opened his arms. "Don't be fooled. We've had excellent sources of information since 1942. I don't know what they are; my guess is that our people broke the German code. The information is so extensive. On top of that, now we know what the Russians are up to. We have the best of sources, but this man gives us the added dimension, the inside. He knows the chain of command inside Moscow Center, who is in favor, what they are after, their seriousness. That sort of thing."

"Who is he?"

"He's top level, one of the new people in the internal division of MGB, Beria's key men."

"An intellectual?"

"Yes," Reed said. "He wrote the operations plan for the Collegium which became the policy paper of the Polituro. It was brilliant. He brought together proposals from foreign residents and chiefs of domestic divisions,

presented the plan to the Collegium and then made it clear
for the Central Committee. He wrote the final draught. But
he's been on the bad list for the last two years, for reasons
we do not know." Reed said. "Istanbul is the penal colony
for their people, the last station, something like Patna for us,
Lima for the Germans. The Russians send their outcasts
here, and the Turks punish them, believe me. That's why we
lick our lips when a high ranking officer is assigned here.
They're usually desperate, and vulnerable. Istanbul is not
the only place they send their outcasts. They go to Trieste,
Delhi, but this is the worst place. The point is, if we were
not sure about Sarkov before, we are now. He's out on a
limb."

"You knew that he was ready to defect?"

"We made some guarded overtures. We did the preliminaries. Tomlinson vetted him and Smythe talked to him.
Mind you, Sarkov has only been here a little over two
months. My guess is that he is under some sort of threat. He
claims that his wife needs medical attention. Could be. It
doesn't matter what his motives are. The point is that he is
coming." Reed stopped then to reflect on the process of
enticement. "The second week he was here Smythe saw
him at a party and dangled some goodies in front of him, to
see if he was willing; Smythe told him what we would do
for him, and let it go at that. Sarkov seemed unreceptive at
the time, but he heard, and now he's taken the bait."

"I remember your talking about that, "Peterson said,
"and I remember thinking how the Russian system produces
as many misfits as ours. Tell me, just for curiosity, what
advantage will it be to have him brought in? He sounds like
a civil servant who has outworn his usefulness and he
knows it. What does he do? He turns traitor, rattles along
about politics of the Center, tells you a few operators you
didn't know at the time, but would know eventually, goes

on about suspicious Russian intentions toward Greece, but what does all this prattle add up to? Nothing. What does he get? Thousands. We support a traitor and his wife in comfort, whisk him around whenever the secret police get warm, and generally treat him like a silent hero. We don't even show him off, can't do."

"That's not true," Reed said. "He's not a misfit like Phillips or Langley. My guess is that he is a high type man who was caught in the proletarian system. It's the opposite of us. Their good people are punished by the system."

"You can look at it that way," Peterson said. "All I know is that these Russian blokes crave the luxury of the West. I've seen it over and over again. I warn you. It will come down to that: the fleshpots."

"He told me that they have already stolen the secret for smashing the atom. How did they do that?" It was a rhetorical question, but Ambassador Peterson answered, "They riddled the Manhattan project with their people. They had more spies in there than they had at home."

"At the end of the conversation Sarkov dropped his own little bomb. He knew it would disrupt me, and it did."

"What was that?"

"He told me that he has the names of three double agents working in London. They're all high up. One of the traitors works in our building. That alone would be worth the trouble."

"How would he know such a thing?" Peterson asked. "The Russians work in their own little boxes. One man doesn't know the other exists, let alone what he does."

"Sarkov knows," Reed said. "He knows because he wrote the checks for all the double agents in England, I would imagine. There's an old service adage: the secret's exposed when the money's exchanged. And Sarkov made out the vouchers. Of course he knows."

"You can't tell me your security people aren't aware that they have traitors, if there are traitors. I can't believe that. If we know it, they must know it. It's their business."

"That's true," Reed answered. "But if security suspects a leak, it's all hearsay. Has to be. Now we present them with a Russian who confirms their suspicions, that is, if they are suspicious at all."

"Here's my view, and it's the worst possible situation," Peterson said. "If there are traitors, I believe McKenzie knows it, but prefers to keep the whole thing quiet." He began to gait, like an actor, his gestures overblown. "He doesn't want publicity any more than we do. What does he gain by exposing a traitor?" He walked around the desk and said softly, "That's my reading. He knows some of his men are talking to the Russians, and maybe taking some money for their information. He lets it be known that he doesn't like it. But he doesn't make a row. The Russians are allies after all. What would the back benchers in Whitehall say if they heard that some of the secret service was talking to the Russians? Half of them would cheer." Peterson picked up the jar of dry mustard and turned it in his hand. Some of the mustard spilled on his hand and he reached into his breast pocket for a handkerchief. "What would you mix in with this?"

"I told you, I don't use mustard."

"Oh yes, you did say that," Peterson answered. "But the scullery won't know what to do."

"Is there any pouille fouisse? It would give it sparkle. I'll tell them in the kitchen."

"Yes do," Peterson said.

He put the mustard back on the desk; both men stared at it until Peterson asked, "Do you have any suspicions?"

"About the traitors, you mean?"

"Yes."

"I have no idea," Reed answered. "We've doubled the staff in the last two years and, of course, I haven't met these new people. I haven't even seen the Broadway station, so I am at a loss."

"But you do know the top echelon. Wouldn't the names be among them?"

Reed nodded. "That's what Sarkov implied. I think you know those people as well as I do," Reed continued. "You know Miles Stewart. He's director of counter intelligence. White and Davies answer to him. Charles Carolyn runs the intelligence gathering section. They've opened a new division, Russian counter intelligence; Sloan's been appointed there. Frankly I don't see any risk among these people. I doubt if it is one of them."

"If you're talking about communist leanings, it could be any of them," Peterson remarked. "I know them all, except this Carolyn fellow. The rest are absolutely first class, but most of them carried commie cards in the thirties. Who is this Carolyn?"

"An outsider," Reed answered. "Sinclair disliked him, but McKenzie put him up there when he took charge. A brilliant fellow, really, from Manchester. He's working class, came up the hard way."

"Just the same, when there's the suspicion of taking money I worry about working class chaps. No offense. But the others are so blasted first rate. I know Stewart from the first war; White and Sloan come from the best of families. Sloan wrote those Spanish pieces for the *Times*, didn't he? And wasn't White decorated for one thing or another."

"Carolyn has no communist leanings."

"I didn't mean to say that any of them were communists, only that you have to understand the atmosphere of Cambridge in the thirties. We were all in the marches.

Labour was in disarray; we all thought that Marx had the answer. It was really quite respectable. I hope they don't keep lists of all the fellow travelers, nearly all of my class would be there, and half of the present intelligence people, the upper half."

"Carolyn wouldn't be on any list, except Labour's."

"If you say so."

"He knew enough to stay loyal even in its troubles. After all, he is working class." The irony was lost on Peterson.

"The last word is that we have no idea whom Sarkov has in his hat." Peterson went back to his original position, knuckles on the desk, head down. "Tell me, if you don't have an airplane, how do you plan to get him out?"

"Do you remember Colonel Tor? He's in charge of the secret service here, such as it is. Do you know him?"

"Is that the policeman who had so much to do with Cicero?"

"The same."

"His father was one of Ataturk's men."

"Yes. You have a good memory."

"I play bridge with Tor now and again. He's brilliant. Why him?"

"He told me once that he felt obligated to us for the Credits. I thought I'd call in the debt."

"Good idea," Peterson said. "I think he's a discreet chap; he is at cards anyway."

"I'll be careful," Reed said.

"I don't like it," Peterson said. "You know that. All this cloak and dagger business disturbs me. The whole thing could be a fake."

"Could be, but I doubt it."

"The Russians are past masters at double dealing, better than the Italians, or the French. My advice is that you keep this fellow under wraps for as long as you can, months, even a year, until the facts can be sorted out. He knows he's going to be interrogated?"

"He asked me who would be doing the questioning."

"He may have been schooled in interrogation. I think you had better assume that he has."

"Why do you think it might be a double cross?"

"Publicity," Peterson said loudly. "It's always publicity." He leaned forward and looked up, his eyes glistening as if he were chemically stimulated. "Suppose he takes us in. We fall for it. He returns to Moscow and makes a laughing stock of us in the Russian press. Our wire services pick it up, and all England knows what damn fools we are. It's the sort of thing the Russians like, the public humiliation."

"That's what you think this is all about?"

"I do," Peterson said. "You haven't given me one piece of evidence to indicate that it isn't double dealing." After a moment he continued, "And furthermore, I'm ordering extreme caution. I want all messages copied, and I want you to do nothing without consulting me first. And at all times I want you to assume that all of this will become public. I want you to be able to justify every move. Hear?"

"I'll make as little trouble as possible."

"It's already been too much trouble," Peterson said. "What I would like is for your Colonel Tor to ship the Russian out tonight. Could that be arranged?"

"No," Reed said. "I haven't talked with Tor yet, but before anything, I have to convince him to fly out Sarkov's wife and sons. That's first, getting the family out. I don't know what I am going to say to him, that helping us with these people discredits the Russians? That will take a lot of convincing."

"You mean there will be two flights, then," Peterson asked. "One bringing out the family and the other the subject himself, in ten days or so?"

"It's quite a lot to ask," Reed said. "But I don't see any other way to do it."

"What will be the destination?"

"Cyprus," Reed answered. "That's the first leg. I'll have to make arrangements for other ports. Ultimately Sarkov wants his wife treated by a Doctor White in Boston. At least that's what he says."

"I hope you're not disappointed. A lot rests on a Turk intelligence officer helping the hated Russian."

"May I come in?" Race asked, coming in.

Peterson waved him in and watched the assistant's eyes fix on the mustard. "It's for dinner tonight. Do you like ham?"

Reed picked up the jar as a preliminary gesture to leaving, just as one might pick up a bill in a restaurant.

"What did you find out?" Peterson asked the assistant.

"We know where he will be sleeping tonight. In an hour I'll know the route he took, and what he did on the way."

The statement was so disturbing to Reed that he jiggled the mustard. The assistant was neither a diplomat nor diplomatic, neither an intelligence officer nor intelligent. He was a mediocre clerk with some gift for order, as long as the order dealt with papers and not with people.

"What the hell have you done?"

"What you didn't do," the assistant snapped. His voice was high; he was ready to shout in his own defense. "I gave the man the name of a hotel and I sent Tomlinson after him to see that he goes there."

"You didn't?"

"The last thing I did was give him the name of a reasonably respectable hotel where he could hide. He told me he had no plans so I gave him some advice. I believe he will go to Casim's. Furthermore, when he left, I thought it best to send someone after him, to see."

"You sent someone to follow him?"

"Something like that, yes. Tomlinson has experience with watchings, and he knew the Russian before, so I sent him."

"Don't you realize that Sarkov will know someone is watching? Have you ever had anyone following you? You can feel their eyes on your neck."

"Don't be disturbed," Peterson said. "It's simply a matter of staying informed. If you had asked him, I'm sure the Russian wouldn't mind someone accompanying him. He may think it's our security. After all, we want him to be safe, don't we? What's the danger in our being certain he's alright?"

"I told him he could trust me," Reed said. "When he realizes he is being followed, he'll know he can't."

"What difference does it make, in the long run?"

"He and I had a pact and we let him down at the beginning. That's the difference."

"Did you tell him you wouldn't send a man after him?" The ambassador and the assistant were conspirators, and their deceit was too complex for Reed. "We've all trusted someone we ought not to have trusted," Peterson said, "and we've all betrayed something more important than a Russian traitor."

There was nothing Reed could do and so he kept silent.

"It's the secret vice of diplomats," Peterson said, his carious teeth showing. "Saying one thing and doing another."

It was like an unknown language to Reed, he could not make it out. He could hear and comprehend the words, but the meaning escaped him.

The ambassador recognized that Reed was not listening so he instructed his nephew. "It's a little like chess," he said. "A pawn is exposed! The question is whether to allow it to stand, how best to use its exposure to threaten a better piece, or simply to wipe it off the board. It's a situation in which we have all the advantages, the Russians have none. We can choose the strategy and when to employ it. Trust does not enter into it."

"No, but betrayal does," Reed answered. "Sarkov is not a pawn." He stood straight, like a soldier at command. "I would rather leave the service than mislead."

"Don't be so serious, John," Peterson said. "It's only a way of speaking. I recognize your obligation and I bow to it. But we have to consider our end, don't we? I'd like to know where he goes, who he sees, that sort of thing. We want to know that he's safe and that he does what we expect, that's all."

"That he doesn't talk to his embassy people, you mean?"

"I won't say that's not in there, yes."

"Suppose he's legitimate?"

"We'll be the first to know, won't we?"

"Have you something up your sleeve, something devious?"

"You'll be the first to know, won't you?"

"I wonder," Reed answered.

"My dear fellow," Peterson said. "It's all a game and it's all in knowing which game it is. The Germans had no idea of our fascination with cricket. If they had, they might have crossed the channel when they had the chance."

"I'm not sure I follow you."

"I'm trying to decide whether the present situation lends itself to chess or bridge? The Russians are notoriously poor at bridge and brilliant at chess. They will want to play chess. I want bridge. They have always gotten their way. Do you remember how they kept Blake under wrappers for months. He was in Moscow six months before anyone knew he had defected? The Russians wanted control, power. That's what they understand. As in any good chess game, force and power determine the outcome. Not so in bridge. Do you understand?"

"I'm afraid I do."

6

Sarkov latched the embassy gate and turned to face the street. Like a robber who had planned, and executed a crime but had made no provisions for escape, Sarkov's fright reasserted itself when he was confronted with the simple decision whether to walk to the left or to the right. Instead he brought out from his breast pocket the slip of paper with the name of Behcit Casim's hotel.

It was as close as he had come to a plan of escape. It had come to this paralysis. Sarkov's luck had been bad for months, eighteen months, and with bad luck came fear. The bad luck began when he failed to respond to Anosov's third bulletin. That failure marked the beginning of the decline of his fortunes. It was not a gross failure, since Anosov had exaggerated troop movements twice before and it had become a scandal in the military that Anosov misrepresented the size and intention of the German forces. But the third time Anosov was right. He sent a bulletin warning that the Germans were about to attack the Russian army near the Austrian border. When he received the message at Moscow Center, Sarkov labeled the bulletin "third class" and no one paid any attention to the warning. As a result, when the Wehrmat attacked, the Russian army was not prepared. After the defeat, the military sought an explanation from intelligence and intelligence found their scapegoat. Sarkov was reprimanded and sent to Analysis, to rot.

In espionage as in womanizing, one failure is decisive. Word got around. The Anosov failure cast a pall on Sarkov's past, even on the times when he showed promise, so that after the failure even the promise appeared rather a hint of his ultimate collapse.

Sarkov's best work had been done in Special Section I, Pure Intelligence, in which he assembled reports, usually radio transcripts, and sent digests of those reports to members of the Politburo. The Anosov investigation charged that even then he was prone to de-emphasize important material.

Six months after the Anosov debacle, Sarkov was assigned to Analysis in Moscow Center. It was a demotion. Too young to understand the full implications of his demotion, and too old to work outside Checka, Sarkov accepted the demotion. Then his bad luck took a turn for the worse.

In the Anosov case he was in the wrong place at the wrong time. Next he was from the wrong family in the wrong circumstances.

More than they would admit, Checka, after the Revolution, relied on the "old boy" system as did British Intelligence. Like the British, the revolutionaries recruited from the university men of patrician families, even though these families were in disgrace, and many of the intelligence officers, like Sarkov, came from these families. However the comrades in charge tried to bypass patrician officers as much as possible. This is what happened to Sarkov. Beria, the commoner, was more than ordinarily disinclined toward patricians; and when the next promotions came due, he ordered the commoner Merkulov to be promoted over Sarkov. Sarkov remained at his small desk in Moscow Center, overlooking Lubyanka.

He had another chance six months later. This time he was given the assignment of overseeing an assassination.

Even though he was not a field operator, had no sense for espionage, Sarkov studied the methods of *mokrie dela*, the dirty tricks section, and planned the assassination in detail. It went off without incident. He was promised a promotion, high level work in a foreign embassy, but, like that man accused of infidelity, the pall of failure followed him like a bad smell. He never received the promotion.

Finally, after floundering in the bureaucracy of Moscow Center for too long, he was assigned to Istanbul, a Checka insult. When his wife's heart problems became too severe for anyone in Moscow to treat, he began to talk to her about defecting. And these issues had brought him to this place.

He had taken two steps to the left when the embassy gate opened and a tall man walked into the street. The tall man seemed surprised to see him, and the man's surprise frightened Sarkov still more. "What's the easiest way to Galatasary?" He asked. "Is it up or down?"

Sarkov turned to face him. He was English and it appeared to Sarkov that he had assumed that Sarkov was English. He waved and the man followed. "The second passage," Sarkov said pointing. "Kiritzantan. It isn't marked, but what street is? At the end, turn right and down the steps. That's Cickek. Better than that, come along. I'll walk with you."

"Thank you," the tall man said. "I wish the Turks would mark their streets. It's so uncivilized, only the natives know the routes. I didn't leave the house for two months when I first came here. I don't know whether I was afraid of getting lost, or being robbed."

A man on the run, especially a new man on the run, generates a kind of paranoia which suspects even friendliness and courtesy. Sarkov's paranoia kicked in and his eyes widened with fear.

"Where are you going?" The tall man asked.

"I'm looking for a hotel," Sarkov said, slipping the paper with Casim's name back into his pocket.

"To book or to eat?" The other man asked. "If you would like to eat with us, come ahead. I'm going to meet Sheldon at the Park around seven. Would you come?"

"Thank you, I have another engagement tonight. But I want to book the hotel first."

"I see," the tall man said. "If you're thinking of a hotel for friends, I call the Panuk. It's so like the Strand Palace. Do you know it?"

"I don't think I do," Sarkov said. Was this a signal from Reed that he was to stay at the Panuk? Sarkov was unused to signals and subterfuge.

"It's below Sophia, near the Post Office. The rooms are better than the Malatye or the Keysin."

"Good, I'll stop there," Sarkov said. "Well, I turn here. Good bye."

The other man was not ready for the adieu. Sarkov offered his hand, but pulled it back quickly, remembering that the English rarely shook hands; it was the Americans who did that, at every opportunity.

"What's down there?" The tall man asked, bending forward like a curious crane.

"A bath," Sarkov answered. "Down there at the end."

"Are you going into a Turkish bath?" The tall man asked. "How can you look at those gross bodies?"

"I don't look at theirs, if they don't look at mine."

"I don't mind looking, but it has to be the right sex. As a matter of fact, I'm going to look at one body before dinner. Care to join me? I'm going to Nina Pilars. Ever been there?"

"No, I haven't," Sarkov said.

"Do come along. It's a brothel, the best in the world. You'll enjoy yourself far more than in that nasty place."

"No," Sarkov said "I'm happily married."

"Oh, I am too," the tall man said. "I'm sure Nina is half the reason." And then he asked again. "You should come along. It's really quite an experience if you haven't been. Clean and exciting."

Sarkov had taken four steps into the passage. He waved and then turned boldly toward the entrance of the bath, and did not look back. However, he was certain that the Englishman was standing and watching, trying to ascertain how he would follow, without being obvious, into the labyrinth of the Turkish bath.

At the entrance an elderly Turk in baggy pants nodded and showed his stubby teeth. The old man did not mistake Sarkov for a Turk, or an Englishman; he knew he was Russian, so he made no attempt to speak, and when he turned to lead, the Turk waved his hand in indifference. He beckoned and Sarkov followed.

The entrance-way resembled a prison, or rather the one prison Sarkov knew, Lubyanka. The arch, the dark corridor in, the hollow sound of keys in locks, all made Sarkov think of the Moscow prison. The difference was that this place smelled of disinfectant mixed with soap.

He heard voices as if in a vault, but there were no bands of bathers, only two: an older man, more massive than Sarkov, wearing only a fez and sitting on the edge of a stool. The other, an adolescent, stood opposite the older man and sprinkled water on the other's chest. The young man caught the water from a spigot in a basin and sprinkled it with his fingers.

The old greeter put on wooden sandals and retreated across the cobblestones into a second, darker tunnel. He had assumed that Sarkov would follow, but the Russian had stopped to watch the bathing ritual.

The older bather was in the stage of drying himself. He walked around the cistern and waved the towel like a tassel, all the while he shook his body like a dancer. Sarkov put his back to the wall and slid along the bricks. He felt vulnerable, isolated, and apprehensive. He knew he was in a hostile setting, and that maybe this scene would be worse than the one he had left. He had never hid before, never had reason to hide, but now he was under threat. He felt that harm was present to him in the next room.

He thought of his wife and their dacha. At least he would be secure there for a time.

Before him were two tunnels. Down the first was a thin man wrapped in a large towel. He was leaning over, cleaning his feet with a metal brush. He was talking with someone in the room, but Sarkov could not see the other man. Sarkov walked by and the man did not look up. While he was edging along between the tunnel and the second arch, the man and the boy stopped and looked at him. Sarkov continued, his back to the wall until he reached the third archway. The fat man in the fez collapsed on a hexagonal slab in the attitude of grotesque indolence and let out a snore.

In the dark Sarkov ran along the tunnel. He turned a corner and there was light and people. He was the only man in the room with clothes on, and he felt naked. He was in the Hararet, the steam room.

As a foreigner Sarkov did not know the ritual of the steam. It was like an Inferno to him, the naked bodies, the heat, and the grey light. He took two steps forward and then stepped back. A huge masseur did not look up from his work of kneading the back of a man who was lying on a bench. The masseur had removed the body hair with paste of quicklime and he was scraping away the residue with the edge of a muscle shell. It looked like torture to Sarkov. The prone man strained to look up at the visitor; his eyes pulsed and his mouth pursed, like a fish recently pulled from the sea. He turned his head back to a comfortable angle and settled into some muted grunting.

Without looking at Sarkov, the masseur said, in Russian, "What do you want?"

"I would like a massage, like he's getting."

"Then why are you standing there with your clothes on?" Only then did he stop kneading and wipe his hands. "Do you want a massage with your clothes on?"

"I didn't see where to hang them."

"Where is the greeter? He should have told you. You have to take a bath first." As if in anger he returned to the man's back with his kese. He hissed and stroked as if he felt some pleasure in inducing pain. "Cok pis. Cok pis," he said, first in Turkish, then in Russian, "Very dirty. Very dirty."

"Must I go all the way outside?"

The masseur stopped his work and stared at Sarkov as one might a pest. His eyes drooped under his bushy brows which arched like a circumflex. At first Sarkov thought he was a bother to this man, but in the long look he saw a victim, a man on the run like himself.

"Take my advice," the masseur said. "Leave now. You can go where you want. You will be safe."

"I can't undergo a message?"

"You didn't come here for that. You came to escape, and it's safe to go. So go. If you stay here you will be in more danger. Go." He made a gesture of exit with his hand, as if he were cajoling a cat.

"I don't want to go the way I came."

"You don't have to. The tall man is gone and the English have given up on you, for now. But this is not safe.

I wouldn't be safe in your dacha in Zhukovka, would I? So, you're not safe here."

"How do you know all this?"

"Russians don't come in here. It's not safe for them. They might come if they were desperate and wanted to hide," the masseur said. "How often does a Russian diplomat come in here wearing an Italian suit? It's not difficult to see he's hiding from someone, maybe it's the tall Englishman in the alley. Hey?"

"Is there another way out?"

"Through that passage. It leads to the back of a Kebabci," the masseur said going back to his work, splashing water on the fat man's back and helping the surface dirt flow off, like guilt.

Sarkov walked past the dirty cloth and into the dark passage. He wanted to stay in that dark place because he felt that he was being watched, not yet by Russians and not at the moment by the British, but surely by the Turks.

He pushed the cloth aside and entered the back of the pastahane, past the chipped marble tops, the out-of-date calendar, the picture of Sultan Mehment torn from the pages of the magazine *Hyat*, until he sat down near the street. Again he thought of food: a green pepper he saw a man eating at the table next.

Across the street, near the entrance to the Grand Bazaar, two attendants wheeled a coffin. They were heading for a mosque in Bayazit. Just in front of the pastahane two porters ate mullet. Next to them a lady poured perfume water on her hands. Then she rubbed the water on her face, completing the ritual. Sarkov watched the feminine gesture and decided, impulsively, to flee to his dacha and his wife.

7

Sarkov startled his wife. She was standing in the living room facing the street when she heard his step crush a particle of sand on the tile behind her. She turned quickly, losing her balance, reaching for the arm of a chair, letting go of the nitroglycerin bottle, but not falling. She asked, "Why the back way? You've seen the English?"

"Yes. How did you know? Have they been here?"

"No."

"How did you know?"

"The valise," she answered. "You always carry your papers. Where is it? You must have left it at your desk. That means haste, something frightened you. You went to the British, even though we said we would wait. And you're back too early. Eleven."

"Yes. I've seen them."

"What frightened you?"

"There's an order from Kiktev," he said. "This. We were right: Victor reported me. But that isn't the worst. Someone followed me out of the British building. I evaded him, but I had to hide in a wretched bath."

"Your clothes are damp, even your jacket. You look like you fell into the Marmora. Who was it? Not our people?"

"No," he answered. "An Englishman. Why follow me?"

"To find out what you're doing, that's all. Did you tell anyone about this place?"

"One."

"Why did you tell him?"

"Because he is sending someone to take you to safety. Did anyone call?"

"No," she answered. "Why would they? I'm trying to understand why the British would follow you when you told them where we live? Who else did you talk to?"

"A second-rate clerk," Sarkov answered. "He tried to put me out, but I persuaded him to let me talk to their agent, a man named Reed. "

"Good," she said. "We know we can't trust him. Do you think the clerk talked to Peterson? Did he have an opportunity, while you were there?"

"I'm sure he did."

"That's the connection. Peterson had you followed." She was satisfied that there were no more conspiracies. She turned back to her original position and pointed, "There are two of our people in a car down there."

He ran to the window. "There's no one there now."

"They're with the *Muhtar*, eating."

"We have *Zaporozhets* at the embassy," he said. "That one looks French. Are you sure they're our people?"

"The tall one is wearing a V-S-R beret," she said. "They must be logging the amount of chrome on the ships. You can measure the tonnage by the line on the hull. D department would want to know how much chrome the Turks are shipping to England, wouldn't they?"

"Yes," he said. "But I don't like those two so near."

"I don't think they'll bother us. If I am right, they'll leave in a few minutes. It's high tide and the ships can't pass under the bridge."

She reached down for her bottle of nitroglycerin, but only held it, did not unscrew the cap, or take any. Like a secret drinker she detested her reliance on the drug, never took it in sight of anyone, even her husband, although it was constantly with her. "What happened with the British? Tell me everything."

"I almost missed Reed. He's been in Ankara."

"But you didn't," she said. "It is always the same. You get away with things, as if someone was watching over you. What did he say?"

"We're all being flown out."

"Wonderful," she said. "Then it went as planned."

"Yes."

"What else?"

"Nothing," he said. "When he saw the information, he gave me everything. No compromises."

"When do we leave?"

"Tomorrow. You and the children go first. The English will pick you up, before sunrise," he said. "I follow in a few days."

She turned her face as if he had slapped her. "I knew you were holding something back," she said. "How many days?"

"Ten."

"Why aren't you coming?"

"Because I can't," he answered. "I have to wait for their man from London. That's how it's done."

"That's how what's done?" She asked. "That's how the British do it, protecting themselves. They let you wander around like a lost child while they decide whether they want to bring you in or not. I detest them. There is no honor, just good manners. You should have gone to the Americans. At least they're genuine, if a little stupid."

"You know I couldn't do that. The British have the resources."

"What resources? What did they do for you? Twenty three years of marriage. I know you can't take care of yourself. You can't find your way to the Ukraina Hotel."

"I knew enough to marry you. You've taught me."

"No," she said. "I don't like this. I want you with me. Couldn't you fly out with us, and talk to the British later?"

"I have to stay and wait."

"I knew you weren't telling me everything," she said. "I'm unhappy that you didn't insist. Why didn't you? That's how we planned."

"He told me I would have to stay until their man comes."

"Could you go back and talk to him?"

"It's all in motion."

"No asylum?"

"Peterson wouldn't allow it. He didn't want me in the building."

"So you have to hide like a fox."

"What can I do? It's arranged."

"What's arranged?" she said. "We'll have to think of something. What?"

He held her. She was the source of his disloyalty to country and the NKVD. If Moscow Center had known how far he would go to protect her, he would have been jailed long ago. Like many traitors, he was driven by a love far greater than country.

"I'm having trouble comprehending this," she said. "Why must we go and you stay?"

"They're protecting themselves," he answered. "The man will come from London, sooner than we expect. They want to know what I know."

"Why not meet him in neutral territory?"

"They're protecting themselves, as you say," he answered. "What I'm doing could be a trick. And they don't want that. Remember what Vidorov did to the Germans?"

"But they didn't give you any assurances, nothing at all. Nothing. Couldn't they hide you in a safe house?"

"My guess is they don't have one."

"So you wander around this foul city, you the innocent."

"They don't know me here. They expect that I could get by for a few days, and I will."

"No, they don't know you. You're not courageous; you're too smart for that. And you're too smart to worry about shelter, or food, or clothes. Remember the trip to Odessa. You packed your socks and pants but forgot shirts. And tooth brush. We had to buy shirts, and you with forty shirts at home!"

She touched his lips with her fingertips. He did not object. He could not deny that he depended on her. The next ten days would be critical, not so much whether the enemies would find and kill him, but rather whether he would be able to survive without her.

The telephone rang. After five rings Irina lifted the receiver and said 'hello.' She said nothing else. She held out the hearing piece so that Sergei could hear. The voice on the other side was insistent, quick, and imperative. After half a minute the voice stopped and the connection was broken.

"It was Vadim, wasn't it?" Sergei asked.

"Yes," she said. "The lisp."

"He's looking for me," he said. "He might come here."

"Not while I'm here."

"He'll bring someone with him."

"No," she said. "He'll call again, hoping you'll answer."

"Tell him I've gone to Beyoglu to deliver some papers."

"You can't tell a lie without quivering," she said. "There's nothing devious about you. Don't worry about Vadim or anyone they send. I'll take care of them."

"They're no match for you, are they?"

She smiled, but then asked, "Who will pick us up tomorrow?"

"The Turk police," he answered. "Early, before sunrise. Stay quiet. They will drive you to a plane field in the south, near Ismit. You don't have to do a thing; it's all arranged."

"I don't like it," she said. "The police are worthless. They ring their sirens and steal fruit from Yuseff."

"It's not the regular police," he said. "It's the second section people, like our security. The man in charge is a colonel, who, they say is brilliant. Our people hate him."

"Isn't it odd that a Turk colonel will help Russians escape from their own security people?"

An automobile backfired, the noise like a gunshot. Sarkov leaped to the window. The old car bucked forward, jolting down the cobblestones to the end of the alley, stopped, turned to the right, and chugged up the hill.

"They're gone," Sarkov said, kneeling on the padded chair. "We're alone."

"It doesn't make your danger less."

"It does for me. I feel safe with you."

"You don't want tomorrow to come, do you? Isn't that why you're not telling me everything?"

He looked away, like a reprimanded child. She continued, "Did anyone tell you where they were taking us?"

"He said, 'Cyprus.'"

"We'd be safer here than in Cyprus. Did you tell them that Lui is in Cyprus, that Grubyakov is there. They'll know we've arrived before the motors have turned off."

"He told me Cyprus was only a stop. You won't leave the airstrip. You'll go on to some safe place."

"Where would that be? Did he tell you?"

"I didn't listen after he said you would be cared for," Sarkov said. "He knew Donaldson in Washington. Remember him?"

"You're better than the whole lot," she said. "They should know what a 'catch' you are. They would have taken more precautions."

Sarkov said, "I won't give them any information until I know you are safe."

"Am I your only worry?"

She had seen their son slink up behind her husband. He was dressed in school clothes, but disheveled, as if he had been playing a strenuous game. The gypsy maid followed, but retreated when she saw Sarkov.

"How's my prince?" Sarkov asked and held out his arms.

"I skinned myself," the boy said, rolling up his sleeve and showing the bruise, all the time struggling like a fish. The father kissed the broken skin and looked to his wife. "It's not too bad." He put the boy down, but kept his hand on his head, to hold him in place.

"How would you like a ride in a plane?"

"Can Udi come?"

"Not this time. Just you, your mother and Georgei."

"Why can't Georgei stay home?"

"Because you're all going. Change your clothes." The boy obeyed like a recruit who had been issued the orders he had hoped for. He had his shirt off before he had left the room.

"He thinks we're going now," Irina said.

"I wish you were."

"I have to think what we should take."

"No, leave everything," Sarkov said. "When our people search, I want them to think we are still here. Leave the lights on, tell the gypsy to go home, that we've gone on holiday. I want the security people delayed as long as possible."

"Where are you going to stay?"

"I haven't decided," he answered. "That English clerk told me about a hotel, but I don't think I'll go there. I'll stay with Russians."

"We have to talk about your plans. You mustn't leave until all your days are scheduled."

"Don't do that."

"You can't find your way home from Silver Grove. Do you remember? You had to call me. And this is the most complicated city—the wrong half is in Europe, and you're going to be alone, for ten days. Eighteen years in the intelligence and you're as guileless as Nathaniel."

"As Who?"

"A nice boy in the Bible."

"Your talk is more seditious than mine," he said, shaking his head. "I'm sure we're on report for what you said to Illyndor Pankov."

"A second rate bureaucrat, like all of them," she answered. "There is no heart in any of them."

"Shh," he put his finger to his lips.

"Never mind," she said. "I hope we are coming to the end of the deception. You say one thing at Center and believe another at home. If any of them ever understood your poems, we would be in Lefortov. Did you tell the English what you were doing before coming here?"

"No."

"Demoted to internal security because you're not 'idealistic' enough. So now you're supposed to spy on your own family. That's what they want, secrets on Tanya. 'Why does she want to dance in Belgrade?' What about her use of cosmetics?' What does she talk about at home?' How good it was before the Bolsheviks! They make me ill. I am happy to leave. I only hope they don't punish our families."

"What more could they do?"

"Harm the children, Vyancheslav's children." She was walking toward the cooking area. "I won't leave until I know where you are."

"How will I do that?"

"Ring twice. Hang up. Ring three times, like we do."

"I'll stay in my room. I'll go out at night to eat,—I know the places—but I'll shy away from people. I'll call on Kiev and Polyanko, if I feel lonely. I'll turn my room into a cell, like a monk. I'll be safe. Not happy, but safe, until we're together."

"I still say you'd be safer in Kilyus, or with us," she said. "Why couldn't you come, and fly back to meet the Englishman?"

"I have no answer," he said. "But I know I can't."

"I should have met with the English," she said, clearing a place on the table for Memboury's map of Istanbul. The map was finger soiled, dark at the folds, and ripped slightly. In a little box at the upper right were the city street names in Russian. She spread out the map with the back of her hand in a gesture as professional as a general. Then she put on her half glasses, humming as if she were alone, scrutinizing the map.

"The best place is about here," she said. "Two kilometers up this hill. There's a *han* called the 'Mouse Hole' which will do."

"Which street?"

"Persembe Pazar. There are bad features about it, but it would be good for hiding. Kurds stay there because it is cheap. There's a back way which you can use, and the area is crowded with local people."

"What about the hotel the Englishman gave me?"

"I thought you didn't want the English to know where you are."

"I have to trust them."

"That's the shame of it," she said. "You have to trust them, but they've given you every reason not to trust them."

"Who can I trust?"

"Me," she said. "Listen carefully. Every Turk on that hill will know who you are and what you're doing. They talk, the men, not the women. The men gossip, but only among themselves. Fortunately they will never speak to a Russian, even under the gun. And they hate the English. The English will not find out where you are, unless you blunder. This is very serious: stay near the rooms."

"I wish you were hiding and I was going."

"I'm more resourceful than you," she said. "And more devious." She touched his arm. "I've always been better at plots."

"If you hadn't suspected Isymbal, we'd be in the camps."

"He wasn't difficult," she said. "Fine friend, making advances to me. It made me suspicious of Merkulov. After Vsevolod's arrest I knew you were next."

"I was never aware of what he was doing."

"I know," she said. "That's why I love you."

He tilted his head toward her, not touching, but close, and not talking. He wondered if these were the last moments with her, whether he would be dead in ten days, whether she would ever receive her medical treatment which precipitated these terrible risks. Like a juggernaut, circumstances had been sent in motion, could not be reversed, nor could the direction be predicted.

"I will stay in my rooms. What else?"

"If I don't hear from you in two weeks, I'll come back. Meet me on the sea side of the Galata at morning prayer. There will be less people. Write it down in your book. The sixteenth."

"How will you come back?"

"It will be easier for me to come back than for you to escape by yourself."

"I'll be waiting," he said. "That relieves me. The hope of seeing you sustains me. Two weeks is not a long time. If the English renege, I will have you to think about. I can stay away from the brigade for that long."

"They're easy," she said. "They have no skill, and they're so obvious: the grey coats, the gloves, even in summer; the slouch, the gold rims. They look like toys. Stay in your room and you'll know it if they're around. They stand out like aching teeth. They're not your worry, the English are."

"Yes."

"If they fail, I'll come back and fetch you."

"I feel much better."

"We have each other," she said. "Nothing more. We mustn't depend on anyone but ourselves, so we have to plan."

"Will we ever see Moscow again?"

"Don't be sentimental," she said. "You never liked Moscow." She put her hand on Sergei's head in a gesture more maternal than conjugal. "Wherever we were you never missed Moscow for one moment."

"I longed for it because you were there."

"We have to think of each other," she said. "It will help us take chances."

"I'll remember that."

She touched the end of his nose. "Be a good soldier. On your way, now. I'll be waiting for you, at the bridge."

He stood up.

"The best goodbyes are the shortest," she said. "Go."

With a failed salute, he smiled, turned and walked resolutely in the direction he had come.

8

John Reed could have offered Sarkov a ride, at least part way, to his dacha, if he had seen the Russian, but Reed was not looking to his right when the limousine passed Sarkov at the Galata Sarayi.

Reed had his own anxieties. Not only was he devising questions for Colonel Tor, but he was troubled that he could not prevent Ambassador Peterson from becoming involved in an affair which he would surely ruin.

As soon as he had finished talking with Peterson, Reed called Tor who summoned him to a cafe in the old section of the city.

Reed had come to depend on Tor in extraordinary circumstances. The colonel had developed, in Reed's estimation, from a comic to a mythic figure. During his first few months in Turkey, Reed believed Tor to be part of the Turkish farce. His first impression was that Tor oversaw the flimsy Turkish Intelligence, such as it was, and that he went about chasing Albanian hashish traffickers and Greek jewel thieves; but then Reed uncovered Tor's involvement in CICERO and his instigating and negotiating the treaty for the Credits which England advanced to Turkey soon after the war. Reed came to believe that the Colonel was not only astute, but clever, very political, and powerful. Reed discovered that Tor's power in the city was nearly complete, the only exception being that he exercised his power anonymously. In the span of ten days, Tor blocked the contract for

German shipping from African ports and rounded up and helped convict a Turkish band of murderers who had victimized foreigners in the city, and did both with only a few knowing the force behind the acts.

In the course of his investigation Reed found out that Tor was enormously grateful to the Crown for the Credits, and would do whatever he was asked for England. So Reed asked. Most Turkish politicians were hostile toward the Crown, but Tor was sensitive to English requests and quick to respond. What disturbed Reed was not the man and his favors, but rather the places he selected for their meetings.

The two never met in a customary place, like Tor's office at Sagmalcilar prison. Always it was at some unlikely, teeming place, like the Kabatas Landing stage, or the hot room of the Galatasaray Mamami. It was unsettling to have to roam the souks, probing for the right street, and then making enquiries, just to find the colonel in a filthy, hot, cellar. The places of assignation were so foreign to a westerner, especially an Englishman that Reed was "put off" so much so that he asked to see Tor only when it was absolutely necessary, like today. He was uneasy at the prospect of meeting Tor in this cafe.

The limousine rumbled through Galatasary Square, down Postacilar Sokak, by the Tekke, the whirling dervish monastery, past the tower, and over the Galata Bridge to the old section.

The Galata bridge not only joins the old section of Istanbul to the new, but it also connects Europe and Asia, West and East. The new section of the city, the Beyoglu, is more fashionable. The old section suffers from a resistance to anything modern. It is old rather than ancient. Once called Byzantium, it was old when Constantine established the capital of the world there in 340. It is full of grandeur and mystery, but mystery of the wrong kind: sudden death. In one expanse of its history Byzantium had 107 califs, 34 of whom died of natural causes! The foreigner would do well to exercise caution.

The limousine bumped along a sokak which had contracted from a street into a road to a footpath so narrow that the limousine could not pass. Reed got out and walked the last hundred yards to the end. A money changer rested his head on his hand on a box while he listened to caz music. He refused to move until Reed shook him. He lifted his head and directed Reed to a rope ladder which seemed to hang down to the river.

The rope did not extend to the water but ended at a level below where there was a native cafe which, like most cafes in the old section, was a poor imitation of La Tour in Paris.

Like all of old Istanbul, the cafe lacked refinement. No care had been taken in furnishings or cleaning. It smelled like a barracks and looked like the anteroom of a jail. Its saving feature was that it was open on two sides to the elements. Reed brushed himself off and sat near the rope, as far away from the center of the cafe as he could, and waited for instructions. They were a long time coming. He drank two rakis before a waiter with split shoes approached and stood too close. Reed would not have acknowledged him except the waiter's greasy napkin reeked of stale tobacco and onions.

"What is it?" Reed asked.

The waiter had large eyes, crops for brows, and a quarter-inch part in the middle of his hair. He looked like a lynx. "What?" Reed repeated.

"You are invited," the waiter said and motioned toward the lavatory.

If toilet facilities measure the advancement of a civilization, as someone has said, then Turkey is neolithic. The large latrine into which Reed walked was not a lavatory by any western standard, but a sewer, a cesspool without leechings. In front was the trough, a standing pool of excrement. There were three defecating poles. On his right and left the walls were papered in pink, on one hung an antique portrait of a sultan, dangling off center, with sayings from the Koran, and on the other the pink paper was soiled where too many men had rested their hands. Behind him a mirror encompassed the entire wall, even the door: Turkish men like to watch themselves evacuate. Tilting back on a cane chair, where one slip would have toppled him into the swamp, Colonel Tor rested his head against one of the defecating poles.

"What's that on your tie?" He asked.

"Mustard," Reed answered, holding out his tie and looking down until his chin tucked into his sternum. He looked like a chastised schoolboy.

"Mustard goes well with *lahana dolmasi*," Tor said. "You shouldn't spill it on your clothes, especially a Leander tie. It's difficult to get out."

Reed swung his head and reached for the door. The Colonel did not seem to be affected by the foul smell or the portly flies, but Reed was nauseated. "Do we have to talk in here?"

"Certainly not," Tor said, righting himself, flicking his cigarette in the pool, and looking around like a tour director.

Outside, he made a gesture of dismissal to the waiter and the one customer. When they were seated Tor asked, "You want a favor?"

"I'd like you to transport a woman and two children to Nicosia."

There was a pause. Tor was waiting for the rest. Finally he said, "What's the favor in that? She could arrange passage in twenty minutes, and you in ten."

"She's the wife of the Russian Vice Consul."

Tor pushed back his chair and looked up at the ceiling. He let out a soft whistle.

"I've told you a great deal in a short time, haven't I? Maybe more than I should."

"What does it mean? My imagination is working." He pointed toward his temple.

"What are you thinking?"

"I don't like to guess," Tor said. "You know that." He was quite serious. "What about the husband? Where is he?"

"Truthfully, I don't know."

"All right, I'll guess," Tor said. "I thought you might have hidden him. No. You let him off on his own and he's run to Edirne or Yalova to wait for negotiations. Was that wise? Anyone can shoot him and be a hero. Anyone. He couldn't be too valuable. Vice Consul. How high in the NKVD?"

"Major."

"Hmm."

"He's the highest ranking intelligence officer to defect since the revolution."

"What's he bringing?"

"Information."

"Be cautious, John. Be cautious. If he's bringing secrets and nothing more, he won't have leverage with London."

"What he showed me was quite substantial."

"Because you hadn't seen it before. But suppose you had? And suppose there was other information that he didn't know, but you did? Suppose his information is useless except to some functionary like himself? Then what would you do if you were London?"

Reed was silent.

"Let's look at it another way," Tor said. "Did he give reasons?"

"He said it was his wife. She has heart trouble. That's true. She does."

"Russians," Tor said with disdain. "It's usually the fleshpots. They acquire a taste for luxury and will do anything to keep it."

Reed held up his hands. "He said it was his wife."

"So he wants to exchange useless information for a new life, citizenship, a great deal of money, and medicine for his wife?"

"Yes."

"There has to be more. It's not enough. Your McKenzie will not go along. It's simple economics, like me doing favors for you so Britain will continue the Credits."

"What more can he bring?"

"I don't know, unless you tell me, or I ask him. Those are the rules. He can't expect you to whisk his wife to the best medicine and do all the rest for him without something substantial in return. That would be bad business. And I submit he knows that."

"These aren't the rules I learned at Bletchley."

"I am guessing again, but I expect that your Russian friend does not expect to survive."

"Then why defect in the first place?"

"I don't know. You say it is the wife. It could be that Checka is chasing him. Any number of things. We'll go along with what he says until we know better. What's the date for the meeting?"

"The fifteenth."

"Ten days from now," Tor said. "Did he select the day?"

"Yes."

"It doesn't give London much time to develop a plan and send someone, does it?"

"How much time do they need?"

"You still don't understand, do you?" Tor asked. "Now listen." He leaned forward like an enthusiastic teacher. "If your Russian is brought in, there will be a trade, a major contingency, like," he waved his hand and looked about. He was enjoying the muse. "Like a public embarrassment, the elimination of a spy, the placing of an agent in a sensitive place, the protection of a secret which London knows the Russians don't know. Something important like that."

"Isn't information important?"

"It's least important. We share one another's secrets. There are no secrets. No, the game has gone far beyond that."

"I don't understand," Reed said. "I thought spying was collecting intelligence."

"I know," Tor said. "Most people do. It's easy to assume that because of books and what you hear, but today the work is about disgracing the other side, any way you can."

"Wouldn't this defection do that?"

"In a small way," Tor answered. "It won't bring Beria down, just soil his reputation, and not for long."

"You're a fox, Colonel," Reed said. "And I never fail to learn from you."

"It's not enough to be sly," Tor said, "when the bear is after you. The fox is no match for a beast like that. What can he do against the strength of such a creature? The bear is king of the woods, and the continent. Who can stop him? A fox? If the bear wants to swim in warm water and plunk his dirty arse in the middle of this city, who can stop him? Do you know?"

"I know it's been bothering you," Reed said. "Isn't it strange about the fox? They say he can hear the squeak of a mouse at thirty paces. He can hear the bear long before the dumb creature knows he's wandering close. Couldn't the fox distract the bear? I mean if he was desperate as well as clever, couldn't he fool the stupid bear?"

"I've been trying to think, thought of nothing else for weeks. Do you know that the bears do not hibernate? No, he sleeps to keep from gorging himself. It isn't hibernation. He has to sleep or he will die from eating. It's the only way nature can stop the brute from killing himself."

"So you think Stalin will have to sleep after gobbling up Germany, and Poland, and C, and Romania, and the ports?"

"Potsdam ended last week and now they are dividing up the minor spoils.'

"And Istanbul is precious to the Russians."

"Stalin has made it known, he wants a warm port, access to the Mediterranean. Here." He leaned forward, "Whatever happens better happen in the next week." He stood. "Today I will make plans to bring this woman out."

"Perhaps our Russian friend will be so desperate that he might offer a solution?"

"Maybe so," Tor said. "But today I will take care of his lady and her children. Babek, I know the section, and the dachas. They will be flown out tomorrow. Is that all?"

"For now, yes," Reed said. "If all goes well, we'll have to fly out the husband on the fifteenth."

"That will be more difficult."

"I know," Reed said. "But I have time to work on the papers and the diplomacy. I think I can do it." Then, "I remember," Reed said, "the childhood story of the fox out-witting the stork. Since then, I've always liked foxes. I hope you have the same success." They shook hands.

"He's no match for the bear. I'm afraid of the bear, my friend, more afraid than I have ever been in my life. What can one do against the strength of the bear? He is king of the woods, and the Baltics. Who can stop him? Who can distract him when he wants to swim in the warm water? Who? Can a fox?"

9

"This is a Mercedes; it can zoom like a falling star," Yuki said. He was talking to the two boys in the back seat. "But I never go faster than twenty." He was Colonel Tor's chauffeur and confidant. "Do you have bad roads outside Moscow?" His chest rested on the steering wheel, his forehead nearly touching the windshield. He was studying the alluvial soil for solid places to drive.

"Where are we going?" Irina asked. "Eskesehir? My husband said the airfield was in the South."

"It is South," Yuki answered. "But we have to go West to go South."

"Of course we have to go West to go South," she said. "This is Turkey." Yuki understood the sarcasm, stared at her in the mirror, but said nothing. "Will my husband be waiting? You picked us up so early. I thought he might be coming with us."

"The Colonel will explain," Yuki answered, cocking his head toward Colonel Tor who was somewhere South waiting for them. "All I know is that your husband is still in the city, at Pazar. I don't approve."

"It's a good place," she said, "if you have no where to go."

"If he is hiding from Russians, why join them?"

"He looks for friends," she said. "You would too, if you were running. Is he in danger?"

"No, not yet."

She wondered how long it would take for Sergei to find out that she had left the country. She was trying to digest the grief of another separation. "Are you watching out for him?"

"We don't walk him on a leash, like a pet," Yuki said. "But we watch him, yes, from across the sokak. He doesn't take twenty steps and we know where he's going. But now we have to protect him from the brigade. Two came in last night. They're like bees. We can handle them, as long as there is no swarm. Two buzzed in from the South, from here, and we tempted them with our sweets. We can manage one or two or even ten, but who can control an angry swarm?"

"The *Istrebitelli*," she said. "The embassy must have sent for them. What are you going to do?"

"What can we do?" He asked rhetorically. "Istanbul is a city of delay. We give directions: one assassin asks a peasant in Suadiye if he has seen a Russian who looks like your husband. The peasant nods, scratches himself, spits, and points toward Ergue. They buzz there for half a day. That night the police stop them for questioning, examine papers; the others stay for support. Two days go by and the sergeant gives a hint where your husband may be, and off they go. It goes on and on."

"But they catch him. He's not good at hiding."

"No, he isn't," Yuki said. He tossed his head toward the right, south, where they would meet Colonel Tor. "But he is good at concealing."

"You think my husband will be safe?"

Yuki looked back at her. The automobile was barely moving. "I bet the lottery every day," he said. "I know the odds but still I the wager. I have as much chance winning as

you do of putting through a telephone call on our Central. I
do it because I am a gambling man. I would wager anything
I own that your husband will survive. Do you want to know
why the odds are so good?"

"You're going to tell me about this Colonel whether I
like it or not."

"You don't want to hear, but I will tell you anyway."

Before he could declaim, Irina asked, "Is he some sort
of divinity?"

"Make up your mind after you have spoken to him and
hear what he is going to do for you."

"Why should I trust him?"

"Wrong question. Right answer: you have no choice."

"Why is he doing this?" She asked. "It has to be politics. I can't understand what it is. How does my husband's
desertion help you? There is something missing, something
I don't know. I will have to ask."

"Yes, ask," Yuki said. "Everyone asks and everyone
receives an answer. He will answer. He will tell you that
you will be safe, that you will be in Cyprus tonight, and that
you must not worry about your husband. He will be safe.
That I know. Why is he doing this? I don't know. I will, one
day. But I don't now. I do know that the Colonel fears for
his city. He is terrified that the Allies will make a deal with
the Russians, a deal where we will lose our beloved city. Do
you think that will happen?"

"We lost six million," Irina said. "Stalin will get what
he wants."

"Like all glacier beasts, the Russians love warm water,
especially the Dardanelles. If you want to know what the
Colonel dreads, it is that. He fears losing Istanbul worse
than he fears his own death."

"Do all Turks fear Russians?"

"Is fear and hate the same thing?"

"They are with me."

"My father was a Kurd from Anatolia. I grew up hearing about the slaughter of the peasants and the famine in Urgurp."

"We Russians were blamed for that, but wasn't it the Rumanians?"

"I was told it was Russians from Orstrecht. They had slant eyes, like Mongolians." As an afterthought he said, "They tortured my uncle, red ants walked over him."

"It's wrong to blame," Irina said. "Russia is so large. There are eleven time zones in my country, eleven. And thirty seven different languages. A hundred years ago the boundary between Russia and Turkey was that bridge," she nodded toward the Galata which could not be seen.

"I have Russian ancestors," Yuki said.

"Most Turks do," Irina said. "I have Turkish blood."

"My father was pure Turk. Thank Allah."

She looked across the water toward the city and the ludicrous architecture, and the filth of the Marmora. They drove past a cement factory and the Florence Nightingale hospital. "Are we going to Ismir, or Ismit?" She asked.

"Half-way between Lake Sapanca and Ismit," Yuki answered. He turned his head and she caught the vapor of garlic. He smiled, showing gold. "Don't worry. You will be safe. This man lives his word. You will be in perfect health by the next rain."

"What do you know about my health?"

"I know that you had a thrombosis, left ventricle, your third attack, and that the Colonel has decided to provide you with the best doctor in the world."

"He has? Who is that?"

"I don't know. I heard, but if I said a name, it would be something I heard, but did not understand. The Colonel has told no one, not even the pilot."

"Will my husband come?"

"Soon," Yuki answered. "He will come at the proper time."

"You're full of information, aren't you?"

"I'm telling you all I know."

"Another question I will have to ask the Colonel."

They drove behind a donkey cart. The farmer remained proprietarily in the middle of the road, even though Yuki sounded the horn and drew close to the cart, and then the fender touched the right wheel of the cart. The farmer did not budge. "These farmers refuse to accept the automobile," Yuki said. "He believes that the path belongs to the donkey and that the automobile is an invention of Satan. How will we ever catch up with the modern world?"

"Why would you want to catch up with the modern world?"

"Why do you say that?"

"He moves from place to place in his cart and never knew the war was on."

"No, and he doesn't know that airplanes fly to Cyprus in two hours either," Yuki said. "In the whole of his life he has never traveled beyond Tekirdag. His father died at thirty, an old man, from typhus, and his mother wrinkled up like a date. It's easy to be sentimental about peasant life as long as you don't have to sleep on cement and smell the goats."

"I've never been accused of being sentimental," Irina said. "I've learned that I could die at any moment. Then I had to accept my husband's problem. All in six months. A person like me needs all the truth she can find."

"You're not going to die," Yuki said looking at the children. "You have too much to do."

"Earth is the place for caring," Irina said, clutching the two boys. "I don't know where it's likely to be better."

"Is it strange for you, leaving your country?"

"I haven't lived in Russia for twelve years. This one was born in Brussels."

"But you won't go back now, ever."

"No."

"The other side will provide. They did for Vodoroff. He lives on Capri, drinking red wine, and doing nothing."

"Vodoroff is a traitor."

"Watch your language," Yuki said. "Treachery depends on your view, on which side of Arrarat you are standing; traitor on the north, hero on the south."

"Aren't we fortunate we're in the South."

"Don't forget, Russians have been the enemies of Turkey since Hector. We have always known our enemies. The West is too young to recognize their enemies."

"I wonder if there are nationalities in the next world."

"I don't want to go if Turks don't live together."

"Most likely you won't."

Following the irony, Yuki was silent. Was he silent because she reinforced his enmity for Russians, or had she placed a doubt in his mind about all allegiances?

He turned off the main road, if it could be called a road, onto a dirt path which led to a barn and a small house. "Go inside the first door and wait," he ordered.

He sped toward the barn, along a section of grass, too close to a pistachio tree. He brushed a defiant goat who wore blue beads to ward off the evil eye, and finally the automobile came to rest in a ditch. The back wheels sunk in the red mud, and the more he revved the motor, the more the wheels dug in. Touching ground soil, the machine jolted out and Yuki spun the wheel dangerously, hitting the right corner of the barn.

"Did you like the ride?" he asked the wide-eyed boys.

"They're not aware of the danger," Irina said. "I hope the pilot has more sense." She said backing out of the rear seat.

"You forgot your luggage," Yuki shouted.

"We're not taking anything," she said.

"Why not?"

She did not answer. The man was right. She should have taken some necessary things. After years of marriage to an intelligence officer without guile, she should have learned that she must rely on her own stealth, and common sense.

Yuki stood near his door as if waiting for further questions.

"Tell me, was our gypsy maid one of your people?"

"Certainly."

"Two weeks ago I found a book by Koy. I said to myself, 'how could a woman who not only reads, but reads Koy be housekeeping for the hated Russians?' Then when she ate pork I knew she was too smart to be a maid. Did she tell you? I asked her where her shells were. She didn't answer. The other day I asked her what 'tipping the goblet' meant and I could see she was angry."

"She was good at watching, but not at deceiving."

"Don't be difficult with her. She did good work," Irina said. "We expect to be watched, so we are watching. Who are more suspicious than espionage people? I wanted to know who she was working for."

"You thought your own people?"

"Does your Colonel watch you?"

"Of course," Yuki said straightening himself. "If I were he, I would watch me." He smiled, then gave the order, "Go inside there. A woman will pour perfumed water on your hands. Rub the water on your face, like this. It is a term of respect, a welcome. Then she will offer you a tulip glass. Drink the contents, very slowly. Understand?"

Irina assented. She knew the intricacies of Turkish courtesy.

10

Irina was distracted from washing her hands, and drinking tea from a tulip glass, by the man and his horse.

Colonel Tor looked more like a military man than a policeman. He wore a khaki shirt with a leather strap extending from his left shoulder to his right waist, riding breeches, and shiny boots. In his right hand he held a groom's brush and in his left the bridle of an Arabian stallion. He was whispering in the horse's ear as if the two were plotting an escape through the sky. Both the man and the horse were expecting her, she was sure. Tor asked, as if he had known her a long time, "Do you know what kind he is?"

"An *asil*," she answered. "In my part of the world we don't see animals like him, except in shows. Why is he here?"

"Do you know the *cirit*?"

"Yes. It's your game."

"Would I have an unfair advantage if I rode him?" Tor asked. "See the curve of the crest, how close the angle is to the throttle? He's made for sport. My friends will complain when they see what he can do."

"They'll be right," she said.

He walked in front and the horse lifted his head. He patted the jibbah. "He has more brains than some men."

"You can tell the pure blood by the nodes on the back," she said walking toward the animal.

"Don't bother counting," he said. "There are twenty three vertebrae. Not the trace of another strain."

"He's magnificent," she said. "I had an Orloff when I was a child, but he was weak in comparison." She ran her hand along the neck muscles to the withers and down to the canon bone. The gesture was so expert that the horse did not flinch.

"You see," Tor said. "He's perfect. I'll never lose."

"Aren't you worried about cold weather?"

"Should I?" Tor asked. "Look at his windpipe. There isn't any heaves. He could breathe in the heavens. Look for yourself."

"They say these *kochlani* can canter for hours," she said, "but always in hot weather."

"Every horse in the world would choose cold weather," Tor said. "It isn't the cold I worry about, it's bog spavins, from the quick turns." He walked around to the side and handed her the bridle. "Ride?"

"I haven't ridden for years," she answered. She did want to ride; she was impatient with the preliminaries. She wanted news of her husband and she wanted to know what Tor planned for her and her children. Although the stallion was exquisite, the only ride she wanted was a plane ride to Cyprus.

"You're worried about your husband?"

"Yes. Where is he? Is he coming with us?"

"No, he's not here," Tor said. "He's taken a risk only a desperate man would take, and he's entrusted you to me."

"It's not you. He's trusting the English."

"Where is the reason in that?"

"He was forced to trust them. And I have no alternative but to trust you."

"Tell me," Tor asked, "why is he staying behind?"

"The English ordered him," she answered. "The negotiations might begin early."

"Why not fly out, and come back?"

"Would he be safer in Cyprus?"

"No," Tor answered, "no safer than here, unless he docs something foolish."

"He does rash things, not foolish."

"Even so, I will watch him."

"How did you get involved in this?" She asked. "Is it because we are Russians?"

"Is it as impossible as it sounds?"

"You won't answer my question," she insisted.

"I will, if you answer mine."

Silently she assented.

"Why this desperate move?"

"My heart trouble," she answered.

"Is that all?"

"Aren't motives always complex?"

"Couldn't you be treated in Russia?"

"The government wouldn't allow it," she answered. "There is one physician in Leningrad, but they wouldn't give me permission to see him."

"So you leave everything—in the hope that Doctor White will help?"

"Yes, White."

"Why wouldn't they allow you to see the man in Leningrad? Is it Gogol?"

"Yes, it is," she said. "They are suspicious of my husband's ideology."

"But there is Redin in Moscow. He knows as much about the heart, and Cabol, the Frenchman, who is teaching at the university?"

"You don't think it's my heart, do you?"

"I'm not interrogating you," Tor said. "I'm not going to arrest you, I'm going to help you. It would be better if I knew. You are a Solanov. I read about your ancestors in Tolstoy." He patted the stallion. "Pure blood."

"Me or the horse?"

"Both," Tor said. "Mehmet knows he's a noble beast. Look at him. You too, you know your blood is pure. But you are in the wrong place with these new Russians. They detest nobility."

"My grandfather was loyal to the Czar. He fought against them, at Manezh. After the revolution they accused him of having the noble blood, of being decent. He came from the old order. After his trial he lived in disgrace in Leningrad, but he was too exceptional. In the recent war when they needed a true general to shut down the Germans, they called on him and forgave him for his loyalty to God and the Czar. When he won the battle they gave him a medal. My mother, his daughter, studied medicine. If you examined my family as much as you researched the heart specialists, you know who she was."

"She corresponded with Osler in London," he said.

"If she were alive, I would not be sick."

"I didn't have time to read her monograph on myocardial thrombosis," Tor said. "I didn't read Groote's response either, but I do know that he based his work on your mother's study."

There was no room for deception with this extraordinary man who uncovered information so quickly. She decided to answer all his questions, even with candor. Most likely he knew the answers, but her answers would strengthen his trust. "My husband was passed over in February. Late April we suspected the authorities were moving against us. They did. He was assigned here in June."

Tor said, "I know. I know about Merkulov and his maneuvering. But the reasons for your husband's demotion were different. It wasn't ideology at all, but an exercise of power, two levels above. Your husband aligned with Shevelov, didn't he? That was a mistake. Shevelov is being eased out, and the insult to your husband is the first slap, that's all."

"How do you know that? How did you find out about me, in, in, such a short time?"

"It's not difficult," Tor said. "You know that. Intelligence is the same in every country. We share information. We have the same problems. It's like business, all of us develop methods of finding out. We Turks have a highly developed system, three thousand years of experience."

"Do you know where my husband is now?"

"At this moment he is sitting in his room at the Panuk Palas."

"He said he was going to Sirkici, near the Post Office."

"That's like your Metropole, full of foreigners. He must have realized that the foyer of the Sirkici is the most dangerous place in Istanbul. People who want to hide make the mistake of drifting toward foreigners, when they should stay with local people."

"Did you warn him?"

"No," Tor said. "No one has been near enough to talk with him. He moved on his own. He will be safe, as long as he doesn't go out."

"I told him to stay inside."

"Yes," Tor said. "I can see that he would be wise if he followed your advice."

"Will you protect him?"

Tor nodded. "But you know about political immunity. We have it here. Embassy people have rights beyond the ordinary; obligations too. We respect them. My men will watch and see, but there may be trouble from the embassy."

"You won't interfere if they arrest?"

"We can distract them. But interfere, no."

"Your driver told me the *Istrebetelli* are here."

"You know them?"

"The young ones," she said, "like Popakov, are sinister. They murder on command. The old ones are drunkards, the residue of Section Two. I don't think they will find Sergei, not, if you help."

"There will be others. What should I look for?"

"I don't know," she said. "Sergei was involved in an assassination last year. Beria ordered one man to do the killing. Maybe he'll do it again, send one man."

"Yes, I know," Tor said. "I'll watch for him."

"I've answered your questions, now you answer mine." Irina said. "Why are you doing this? I have tried to reason to your motives, but I can't imagine what they are. It starts with politics."

"Don't all motives begin with politics, or money," he said. "The truth is I have been trying to establish an advantage. It is here, but I don't see it." He patted the horse.

"Against the Russians?"

Tor nodded. "I play Bridge with your Ambassador. He is not a good bridge player; he is a chess player. He understands force and facts, but bridge is finesse. He's not good at bridge. If I have an advantage against Russians, it will be with finesse."

"Would you tell him you are protecting Sergei?"

"To tell would be reward enough," Tor said. He pulled on the bridle, as if it were a light switch. "But is it wise to reveal finesse?"

"Your driver said that you are worried about a Russian occupation," she said. It was a statement, not a question. He stopped moving and stared at her. "You asked me why I was frightened!"

"Now I'll tell you what torments me," Tor said. "Stalin craves Istanbul, more than Berlin."

"Berlin has no access to the Mediterranean," she said. "What can you do to prevent him?"

"Someone asked me that yesterday," Tor answered. "What can a little man in a poor country, which was on the wrong side in the war, do to stop the Russians? What can he do?"

"Are you certain it will happen?"

"This morning a Russian cruiser the size of a mosque steamed through. It was a warning of what's to come."

"In Germany the Allies are dividing the spoils."

"Would that they were dividing," he said. "As you said, Stalin will get what he wants. There will be no restrictions on his pillage. Who will stop him? The new man, Attlee? Truman? Amateurs. The old thief will usurp the continent, and my beloved city with it. Who can stop him?"

"You are so remote here, vulnerable," she said. "Istanbul will be like the sweet after the borscht."

"You are very wise," Tor said. "You see what I see, but you also have the advantage of being Russian, of knowing how these thugs reason, and now I am doing you an incalculable favor."

"And?"

"I want your advice," he said.

"First, ride the horse." She ordered

"You want a few minutes to think?"

Without waiting for an answer, he mounted the stallion, directed him down the path at a quick gallop, turned after an hundred yards. On the return Tor did a foot stand, like an acrobat, and then stopped and dismounted within a foot of where he began. "He was slow on the turn, because of the sand."

"If a *gifit* rides him, he will learn about sand quickly," she said. "More you should worry about the stigmatism."

"What?"

"Most Arabians have it," she said. "It is easy to correct. Ride him straight, not from the side, and don't extend the stick too close to the eyes, no more than this," she extended her hands about eighteen inches. "He'll bolt."

"What about the stigmatism?" he asked.

"It's good," she said. "It helps him focus. That's why he keeps his head so straight in the run."

Tor looked at the horse's eyes, then looked back at Irina and smiled. "Before you give me advice, may I give you a warning?"

"What?"

"How long were you in Washington?" He asked. "Four years?"

"Three."

"I was adding the nine months in New York," Tor replied.

"Yes, four altogether."

"While you were in the US was LA Byzov your contact?"

"Yes."

"He is still there," Tor said. "How long will you be in Boston before Byzov knows? Would you say?"

She was becoming reckless in response to Tor's inexhaustible information. "A matter of weeks."

"Byzov works for Abel, am I correct?"

"Abel is chief of operations." She had never spoken so openly. Her husband would not like her telling these secrets.

"What is the code name for the network in the US? Is Myaznikov part of it?"

"I don't know what they call it," she said. "But Myaznikov works from New York."

"And he was instructor of extermination for Checka," Tor said. "Did you know that?"

"I knew he was involved in that, yes."

"If you go to Boston, Myaznikov will come after you with a pellet gun. How long would you hide from him? Hmm. I won't allow it."

"I won't be safe anywhere."

"Maybe not, but there are more isolated places than the United States."

"Where?"

"I thought you might have reasoned to them, by now," Tor said.

"If it isn't White, it must be Doctor Groote," she said.

Instead of assenting, Tor took her arm and beckoned to the boys. He led them between the barn and the house. "Take the boys in there and prepare them. It will be a three hour ride."

"We won't see you again?" She asked.

"No," he answered. "You must not think that my resources are unlimited. They aren't. When you reach your destination I will have no way of protecting you. But I am not worried. You will do well."

"You're like me," she said. "You prefer short goodbyes," she walked up to him. "Before I leave I want to say this: the solution to your problem lies in a public embarrassment, something monstrous that will capture the attention of the world." She turned in a circle, but continued to talk, as if he was not present. "It should be so horrible that all the newspapers will publish it, on the first page, all over the world. The leaders in Potsdam will read it, and perhaps, just perhaps, they will delay the usurpation for a few days. If they stop and reflect how magnificent you are, how precious." She was nearly finished, but said, "You need time. If you're not part of the spoils this week, it could happen that you will never be."

He was wide-eyed.

"Now here is the key," she continued. She put her finger on his tunic, as if he were a school boy. "The brigade is the arm of the Central Committee. Humiliate them in front of the world, and your work is done."

Without waiting for a response, she turned her back on him and walked between the buildings toward the airfield. She could hear the plane, but not see it, as yet. She might have stayed and devised a plan, but it was not her place, and she knew it. Near the end of the corridor she did look back. In silhouette Tor seemed taller, and, with his legs spread, he resembled an ancient hero. Although she could not see his face, she knew he was smiling.

PART II

LONDON

1

Sir Alfred McKenzie, the Control of MI5, had arranged his London office to suit his interests, which were investigation and analysis. He had positioned his Second Empire desk four feet from the two windows which were wide and long. On either side of the desk he had placed his Windsor chairs so that, on bright August mornings such as this one, the sun beamed on whoever sat in those chairs. Like criminals under klieg lights, the subjects could be examined and analyzed. They might squint and, as their eyes adjusted to the glare, might be able to make out Control's silhouette, the shadow of paper on the desk. The four phones, but they would not see him as he saw them.

The rest of the room was spare. Maps, drawings of airplanes, and cheap prints hung on the walls. Next to the door was a shelf of bottles: a blue one, a lavender, and a red, but all of these were relics of the last Control, Sinclair. McKenzie had not bothered to take them down.

McKenzie was not idiosyncratic like Sinclair, who affected green ink and long pauses in his speech. He had been fascinated by airplanes, and aspidistra. McKenzie's one interest was people, his one obsession, their reactions.

This day he was standing behind his desk, his fingertips resting on the desk pad. Two other men were in the office, but neither sat. One stood in the darkest recesses of the room, and the other faced Control from the left.

McKenzie was not looking at either man, but down at his pad. He was waiting for their tempers to cool.

"It's not necessary to rifle through wastepaper baskets looking for suspicious material," the tall man in the dark said. He spoke in a moderate tone, his lips set in prolonged skepticism. He stooped slightly, as a man might who had an old breathing problem. He was not belligerent; he hadn't the energy.

"I'm not allowing any further leaks," the man near "C" said. He looked for reaction from "C" and then continued. "No more unlocked filing cabinets, and no more brief cases going out unopened. That will be the rule." This man had a bulldog face, frozen in ferocity. Unlike the man in the dark, he was inclined toward rage. He found many reasons to be provoked, and he expended his energy injudiciously. He was one of those people who chose their skirmishes unwisely.

"C" raised his hand as an umpire might, for a recess. "Gentlemen," he said twice. "I did not summon you to haggle over security." After a few seconds he continued. "I want your advice. A pouch came through Section F this morning, containing the news that a major in the NKVD has approached our man in Istanbul, to defect."

As expected, the news of the defection diffused the anger like a spark of sulfur diffuses a rank smell.

"Have either of you ever heard of," "C" asked, picking up a sheet of paper and turning it over, "Sergei Sarkov? He's NKVD, transferred from second directorate Moscow Center to Vice Consul Istanbul four months ago." He looked at each man for a response.

"There was a Shahkov, Geli, in Kenya during the early thirties while I was there," the tall man said. He coughed slightly.

"No, this is Sarkov, with an 'r'. Sergei," "C" answered.

"We must have a file on him," the short man near the desk said. He was still angry. "If he was an operator, or if he worked in Moscow, we'll have a biography." He was Charles Carolyn, recently appointed chief of security, Section C. Carolyn was conservative, but it was not from inclination or interest. He had been driven into conservatism by the bewildering folly of the men in his family. Nearly all of them ended up rebelling in some unfashionable way. His father tried to live by Walter Pater's principles, but had died, exhausted, at an early age. An uncle championed Hitler, and a cousin became a yogi. As a boy Charles was confused by what he judged the foolishness of these men. He rebelled into conservatism and, like all converts, practiced his new faith with more vigor than those who are born to it.

"Would you collect whatever materials you have?" "C" asked.

"'Consul' you say?" the man in the dark asked. He sat down on a bench which was hidden. "Why would a diplomat of that stature leave his position? What does he stand to gain?"

"Vice Consul, actually," "C" corrected. "He's not asking for much, really. Twenty-seven thousand five hundred and the usual security. There are usable items in his gloss and hints that he might have more substantial information. I have already decided to go ahead with the transfer. I want your advice on method."

"What I don't understand is whether we are allies with the Russians, or not?" The tall man asked from the dark. He mumbled through the lozenge and then clicked it against his plate. Carolyn reddened again.

"C" saw the red.

"I know that the Russians are not allies with us. I am certain of that."

"C" held up his hand again. "There's nothing here about reasons "

"Could be a ruse," Davies said from the corner of the room. "It's difficult for me to believe that a consular official would give up his position for pounds sterling."

"It's not here," "C" said. "We'll find out. After we keep him under cover for three months, question him, what he knows, we'll have a clearer picture, I'm sure."

"I'm more afraid that the Russians are setting us up for a trick. How they love the public humiliation!" Carolyn said.

"C" answered, "Sarkov will have less freedom than if he were in Dartmoor. If it's a trick, it will be a dull one."

"Let's assume he's legitimate," Carolyn asked. "What's he bringing?"

"The outlines are here," "C" answered. "The geography of the new NKVD buildings: blueprints, key impressions, position of alarms, office plans."

Carolyn looked over toward Davies. "Looks like the Russians could tighten their security."

"C" went on. "He lists the network in Western Europe. On the last page he hints at the most important item. I'm sure you'll be interested."

"What?" Carolyn asked, seriously curious for the first time.

"He told Reed that he has the names of three Soviet penetration agents working in this building. They're top level people."

Carolyn walked around the desk and tried to read.

"It's only a hint," "C" said. "Just enough to make us curious."

"Well, he's done that," Carolyn said.

"Why should three names make Comrade Sarkov so important?" Davies asked. Though capable, he had fallen into saying things rashly, as a man might who had a prolonged spell of bad health. "Registry has the names of two hundred communist party members. Undoubtedly some of our people are on those lists. As a matter of fact, I'm probably registered."

"These are NKVD agents," "C" said. "Not sympathizers, or even card carriers."

"Some people hold to the communist theory quite seriously," Davies said.

"Any traitor can plead theory," Carolyn snapped. "I know there is information going out to the Soviets, have known for months. I also know that we treat communists in the firm like spoiled children, but if I find out they are working for Russia, they will be subject to the Emergency Powers Act just like the Germans. I like to think that I know my enemy." Carolyn slipped into his North Country accent, which he did when excited. It reminded the other two of his private school education and his Roman religion. In these moments Carolyn had as much authority as the janitor.

"Have you talked with Alexander about this?" Davies asked.

"B Section has been screaming about subversion. Here's their chance to prove it."

"I say we keep this quiet," Carolyn said. "Talk will drive these traitors to ground."

"I haven't talked with Alexander, but I have explained the situation to Sloan," "C" said.

"I wish you hadn't," Carolyn said.

"It's his area, double agents," Davies said.

"I'd rather have Alexander," Carolyn said. "He knows Russian, and his loyalty is not suspect."

"Inferring that Sloan is suspect," Davies said. "He was as thoroughly vetted as any man in the service." Davies walked back into the shadows.

"His file states 'nothing against'," Carolyn said. "Even though we know his sympathies, his communist friends, his activities in Gerard Street. He makes no bones about it."

"The man is absolutely first class," Davies said. "Westminster, Cambridge, a second in history, and the Athenaeum. I think it unfair to leap from socialist leanings to membership in the communist party," Davies said.

"I've already summoned him," "C" said. "He will do the planning on the Sarkov transfer."

Carolyn straightened and looked at "C" for an explanation. This time "C" looked away. Carolyn felt like a tradesman with a skill, and these men his employers. He was lionized in MI5 because he was efficient, and parsimonious. He had risen to director of security on ability, thoroughness, and a genius for detail, but not on class, education, or friends. Despite his suspicion of a class conspiracy, Carolyn was certain that their prejudice would not impede his work, but he was equally certain that "C" would never invite him to his home.

Davies coughed in earnest. After the clearing of the throat, the handkerchief to the mouth, the fumbling for a lozenge, the older man rose from the dark bench and took his leave.

The other two stood in deference.

"He should retire," Carolyn said just before the door closed.

"He has impeccable contacts," "C" said. "Even the backbenchers pass on the ledgers if they see Davies' initials. In his day espionage was all diplomatic. He thinks it degrading to round up sources."

"He wants espionage to be nice, as he is, but it's nice in the Latin sense, nasty."

"What have you found out about Sloan?" "C" asked. "Davies is on his way to tell him what you said."

"I have traces on all our people, even you," Carolyn said. "What I have on Sloan is strictly circumstantial, like the Walter Krivitsky list and the Sissmore report."

"Surely you wouldn't base an accusation on those?"

"I began there," Carolyn said. "But there are all kinds of suspicious activities. His name came up in the Springhall trial. Urens admitted to the prosecutor that he had a contact high up in this building. He didn't know the name, or so he said, but he said that the contact knew Gorski. Sloan entertains Gorski."

"It's hardly enough for an investigation," "C" said. "Sloan has been successful at Bletchley, and enormously successful in smoothing over the difficulties with the 'Indians.'"

"They're only suspicions," Carolyn said. He placed his right hand over his left and wiggled his thumbs in an imitation of flight. "But they made me fly back to his school days. He was in the marches," he said as he held up his hand to stop "C" from answering. "I know, you all were in '31, but this fellow did a curious thing: he went to Vienna, to a Soviet training school there, stayed for six months, took a wife who is a genuine Soviet agent, now working in Germany."

"His father married an Arab," "C" said, knowing it was not an argument. He added wistfully, "Even old Keynes was disillusioned with Labor in '31."

"As it goes on, Sloan's story becomes bizarre," Carolyn said. "He never bothered to divorce the woman, but took another when he came back here, and has four children by the second one."

"All the children are bastards."

"He doesn't care about that," Carolyn said. "These people have different standards. The first woman came here three or four times and stayed with the second woman and her children. To complicate the whole ménage, Sloan is currently seeing another woman. This one is the wife of a friend of his, a civil servant."

"You have been watching, haven't you?"

"I think treason is first, personal," Carolyn said, pointing to his heart, "then marital;" he pointed to his genitals, "and then national." He pointed to the flag. "One does not become a traitor without deliberation. Dante said that about Branca D'Oria. It's my work to vett all these people. Let me tell you, Sloan's file should be yellow."

"C" moved from behind the desk. "Suppose," he said, "this Sarkov exposes a leak here. What would you recommend? What should we do?"

"We cannot afford a trial *in camera*, can we? No more bad press."

"C" forced a smile. They had never spoken about leaks before. Carolyn had wanted to talk about treachery in the firm, but "C" skirted the issue, up to now. Leaks were inevitable, they both knew, as were their uncovering. "What else?"

"Train executioners, like the commie brigade from Karlshorst. I'll wager Sarkov has given those boys some thought."

"Publicity is no longer acceptable," "C" said. "That's the assumption. No trials, no parliamentary investigations, no headlines, no confessions. We are left with silent execution. There must be something else."

"Tolerance," Carolyn said. "Simply let the blighter know you're on to him and let him rot."

"Do nothing."

"Give him less and less to do," Carolyn said. "Now and again slip him false information to keep him and his friends happy, but always let him know we're on to him."

"Then what?"

"When he realizes what's happening, he slips off to Moscow and no one's the worse."

"It is dangerous, allowing a traitor to snoop around the files until he becomes bored."

"You know better than that, Alfred," Carolyn said. "Do we have any information the Russians don't have? There's a rumor going about that the Russians have the secret to the Atom, got it in Ottawa with no trouble." He walked to the window and looked out. "I'm fairly certain Austria was on to Redl for a long time. They let him stay on. Gave him less and less to do until he and his friends decided the game was up and he went to Moscow. He made a small fuss when he surfaced, but it was all anticlimactic."

"Intelligence was once a game of checkers," "C" said. "Now it's chess."

"It was always chess," Carolyn said, "which evolved from war. Some Chinese warlord hit upon it while he was waiting for a city to capitulate." He turned and pointed to a dossier on "C's" desk. "Is there anything in there we don't know? We know about Center's buildings, the abstelle in Western Europe, even the safe combinations, as if they were any use. What we don't know are those names. That's why this man is so important." "C" indulged himself in Carolyn's talk. "C" had more information than Carolyn, of course, and he rarely told his associate more than was necessary, but he found Carolyn's wit engaging, his judgment accurate, even with sparse information. "C" recognized Carolyn's sensitivity to university men, and tried to soothe him. Being first class himself, "C" thought his judgment on this matter impartial. He was mistaken. It was one of several areas where his prejudice interfered with his judgment.

"How should we proceed with Comrade Sarkov?"

"Get on with it," Carolyn said. "Gather the files, even though we know what they say. Contact the FO and get their approval. Two: brief the liaison. Who will it be? No matter. Three; make arrangements as quickly as possible. Get our man to Istanbul by Thursday. The Russian can't last much longer than that. We have no idea what's going on at their end. It must be dangerous for him. After that, sit tight. I am excited by those names. As long as we handle this as quietly and quickly as we can, it might work. It could be an enormous victory for our side. For heaven's sakes, don't bring anyone else in on this."

He said it as if it was a logical conclusion, but "C" had already summoned Sloan.

2

Philip Sloan walked a circuitous route from his office through Berkeley Square to the restaurant, even though he was late for lunch with his mother. He liked to walk through Berkeley Square because he had pleasant memories of the area. As a child he had taken lessons on the French horn from a musician whose lodgings were on Curzon Street. As a schoolboy he had sat under a plane tree in Berkeley Square waiting with his mother for the diplomatic bag, and letters from his father.

The truth is that his childhood was harsh; he filtered the harshness through his imagination. He did not remember the music teacher's knuckles and his father's unflagging negligence. He rarely sent letters.

It was the surface of experience which Sloan remembered, like standing in the park cheering the royal family when their first child was born on Bruton Street, number seventeen, in nineteen twenty-six. It would be difficult to convince him that he had been a lonely child, troubled, and fearful, and that his mother had shouted at him, in a terrorizing way, moments before the royal birth, that the cheering was a welcome distraction from his anxiety. The house on Bruton Street was still there to trigger the surface memory.

He crossed over the square and walked half way down Charles street before he stopped in front of a shop which specialized in milk fed veal. The name of the shop was "Viands and Victuals." There was a brass rail bordering the window, and inside the rail fleur-de-lis. Shanks and quarters, veal steaks, real hay, grass, even a live lamb, crowded the window. There were no prices on the meat. It was a shop out of Galsworthy.

When the door of the restaurant closed behind him, he did not walk into the main section, but stayed in the foyer to wait for service.

"Your mother is in the Surrey Room," the maitre d' said without moving his lips.

Sloan nodded, like a conspirator. He accompanied many women to lunch here, but never his mother or the woman he was living with. It was an aspect of the maitre d's skill that he knew the dating habits of his regulars, when to warn them of the unexpected.

"I see her," Sloan answered. "What's on the bill?"

"If you hadn't eaten the best in India, I would recommend the mulligatawny soup. We can't import the right ingredients. The curry comes from the midlands." The maitre d' picked up a pencil and began crossing out names already crossed out. "Have a few gins and you won't know the difference."

"Who else is inside?"

"Mr. Dunne and Clark-Henderson are in the first box. Right now your mother is giving you the stare."

And so she was. She had taken a chair at the center table so that she could watch the door. There was no one else in the room, neither customer or server; the restaurant closed the room after one o'clock so there were no settings on the tables, and only a cloth on hers.

She wore a wide black straw hat which was held on by a black veil, tied under her chin. Her collar, which seemed to hold up her head, and the cuffs, were white; the rest of the costume was black. She seemed not to breathe, so tight was her corset.

As her son walked toward her, she moved her head. At the same time she grasped her cane and moved it in a circular motion, regally, as if she were about to bang for order and make a pronouncement. Sloan did not kiss her for fear of toppling her hat, so he hugged her awkwardly, and her hat capsized anyway. She gasped, as if she had seen a rodent, and dropped the cane. She had not expected an open show of affection, even from her son. He had been taught that signs of affection were unmanly. Sloan's father rarely showed any emotion, except anger, and Philip could not remember a warm welcome even after the father had been away for years. He had recently divorced Sloan's mother and had taken an Arab wife.

"I'm sorry, mother," Sloan said, picking up the cane.

"I wish you wouldn't do that," she said. "And I wish you would be on time." She had taken the train from Islington for an appointment with her solicitor. The meeting with her son was part of that transaction. When she was composed, she continued, "I know it is your boy's birthday, and you must be on your way, but I want to talk with you about a legal matter."

"It's not Josh's birthday," he said. "Eileen would have told me."

"Well, it is," the mother said. "The ninth."

"No mother," Sloan answered. "It's later. Near a holiday."

"I think you're wrong," she said. "Call and find out."

"I will," he said. "What's the trouble with the law?"

"You're the first person in our family to flaunt convention," she said. She introduced subjects obliquely, often beginning with a criticism.

"To which convention are you referring?" He asked, although he already knew, the subject was a constant source of irritation to her, and to him. But he wanted to hear her say it. "I didn't support Hitler or attempt to lead a lion into Parliament, or help Ibn Saud buy the Connaught." Sloan's father had done all these.

"Marriage is a sacred institution," she answered. "Only a bad issue can come from not observing it," she continued, imperiously. She sounded like a canon in a vestry.

"The exchange of vows did little to keep your marriage intact."

"Wouldn't you call forty years of marriage substantial?"

"Mother. He neglected you for twenty, and it wasn't forty, more like thirty. He's been gone for five, never to return."

"An old woman ought to be heard."

"She shall. She shall."

"What are you going to do about your situation?"

"You mean my marriage situation," Sloan said. "Eileen and I are going to be married, and soon, because you want it."

"Doesn't she want it?"

"Of course she wants it," Sloan said. "All women want marriage, don't they?"

"Whom will you invite?" She asked, suddenly secretive.

"I haven't thought about it. Anyone you like."

"You mustn't have outsiders," she said, "and don't notify the papers. There should be no acknowledgments."

"I'll do as you say."

"Will you tell the children you've been married before?"

"I've never been married, you know that. I told Josh about Eileen and me; he likes it. I told him it was like Halcraft's handshake with Brighton, nothing written down. He liked that, and he likes the idea that he is different from his friends."

"You mean that he is a bastard."

"That's harsh, mother."

"It's a legal term," she said. "If there is ever a question of legality, that's the term in the law." She pronounced every syllable, like a judge delivering a verdict.

"Josh may not be eligible at Manchester, and he certainly won't go up if he cannot trace his lineage. There's more ramifications to your living in sin than politics."

"Politics has nothing to do with it."

"You were dissatisfied with Labour, we all were, but you went too far. You turned communist."

"Yes I did."

"What is so strange is how close your views correspond to your father's."

"What a terrible thing to say."

"You may visit him before you like. There are spies in Arabia, aren't there?"

"I'll make it a point to send someone else."

"Are you in charge?"

"Of some things."

"The government has not been right since Percy left the Foreign Office."

"I don't work for the Foreign Office," he countered. He was looking for a diversion. "I've been thinking of returning to the *Times*."

"You were always a good letter writer. Do you keep a diary?"

"I write quite a lot, yes."

"The better reason to be married. I understand the *Times* is quite respectable."

"Washburn, the editor, is not married to the woman he is living with."

"I suspect he wouldn't tolerate such a thing in underlings."

The son looked for ways to terminate the conversation, or, failing that, to turn the topic so that they would not talk at cross purposes.

"I hope your son will never be forced to live with me," she said.

"Why would he have to do that?"

"They take illegitimate children away from those who sired them. In a case like that, I would have to support him. It would be an unfortunate necessity."

"Is this the legal matter?"

"It is. I am revising my will, and your son's legitimacy is the issue," she said. As an afterthought, she added, "I don't want him to be dependent, as you were."

"How so?"

"You were too ready to defend your father's position," she said. "He was away too much. You developed an excess of piety, hero-worship,—undeserved,—I might add. I remember you came home with a bruise on your cheek from defending your father's silly position that the Arabs should share in our national wealth. A Jewish boy hit you."

"I have always stood for my views," he said, lamely.

"I hope you are more aware of them now than you were then. Your father had more cockeyed political views than the French government. It was difficult to keep up with them all."

"I'm holding to one philosophy," he said, "and I understand it better than I know my own bloodline. For this I would gladly risk a black eye."

"It's the strangest view of them all. You want to redistribute the wealth. Why is it that so many of the rich want to do that?"

"They've lived the inequity," he said, but he knew it was not true, and he knew that she saw the error.

"That's talk," she said. "You don't suppose your cousin Harold would dismiss the servants for the world. His Communism is all talk."

"That's the difference. I would."

"I know, and that's what worries me."

"What do you mean?"

"You adhere too closely. You always did."

"I have finally found a cause for which I would give my life."

"You don't mean Communism, do you?"

"Yes, Communism. It's my life." He tried never to quote Marx, except in derivatives, even though he knew much of the doctrine from memory. He wondered when he would be able to speak openly. Like a novice, he wanted to preach from the street corners, like a first century missionary.

3

At three thirty Sloan was leaning against the wall outside "C's" office on the fifth floor of 54 Broadway, staring up at the yellow light, anticipating it's turning green. The corridor was dark because there was only one bulb, too close to the high ceiling, and one window, too close to the adjacent building.

An anemic Palm and an uncomfortable court bench guarded "C's" door. Above the door, and to the right, were the three lights, like a traffic signal. The red meant that "C" was not to be disturbed, or that he was out. The green signaled entry and the yellow, caution. Usually "C" turned on the yellow when he was on the phone. It was rumored that he spoke with the Home Secretary every day, and with the Prime Minister once a week.

When the yellow extinguished and the green lit up, Sloan knocked lightly.

"C" stood, beamed, and came around his desk when Sloan came in. "Congratulations," "C" said, "on the OBE. I've been reading the citation, which didn't say much. How could it?" "C" was not an expressive man, but he smiled now, and patted Sloan's shoulder in a gesture of 'job-well-done.' "We couldn't tell the Home Office how you secured the double agent, gathered all that information. It was a grand job. Be sure the others receive some recognition, will you?"

"Yes, of course," "C" said. "It was brazen of you to convince the agent, what's her name, Pope, to steal a transmitter from the Germans. Imagine? Sending information to us over a German machine."

"We couldn't give her one of ours, now, could we?" Sloan asked. "The only proper move was for her to approach her own case officer and ask."

"Damn bold, I'd say."

"It accomplished two things. The Germans gave her the transmitter and she had proof that she was not under suspicion. Let me tell you, she felt much better, and we felt much better. Her information was much more solid after that."

"What did the German officer say about her traveling? Did he ask her why she wanted a faster machine?"

"That was the most dangerous part," Sloan said. "She had no solid answers to questions he should have asked. He never asked. He should have asked her about sources, or codes, or money. Such is the power of seduction."

"What did he ask? He must have had some questions?"

"He asked her to stay the night," Sloan said. "The next day he gave her the Halicrafter and a 1200 bracelet."

"That's not in the report."

"I know," Sloan said. "There are other addenda not added. She's obsessed with money. We neglected to pay her one month and she was so angry that she didn't send. Her material was so good that we had to insure her retirement. It cost a pretty sum to keep the information coming."

"Money?"

"Money."

"She knew the game, didn't she?" "C" asked. "Where is she now?"

"Cornwall, in quiet cottage with her husband and children."

"She was invaluable."

"And expensive."

"It was a brilliant move, sending her to Lisbon. Your commendation is well deserved."

"Thank you," Sloan said. "I wouldn't let that file out to anyone. If it got out, Special Branch would resent the intrusion."

"Do you think we need a link with them?"

"Not a subsection," Sloan answered. "But I don't like cleaning up after them, and their pettiness with sources."

"Speaking of information, we received a pouch from Istanbul yesterday," "C" said, shuffling in his drawer. "A certain Russian, Sergei Sarkov, has defected through our embassy. He was working as Vice Consul, but really high level NKVD."

"It's the wrong time for a defection."

"Wrong for whom?" "C" asked. "True, we have to be cautious, and quiet. We don't want an outrage in Potsdam. The talks are in a sensitive stage. And Istanbul is part of the negotiations. Even Nuri Pasha admits the Russians want Istanbul, even more than the Kuriles. But the Russians have more to lose from a disruption than we do."

"I wouldn't count on the Russians being sensitive," Sloan said, "especially about taking over Istanbul."

"Have you ever heard the name, 'Sarkov'?"

"I haven't. Who is he?"

"We have a file on him. He's rather substantial. Vice Consul in their embassy, but Major in the NKVD, as I said. John Reed claims that the Russians have broken our ciphers. That's the reason for the pouch. It took so long that we will never meet Sarkov's deadline."

"Deadline for what?"

"The Russian wants to be brought in on the fifteenth."

"It will be another four days back, even five."

"And we've wasted one day already," "C" said. "I don't think we can begin tomorrow, either."

"If the Russian set his mark on the fifteenth, his risk multiples every day after." Sloan said.

"I hope we're not too late. But we can't make that deadline."

"What can I do?"

"I'm asking you to drop everything and gather all the necessary materials. Will you?"

"Should I bring Randolph in, or do the scurrying around myself?"

"The fewer the better. I promised Carolyn that I would keep it as quiet as possible."

"Protecting our backs again."

"Correct," "C" said. "But this time there is reason." He looked up, but Sloan did not respond.

"I'll lock these in the safe," Sloan said.

"Read them first," "C" said. "You'll find them invaluable. Imagine! The floor plan of the new KGB building. And keys, and locks, even the pull of the guards. Sarkov must know some of the information in their purple files, wouldn't you think? If I were Beria I would be more than a little apprehensive. Like us, they've tightened their security in the past month."

"Who will you send to Istanbul?"

"Brigadier Thomas," "C" said. "I haven't asked him yet, but I don't expect any difficulty. I want you to brief him tomorrow, early. Be here at nine, will you? Have as much local information as you can."

"What areas, particularly?"

"Oh, information on people who might be helpful, people like Ismail Akhmedov-Ege, if Thomas needs a liaison with the Turkish police. Who are the Russians living there, the long term people, especially those who might give him trouble. Let me see. A Letter of credit for the money, arrange for a move-out to Cyprus, naturalization papers, passports,—three,—that sort of thing. You might even round up a questioning team. I can't think of anything else, but you might."

"Does Thomas know he's going?"

"I'm seeing him at my club. He knows his leave has been cancelled." "C" stopped and sat down. "This fellow Sarkov is either bright, or lucky, come to think of it. If there is a scene with the transfer, the Russians will look bad. And coming after that boorish incident in Canada, they can't afford any more bad press."

"Will there be a scene?"

"There always is, lately. It isn't the service it once was," "C" said. "In the old days we dug for information—ruthlessly sometimes—but now the information is secondary to the embarrassment." "C" was smart enough to be suspicious of his praising the past; nevertheless, he often indulged himself in nostalgia, but only for a few moments. "Defectors like Sarkov do more harm to both services than loss of information. Think how romantic it once was! The code breaking in the Mediterranean. Pure intelligence. Now-a-days there is no mystery to espionage, just embarrassment. There are no heroes, just operators, no information even," he said. "Espionage has shifted from Bridge to Chess."

"A Russian game, chess," Sloan said. "The Russians don't like Bridge."

"Chess is grimmer, and has something of mayhem about it. The Germans were Bridge players. They would overrun you with strategy, expertise, brute strength, if they had it. When the balance changed, and the Allies had the strength, the Germans conceded. The Russians would never do that. It's all anticipation with them, the grand anticipation. That's why we must think ahead: four, maybe five moves ahead."

"What moves do you anticipate?"

"I agree with this Russian, Sarkov," "C" said. "Quickness and preparation will win for us." He stood and looked out the windows, turning his back to Sloan. "He dropped an alarming piece of information."

"Sir?"

"He promises to reveal the names of three penetration agents working here. One has a desk in the firm, probably right in this building. He's high level from what I can make out. Another is close to Whitehall, and the third runs errands for an ambassador."

Sloan stood still in fear. Fear immobilizes. Terror makes one run, or scream. Terror strikes, like a blow to the face, and activity is the natural response. Not so fear. Fear provokes a subtle excitement, like the allurement of illicit sex,—to which it is insidiously intimate,—and it is this excitement which freezes the person in place. Sloan was not terrorized; he was paralyzed.

His back to Sloan, "C" was looking down to Green Park. A band was playing the march from *Athalie*. "C" continued. "The mole in Whitehall is a sissy who wears a cape. We ought to be able to ferret him out with that information alone." He moved his hand to his lips and said, rhetorically, "On second thought, that might fit any number of people." He smiled, but Sloan could not see the smile.

"What else did he say?" Sloan asked weakly.

"Nothing. What more could he say? Reed tried to pry the names loose, but nothing. All the more reason for dispatch. I think this Sarkov is smart. It is upsetting, though, isn't it?" "C" asked. He continued to look out, his back to Sloan.

"Sir?"

"To think that there is a traitor working here. Carolyn insists we ought to have the man killed. No, that wasn't what he said. 'Assassinated quietly,' that was it. How unromantic this all sounds to an old man. I'm reluctant."

"What information does Carolyn have?"

"No more than you have there. He is a suspicious chap. No one is free from his scrutiny. Even you."

"C" turned then, and faced Sloan. As he did, the sun, like truth, fell on the traitor.

"Me?"

"Don't be surprised if you notice signs of a trace. It's just a warning. Carolyn is suspicious. It's his job. Now he's obsessed with these names. He won't rest until he finds out who they are."

"It doesn't make the work easier."

"What's that?"

"Knowing there's a trace."

"I believe Carolyn has a resentment against University men: you and me. That is there, no question. But he is a thorough man, completely dedicated, and loyal to the extreme. Perfect for this sort of work. I'd worry if I were you. He's going to find out things about you that you didn't know yourself."

4

Ten minutes later Sloan hurried from 54 Broadway like a convict running from the police. Ordinarily he left his office after six and walked to the Underground Station at St. James Park. This afternoon he ran, impelled by urgency, the other way to Victoria, and boarded a number 8 bus for Piccadilly.

From the second deck he studied the excavating machines under the name of Swan and Edgar removing rubble from the bombing of the Tailor building near Sackville street. The machines were also widening the street. What the London City Council would not do, Hitler's bombs had done.

On the other side of the excavation, Sloan stepped off the bus at Simpson's on Piccadilly. He appeared to be admiring the calfskin brogans on display, but he was examining the reflection in the window to see if anyone was following. For the first time since he was recruited as a Soviet agent in 1932, Sloan was in panic that he might be found out and exposed: the result of Sarkov's defection and Carolyn's suspicion. Like a man diagnosed deathly ill, he was doomed to detect signs of menace, even when there were none. Satisfied for the moment that no one was following, he hastened past Lloyd's on the corner, and into the Circus.

He stood on the corner of Shaftesbury Avenue and glimpsed back toward St. James' church. A man in a raincoat had followed part way, but turned up Regent Street. All the Piccadilly cabs, but one, circled Eros and went down. The one cab let out its fare near a theater and the man went in.

When a number 10 bus turned into Shaftesbury Avenue, Sloan ran and boarded it. He hesitated in the closet to see if anyone followed.

When the bus reached Oxford Street Sloan was convinced that no one was following. He stepped off the bus and walked across Argyle Street to the Underground Station. His suspicions returned, so he waited, watching.

After five minutes, he ducked down the stairs to the telephones. He had memorized the number and he had the money ready. The line rang six times before it was picked up. Sloan recognized the gruff greeting and interrupted the salutation, demanding, "I have to talk with Anatoli. Tell him I must see him in twenty minutes." He looked at his watch. "No," he corrected, "make it half an hour. I'm at Oxford Street. Tell him it's urgent. Meet me at the newsstand in fifteen minutes." The voice on the other end assented and Sloan clicked off.

Traitors and their contacts are like embezzlers: they have to maintain the fraud, daily. Otherwise they might miss an audit and be exposed. Anatoli, Sloan's contact, lived off the interest of Sloan's stolen secrets. He had to keep the thief happy, and he had to be available. Sloan could call Anatoli away from a state dinner, and did, on a whimsy.

After speaking to his contact, Sloan called home. Aileen's greeting was more laconic than the Russian's. "I have to stay late" he said. "If I do come home, it will be after ten." She assented with a shrug in her voice. "Is it Josh's birthday?" He asked.

"No," she answered. "His birthday is the day after Christmas."

He said, "I'd forgotten," and hung up.

A small crowd had gathered on the platform while Sloan was talking. Among them an elderly couple and two young girls in school uniforms who were waiting for a train which rolled up to the platform. When they got on, several people got off. The commuters walked, as one, toward the exit. One man stopped before going out and walked back toward Argyle Street. When the station was empty, Sloan followed the crowd up the stairs.

Outside, he hailed a cab and told the driver to continue up Tottenham Court Road, out City Road toward Islington. Across from *The Angel* he tapped on the driver's shoulder to stop, left the cab, walked across the square, and down Groswell Road.

At the newsstand he asked the proprietor for a pack of Partagas cigars. The Russian "watch" was standing next to the kiosk. His appearance was as conspicuous as his accent, Sloan thought. He wore gold-rimmed, Eastern European, glasses which accentuated his heavy, Mongolian, cheeks. Ordinarily a sedentary man, he stood awkwardly, shifting his weight. He wore a new hat, pulled down low in the wind, and the collar of his Burberry tucked around his neck.

The news dealer was lighting the stub of a used cigarette when Sloan asked for the Partagas.

"I can't get regular cigarettes, and you want Partagas," he grumbled and disappeared behind the leather curtain without offering any further service.

The Russian said, "I have Kensitas. Would you take one?"

Even though there was no one near, Sloan took the cigarette. It was part of the drill.

"Were you reading the scores?" Sloan asked. Although they knew each other, they continued the ritual to the end.

"Yes."

"Was the Nottingham score in?" It was the "closing" which the Russians liked. It was their method of making certain the contact was valid.

"No, just Leicester," the Russian replied. The signal completed, he turned and walked down Goswell Road. Sloan waited until the Russian was fifty paces ahead and then followed. He heard the automobile start up behind him, and he knew it would follow.

The line drew out for ten minutes. The Russian stopped before a house on Collier Street, lit a cigarette: the signal that this house was the one.

The house was broader than the others on the street. Three foot spaces separated it from the next house. The steps were scrubbed and the doorknob gleamed. While he waited for the door to be answered, Sloan looked back, but both the Russian watch and the automobile were gone.

A young man came out of the house without looking at Sloan. He left a suitcase on the bottom step and scurried back inside. He came back in less than a minute, this time with a young woman.

She slammed the door and the young man said, "Don't give her any grounds for complaint." The girl was tall and slender and had a large picture hat which was pinned on.

The door opened again and an older woman, a woman of authority, said from the threshold, "All your things out in ten minutes or I call the police."

That done, she turned her attention to Sloan and said, as if it were routine to switch from anger to hospitality,

"Come in." Her voice changed from sharp to familial. Sloan handed her a card with Anatoli's pseudonym on it.

Without a word, she led him along a crimson carpet and then left him alone while she fetched her keys. The wallpaper was grey satin embroidered with coronets and harps; small gilt-framed mirrors hung on each of the three levels. Each of the mirrors was headed by oversized stag horns. At the top of the staircase a chandelier hung down half a floor.

While Sloan was waiting, an old lady in a wheelchair came out from one of the rooms on the second landing, gave Sloan a cold stare, and went back in. The mistress came with the keys, walked briskly up the three levels, unlocked a door which led into a bleak corridor, hurried up more stairs which were narrow and twisted. All along the corridor, the names of the people living behind the doors were written on little cards.

The top landing was a closed box.

"Here we are," the lady said and flung open a baize door without knocking. The colors of the room were crimson and purple, the wallpaper plumy, the armchair and antimacassar red, the heavy curtains vermillion.

"I like the view," Anatoli said from the dark. Sloan could only see crowded roofs from his vantage, and beyond the roofs, the top of trees. The room was long, but not wide, with a sloping cornice which forced the occupants to move to the right, where there was a dormer window.

Beethoven's string quartets were playing on the phonograph.

"I was listening to Mozart and feeling melancholy," Anatoli said.

"That's not Mozart," Sloan corrected. "Never mind. Do you know an operator in Istanbul named Sergei

Sarkov?" He spoke hurriedly. Before Anatoli could answer, he continued, "He's defecting on the fifteenth. We've got to stop him. He's bringing my name, and Tony's, and David's."

Anatoli stood up, pursed his lips in concentration. "No," he said, "I don't know the name. Five days from now. That's the explanation for the intercept: 'We've brought the woman out.' We were wondering what that meant."

"It's Sarkov's wife. She's ill. Our man in Istanbul had her brought out."

"Your people have been quiet for a month," Anatoli said. "Now this wire. It's curious." He was still puzzled, but Sloan wanted him to concentrate on his problem.

"Did the message say anything about Sarkov?"

"We had no idea who the woman was, until this moment. Athens. The wire said they brought her to Athens."

"No," Sloan said. "Not Athens. They flew her to Cyprus. She has heart trouble." He stopped until Anatoli looked at him and he said, "Forget her, will you? She's not important. It's him. We have to stop him."

"I'm sure the wire said Athens. Curious," Anatoli said.

"Who sent it?"

"The Greeks," Anatoli answered. "Why would they say it was Athens when it was Cyprus?"

"I have no idea," Sloan said. "Please. Can we talk about Sarkov and what can be done?"

"I'll send a 'red' under Kharlimov's signature right away. Moscow will alert the brigade."

He reached for a package of Player's, offered one to Sloan, and took one himself. As he was reaching for a pad, he continued, "Istanbul. A difficult place."

"The odds are that he will make it," Sloan said. "The possibilities are all with him."

For the first time that day Sloan allowed himself a show of fear. He looked down and saw that his hand was shaking. "We have to be careful," he said. "There must be no mistakes." He had understood the danger when "C" had broken the news, but it was only now that he appreciated the force which would be necessary to stop Sarkov. It was all in the solemnity of Anatoli's face.

"We have to make plans for your escape," Anatoli said, and Sloan's anxiety increased.

"You don't think it's possible?"

"I'm not certain," Anatoli answered, "That's all, but I want to protect you. In case."

"What's wrong with the escape we planned, the Marseilles-Trieste-Prague route?"

"We assumed that the authorities would not be looking for you. If they alert Marseilles or Trieste, we can't go that way, can we?"

"You're right about that," Sloan said. "'C' told me that Carolyn has a trace on me. He's sure to uncover my work in Vienna, and who knows what he will find out from Spain. I was careless. I have a lot of enemies there. Carolyn's a thorough bastard. I'll say that for him. He gives me the chills."

"Then it's settled," Anatoli said, holding up his hands like a referee. "Ivan will arrange your escape. Call him if you think it's necessary. He'll have a plane at Bristol, with private stops. It's there for all emergencies."

"I don't like Ivan. He's so obvious, and so criminal looking."

"He's the most loyal man in the organization," Anatoli answered. "I don't believe you'll need an escape, but I want you to feel secure."

"Well, I don't," Sloan said. "I've never felt so insecure."

"Let's talk about the extermination of Sarkov," Anatoli said. "That is, if you are satisfied with the arrangements?"

"I am believing more and more that I will have to run," Sloan said. "We must be careful. Even if we eliminate Sarkov, there can be no suspicions of a warning. Do you see? He has to disappear completely," he said snapping his fingers, "or they will trace his disappearance back to me. From this end it will have to look like Sarkov changed his mind." He held up his finger. "That's number one."

"A simple disappearance. No violence." Anatoli made a note. "What date?"

"We've already talked about that. He has to be annihilated before Wednesday."

Anatoli frowned in concentration. "The cable goes tonight." Seriousness was his normal state, Sloan thought. "Switzerland is alerted tomorrow. It's two days to Turkey. Wednesday? That's not enough time. Our people in Istanbul will have to kill him."

"Are there people who can do that?"

"What? Of course. Any of our people could do it. They're all trained."

"What if he drops out of sight? Can they find him?"

"Why would he hide? He's at his desk—now. We simply reroute a message and he is taken from his desk two days from now."

"If I were him, I'd hide. It makes sense. Especially after his wife has left."

"She's in Cyprus, you say?"

"Yes, Cyprus. Not Athens."

"That's better. We have excellent operatives in Cyprus. Even if he makes it out to Cyprus, we can handle him, easier than in Istanbul."

"Can you put an end to this? Are you certain?"

"I think we can."

"Suppose Bletchley listens in to your 'red' tonight? What then?"

"Who would be the first to know tomorrow morning? You. Am I right?"

"I wonder," Sloan said. "'C' is such a sphinx. He might not say anything to me. No one knows what he's thinking, what's on his mind. Make no mistake, he tells me only what is necessary."

"Don't worry about the cable," Anatoli said and took two steps toward Sloan. "We have a closing which is impenetrable."

"The Germans thought theirs was impenetrable, and we broke it the first year of the war."

"We change pads every day."

"I know," Sloan said. "I worry about everything. But I do feel better talking to you." It was a sincere statement, if more emotional, even sentimental. Sloan was not an emotional man, couldn't be. He knew that emotions endangered his secret, and the secret was more important than any human association, even Aileen. He was wedded to his secret. It was the love of his life. He could be kind to Aileen, and to the children, even when they were angry with him, or distraught, or even when Aileen indulged herself in self-pity, which she often did. He could be kind then because his whole life with Aileen was an act, just a pose. He had kept his secret for so long that he was able to dole out his emotions, like fluid from a spigot. He could turn them on and off as he wished. He had controlled his emotions for so long that he was surprised by his small outburst. "I used to think that I missed Nikitin," he said. "We talked history. But I don't miss him, really."

"That's kind of you," Anatoli said. "Thank you. I see Nikitin. He talks about you. I wish he could be here with us, to make the arrangements. He knows your case better than I do."

"No," Sloan said. "We don't need him. You're doing fine. I'm satisfied."

"If we survive this, I'll see to it that you get a promotion."

"I don't work for promotions," Sloan said. "Do you think it will be difficult to stop Sarkov?"

"It would be easier if he was in Paris, or London—like Krivitsky—but it will be done. We find him. We end him. I am sure the people in Istanbul will take care of it."

5

At 7:30 Sloan sat in his kitchen, something he seldom did, talking to Aileen, something he rarely did, about double dealing, something he never did. Although he brought communists back from the Benedict street to the house where they talked openly about Marxism and their involvement, he never mentioned his traitorous activities, to anyone. That was his secret. He was wedded to that, his secret, so he maintained good spirits around Aileen, the children, and his friends. He posed with them, and it came easy. Like an actor he put on the *persona* of lover, of father, of friend, even when it should have been difficult. He played his parts well because his true self was safe with Anatoli. He was a professional in the craft of deception, double appearing, as well as double dealing. But the threat of the Sarkov exposure was melting the mask and it was less easy to maintain the pose.

"Something is terribly wrong," Aileen said.

"Yes. Very much so."

"I knew it. I knew it over the phone."

"I've been seeing people, talking, trying to prevent a catastrophe," he said. "I'm afraid it will take more than I have. I don't know where to turn."

"Is there anything I can do?"

"I wish there were."

"Before we talk, would you like some dinner? We had lamb, your favorite."

"I suppose I should, but I'm not hungry."

"You might feel better," she said, rising. "I'll fix a plate."

"No, not right now," he said. "Come in the study. I want to talk."

He walked ahead of her into the study, a planned room, planned by someone who did not live there. The Gibbon had never been opened and the Thackeray was brown, not from usage but from age. It was a cold room, although stuffed with leather, pine, gold, and family furnishings, all too little used. A portrait of Sloan's father hung over the mantle. The old man had that Victorian look of confidence, as if he were at home in the world and knew what he was about. Neither Aileen or Sloan sat down. She put a hand on Sloan's sleeve and he recoiled, as if struck.

"What's the trouble?" She asked. "Is it work?"

"No, not the work," he said. "Well, it is, but something else."

She waited, without talking.

"Do you remember the Russians that used to come, the ones when we first moved here?"

"Yes," she said. "I like Erzin. He did that magic trick."

"There was more to their coming than friendship. Did you know that?"

"You told me."

"I told you that I was associated with them," he said. "But I didn't tell you that I work for them. Did I?"

"Yes, you told me that. That's not a secret."

"You don't understand how much I've helped them," he said. "We talk Marxism, but some of us hold to it very closely."

"I know that," she said.

"I've been giving them secrets, information which helped them to destroy people, even towns of people."

She stood silently.

"Our security looks on that as treachery."

He had believed that he could keep his treasonable activity from her. He had revealed more to her in the last few seconds than he had revealed in the five years of their life together.

She said, "If you're suspect, won't David and Anthony be questioned too?" She walked behind the desk. "Is that buffoon, Carolyn, making charges?"

"No, McKenzie," Sloan answered. "Of course, Carolyn plays his part. But McKenzie said some things. I don't know which is worse."

"What?"

"He told me they were tracing me. If Carolyn looks at all, he will find out about Vienna. I was not careful. It's all in the records. I don't want him to find out about my joining the party and other things."

"Is that when you met Litzi?"

"Yes."

"Is that what you're afraid of, that they'll find out about her?"

"She is very powerful," he said. "She's in charge of the party in Bremen. She was in the forefront in Vienna. There are records all over the place. I signed petitions, pledges, the marriage register. I'll be as easy to follow as a fox by the hounds."

"He'll have to call Vienna."

"No," Sloan said. "All he has to do is phone Childreth. The records are there. There'll be no hiding."

"Can you stop him?"

"I've been trying to think of ways to distract him, at least for a while. He's like a bulldog. Once he latches on, he won't let go."

"Could Anthony help?"

"He's more suspect than I am," Sloan said. "If he interferes it will go bad for me."

"Is there any way to stop Carolyn?"

"I'm afraid not. He may have already seen the lists."

"What would happen if they found out everything," she asked. "I mean, what would happen if they knew you were working for the Russians, getting paid, the secrets, all that?"

"The worst would be a trial," Sloan said. "I doubt they would do that, the publicity. They hate publicity worse than secrets going out."

"It wouldn't be in the papers."

"No," he said. "They'd suspend me. They'd reshuffle staff. They might suspend other people, but that's unlikely. Certainly they would force me to resign."

"That the worst: that you would resign?" She asked. "Even if it all came out?"

"Yes."

"Is that so terrible, that you stop working there?" She asked. "What about Anthony and David? Would they leave? How many work for the Russians. I mean in all?"

"Six that I know of," he answered. "In the RSLO there are four. I don't know how many others, maybe two. I don't know them all, but there are more, I'm sure."

"Don't you think Carolyn had better leave the issue alone?"

"What do you mean?"

"There are too many people in this," she said. "If it all comes out, the service would suffer. You said that yourself, they won't tolerate a public hearing. But there are too many involved, it's bound to get into the papers. Then what? No, McKenzie can't let that happen. It may not be patriotic to be a Russian sympathizer, but it is better to tolerate communists in the firm than risk an investigation of the whole service. Don't you think?"

"It's a little different on the fifth floor," Sloan said. "We talk about the Marxism as a system of living, but the Russians are enemies inside those doors, make no mistake."

"All the same, Carolyn had better be careful," she said. "Loyalties change, all the time. Two years ago you told the Americans everything. Today, nothing. C P is in trouble for what he told them two years ago. You said that yourself. Who knows, two years from now the Russians might be our closest allies. Carolyn better be careful. He might be caught behind the times," she said. "Are you expected to change loyalties the way you change your coat?"

"There's something else," Sloan said.

She waited. It was the most he had ever told her about his work since they had come together.

"I'm afraid," he said. He almost called her name.

"Of what?"

"A Russian operator is defecting," he said. "He promised to expose me and two other agents working in Five."

"It's getting frightfully complicated, isn't it?" She asked. "Why don't you just get out?"

"Because the work is important to me," he answered. "It's my life."

"More than us?"

"I wish you hadn't asked that."

She tipped her head crookedly, as if her mind had slipped a notch. Her eyes crossed, at a crazy angle.

He was like that, cruel, in a cold way. He had always used his secret to keep her at a distance. At a critical moment, when she needed him, he would push her away with a stinging remark, like this one, which laced her fear with the threat of abandonment.

"You would leave us, wouldn't you, without a word? And what is worse, without a thought?"

He showed as little reaction as if she had asked for a cigarette. She turned away, more to relieve her anxiety than to avoid his response. He did not look at her, and he did not respond.

He practices remoteness, which often looks like indifference, even when they make love, she thought. He may show affection to other people, his mother perhaps, or to those with whom he works, but he showed little to her, or to the children. She felt as though she were in contact with one of his substations, the high Scandinavian one, and the rest of him belonged to another command.

It was no time to start an argument, he said to himself. He needed all the friendly forces. "I've never given the slightest thought to leaving."

"But if it came to that, you would."

"I might have to."

"Is that why you never married me?"

"You know I don't believe in marriage," he said. "Mother asked me about that today. I didn't have an answer. I told her that we would be married next Saturday, in Marylebone High Street. Would you like that?"

"You will?"

"I don't mind," he answered. "The ceremony means nothing to me, one way or the other, but mother tells me the children's legitimacy is in question. I don't care one way or the other, but you do, don't you?"

"Yes, I do," she answered as if she were responding to the registrar's question whether she took this man to be her husband.

"It protects us," he said. "If it came to an arrest, I might have to leave in a moment, and you wouldn't have anything, if we weren't married."

"What would happen to us?"

"I would have to leave, to avoid the police," he said. "I couldn't take you, but they would fetch you later."

"Do you think that will happen?"

"No, I don't," he answered. "I don't. I think this man in Istanbul will be stopped. And I think what you say is true: Carolyn will be silenced, especially if he goes too far, which is his way."

"Would we be happy in Russia?"

"I would be a national hero," he said, "and you will share in that."

"What about our families?"

"You wouldn't miss them," he said. "We don't see them as it is. In Russia you would realize that the state is more important than family."

"But I don't know the state. I know the boys and you, your mother, and my parents. I don't know Russia, except your friends, and they are so different from you and me."

6

embers of the Carlton and the Reform each argue that their club is the best on St. James Street. The Army and the Navy object, as do the Athenaeum and the Traveler's, but the fact remains, either the Carlton or the Reform is best.

The Carlton was built with Caen stone, which is not suited to the London atmosphere, so it had to be refaced with Portland stone. The new facing did not match the old. Members of the Reform point out the contrast whenever comparisons are made. The architecture of the Reform is an imitation of the Farnese palace in Rome. It is a lovely copy, although members of the Travelers insist that the Farnese is no match for the Palazzo Pandolfini, which is the model for their building.

If one were to judge a club by blood and ancestry— not architecture, then the Reform would win. If the norms were food and furnishings, it is the Carlton,—plates up. The manager of the Reform tried to bribe the chef of the Carlton to come and work in his kitchen, but the plot, like so much in espionage, failed. However, the attempt did accomplish two things: members of the Carlton began complimenting their chef, and boasting to members of other clubs that the plot proved that their food was the best.

Although he was taking his dinner at "C's" club, the Carlton, Brigadier Thomas belonged to the Reform. After the meal he stood and the two made their way to the clubroom. "C" guessed that the Brigadier would praise some part of the meal, but compare the whole unfavorably to his club.

"The grouse was excellent," the Brigadier said. "A bit too much flavoring, wouldn't you say? Was it left hanging a day too long? But it was done quickly, and well, as it should be."

"And the gravy?" "C" asked. He was an excellent interrogator.

"Made from the meat. No complaints there. But the vegetables are always out of a can here. Why is that? Can't the help find their way to Covent Garden?"

"C" smiled. "Would you care for a mint?"

By then they were seated in a clubroom noted for its heavy chairs, Havana cigars, and daily papers from places as remote as Patna and Bogotá. On either side of the room were windows which looked out on the one hundred and forty Elms which Cromwell's working men had planted "in a very decent manner."

"No," Thomas said, "the Courvoisier is enough." He placed both hands on the knuckle of a walking stick which was made from the shaft of a golf club.

"Is that a golf stick?" "C" asked.

Thomas held up the stick. "My father's niblick," he said. "It was given to him by Henry Cotton on the Old Course, St. Andrew. Cotton stroked a ball a hundred and fifty yards with this," he continued. He set the stick on his knees for examination. "If I can't play in Cairo, at least I can carry a remnant. Do you play?"

"No," "C" answered. "I'm with Shaw. 'Golf is a long walk ruined.'" Thomas had heard that comment before and liked it even less now.

"C" went on: "Whenever I think of exercise I take a nap. Shaw's nemesis, Chesterton, said that."

"Too bad you don't play," the Brigadier said. "Golf's a great leveler. There's no one to blame for the shot. You alone are responsible for the outcome. No other sport, or enterprise, even combat, is so responsible. I maintain that I can tell the cut of a man by the way he plays the game. It reveals character."

"Well," "C" said. "For that reason alone, I'm glad I don't play."

Brigadier Thomas did not laugh, but he caught the whimsy.

"C" continued, "Besides no golf, how is Cairo?"

"The Egyptians insist that we withdraw from the Nile Valley back to the Canal Zone, and they want the Union Jack down from the barracks, but otherwise, Cairo is peaceful."

"Will there be trouble?"

"They've resented our presence since Stack's murder in '24. I don't think there's any more strife, but it is explosive. The Communist Student's Committee could be troublesome, if they were united, which they aren't. They're always fighting among themselves." He stopped talking in order to ponder. "Egypt has never been easy for us. The city has been peaceful during the duration, but the economic problems are just below the surface. There are too many educated people for too few jobs, and it's our fault. The smart people have turned to selling. Then we place such heavy duty on their goods that they can't compete. Angry, of course they're angry."

"The strain's worth it, though?"

"The Canal has dictated policy since the beginning," the Brigadier said. "But, my-oh-my have we been neglectful. We have never dug one artesian well. Half of the children do not live past five, and there are more blind people in Egypt than any country in the world. Eighty percent of the *fellahin* have *bilharzia* or *ancylostomiasis*. Few schools, no health services. Trouble, there has to be trouble. Surely."

"And Farouk?"

"People at home think he is the caliphate incarnate. He's anything but. He's a simple vulgarian, a sexual vegetable, and overripe, I might add. Look at the size of him! And his friends! Especially that factotum, Pouli. Nothing but a limpet lackey."

"It sounds explosive."

"We are trying to maintain the status. The Egyptians want us out. So what do we do? Our Tommies flock to Clot Bey's brothel, Shepherd's is always full, the Continental bursting, and we wonder why the natives want a revolution. I'm glad to be out for a few days, happy for the respite."

"I spoke with Douglas today."

"I know," the Brigadier said. "He told me. You have instructions, and they're not about Egypt."

"C" shook his head. "Sorry we cut short your leave."

"That's all right, old man. I'm interested."

"C" explained the situation in Istanbul and the Brigadier's place in the transfer. "I believe you are the one to handle the negotiations. Sarkov asked for you."

"Yes," the Brigadier answered. "I know him. He's a big fish."

"Do you know Peterson?"

Brigadier Thomas nodded yes.

"I'm not sure he would allow anyone but an Indian to interfere with embassy routine. Of course you have seniority and you've done this before."

"I'll do what I can."

"We'll brief you tomorrow. We'd like you to leave mid-afternoon. Will that be all right?"

"That's fine. I should be in Istanbul in two weeks."

"No, no," "C" said. "You have to be there Thursday."

"Oh, I couldn't do that. I go by ship, or rail."

"Impossible. Sarkov has to be out by the fifteenth."

"I couldn't possibly make that."

"The plane takes three days, most."

"Oh, my dear chap, I don't fly."

"Don't fly?"

"No, I have acrophobia."

"Hmm."

"I don't blame you for wondering," the Brigadier said. "It's a recent phobia. Not with me, mind you, but with the age. They made up a word for it. Inaccurate, as most recent words are. Take the word 'astraphobia.' If you analyzed it, you might think it means fear of the stars. But no, it means fear of lightning. Like my word, acrophobia. It could mean fear of the crown of one's head, or fear of the crest of a wave, of end time, or the end of an evening, and God knows what other end. *Acro* is such a versatile word. Simply to say, 'Fear of Flying' is so much better."

"Is that so?"

"When you consider that Freud defined phobia as a persistent and ungrounded fear, my fear is not a phobia. It's quite sound."

"Is it?"

"The Greeks had no word for 'fear of flying' simply because they didn't zoom about as we like to do."

"We have good reason for zooming."

"I'm sorry, old boy, but I am quite adamant in my refusal. Freud said that phobias are compromises between instincts, like the compromise between sexual excitement and guilt. I can't ever remember thinking sex was wrong, but I do know that I will not fly, under any circumstances. Understand?"

"I'm afraid I do."

Part III

MOSCOW

1

V ladimir Basilevich Bakov began deciphering the message from London at ten-ten, Moscow time. He had been waiting for the tick since eight. The London station had alerted Moscow Center that an urgent communication would come over the wire before midnight. The sender was Rear Admiral Nicolai Kharlimov, head of the Russian military mission in London, but more to the point, chief of NKVD operations in England.

The message began with the brief mark "red" which signaled a communication so important, and so secret, that it was to be hand-delivered to Beria's secretary. In the three years he had been head decipher clerk, Bakov had never seen Beria. Twice he had delivered "red" messages, but both times he had been peremptorily dismissed by Merkulov, the secretary, without catching a glimpse of Beria.

Beria and Merkulov were Georgians, as was Stalin. At the beginning of their association there had been a conspiracy of camaraderie among the three men, although Beria, unlike the other two, was admired all through the NKVD. He paid special attention to the personal needs of his people, although he knew only a few by name. He took care that they had luxuries: the NKVD restaurant was excellent, and when epaulettes were introduced into the army, Beria raised the pay of his staff to fourteen rubles a month, three more than the parallel staff in the army, and he arranged for holidays at Sukhimi, something the army could not do.

He had a reputation for licentiousness outside Center, but inside, Beria was liked and respected for his industry and concern. Bakov had stacks of signals all of which had been initialed by Beria. It was known that he rarely left the building before nine.

This evening, at ten, Beria was standing outside Merkulov's office waiting for the Kharlimov wire.

"I wish we had more time," Beria said. "I don't think we can stop him."

"I do," Merkulov said. "Three of the brigade speak Turkish. First they'll ask the Russian nationals. They get help from the local police. They fan out. They know that Sarkov knows very little about Istanbul, where to hide. They arrest the family, and use them. At most it will take two days. Two days."

"I'm wondering what London's up to," Beria said. "If I were McKenzie, how would I use this to my advantage? He's as clever as a lynx."

"He can't be too interested," Merkulov said. "If he didn't hide Sarkov the first day."

"You're right," Beria said. "Except McKenzie didn't know about this until two days ago. He suffers from the same kind of fools I do."

"Why didn't they fly Sarkov out when they had the chance?" Merkulov asked.

"How would I know," Beria said. "We can only guess. It could have been any number of things, but in most cases, it's incompetence. I am sure of one thing. McKenzie will pluck Sarkov from the Istanbul streets just as soon as he can. So, now it's a foot race."

"And we have the advantage," Merkulov said. "If there were no wires going out of Istanbul, most likely there will be no wires coming in. He has to send a man, and that takes four days, at least. No, he won't make it. We'll have Sarkov by then."

"I hope you're right," Beria said. "But I'm not as confident as you."

"I'll take full responsibility," Merkulov said. "I'll oversee it."

"It could be that London has taken another view," Beria said. "They may use him as a pawn for something more important."

"Sarkov unimportant?" Merkulov asked. "He worked in this building from the first day. He knows the Green Room, the combinations in the halls, the whole German network," Merkulov said. As he spoke he looked more and more sad. "He knows all the music from Canada, the codes, the books on all our men. He knows where the money is."

"Suppose London knows all that?"

"How is it possible?"

"It is more than possible," Beria said. "We know at least that much about London Central. Do you think McKenzie scrutinizes our wires the way we do his?"

Merkulov did not answer.

"It's the nature of intelligence to know more about your opposite than you know about yourself. It's like deployment in chess. You study your opponent and you forget that your rook is exposed. Sarkov is out there, waiting to be captured, and it's the English turn to play. If Alekhine was sitting across from you and he had exposed his rook, what would you do? Would you capture the rook, or would you suspect that he had a future motive, something long-term, which might damage you more than a simple rook?"

"But if I were Alekhine and my rook was exposed and the other player allowed me to pull back, what should I do?"

"Pull back, of course," Beria said. "That is, if the game was chess and the opportunity presented itself."

"Our first thought must be to remove Sarkov," Merkulov said. "Just the way we removed Redens."

"Redens? Do you think Sarkov is an imbecile like Redens?"

"Why should the method be any different?"

"Are you so slow to understand?" Beria asked. "Even if we find him, we have to eliminate him without violating Turkish law. You and I both know Istanbul is the easiest place in the world to hide. Turks hide their names, their faces, their wealth, their intentions. They are more deceptive than the Syrians. You never know what a Turk is thinking, because he doesn't know himself. One thing they don't hide is their hatred for Russia. They are clever people. Make no mistake: we must not underestimate what might happen in Istanbul."

"Our man stands out like an alien."

Beria knew more about the politics of intrigue than Merkulov, but less about the details of espionage, so he sought Merkulov's counsel in running the day-to-day operations. Merkulov mistook Beria's questions as signs of weakness. It was the beginning of his undoing. Beria had come over from government to the NKVD and knew little about the inner workings of the NKVD. Merkulov explained the intricacies of the Rote Kapelle, the roster of personnel in Bvilisi, as well as the method of extricating information from an informant: the process of espionage. As time went on Merkulov stepped beyond his limits with Beria, sometimes correcting him, sometimes criticizing him, often interrupting him. He began to advise Beria as to the best operators in the field, what their compensation should be, but also the best policy toward the Central

Committee of the Politburo, and which officers in the building should receive which vacation packages.

Beria seemed docile and took the advice with good
humor. Late at night, when Beria was leaving, he would
stop at Merkulov's office and say 'good night.' After eighteen months as his secretary, Merkulov invited Beria to his
home. A few weeks later, Beria arranged for a dacha in
Zhuckovia for Merkulov, although Beria, not married,
would use the dacha for his affairs. Merkulov knew about
Beria's profligacy, but never mentioned it either to his superior or to people in the building. He did mention it, however, to a member of the Politburo, and therein lay the second
stage in his downfall.

The third stage was the trap which proved that Beria
was more adept at intrigue than Merkulov. One day, when
they were alone, Beria admitted to Merkulov that he had
shifted a substantial amount of money from 'planning and
analysis' to 'technical support,' a clear violation of procedure. It was not true: he had not done that. It was a simple
trap to uncover who it was that Merkulov talked to in the
Central Committee. Beria told Merkulov not only the
amount of money but also the number of the voucher.
Merkulov did not respond, although he knew it was felo-
nious to move money and should have advised Beria of the
consequences. The following Tuesday Beria intercepted a
memo—the contents of which demanded an investigation
into the transferred money—from Merkulov to Shavsky, the
member of the Politburo.

Beria knew that secretaries turn traitors in a moment
of opportunity. It was the nature of the system, not only in
the NKVD, but in all Soviet politics. Beria had risen to
power by such treachery and deceit, and he expected others

to do the same: it was the nature of the system. But Beria was a professional.

He need not have devised the trap. In the following weeks Merkulov showed his betrayal, in a crude manner. A clerk in the Politburo told Beria that his office was being monitored, that all his office conversations were on tape. The clerk told Beria that the worst offense against him was that Beria was working for Shevlov's demotion, although Shevlov was a favorite of Stalin. The NKVD came under the direct supervision of the Council of Ministers, but the Politburo maintained a close interest in NKVD affairs, and they were unhappy that Shevlov was being demoted.

The clerk also told Beria that the dacha in Zhuckovia was being watched. Merkulov had set that up, too.

Beria was waiting for the opportunity to spring the trap on Merkulov. The Sarkov affair, he thought, would be the clamp.

"I don't think Sarkov is any more clever than Ubarevich, or Kork. Do you?" Merkulov asked.

"They were fools, like Redens," Beria said. "Sarkov knows what he's about. We have to assume that he has a plan, and that it will work."

"You're too pessimistic."

"I am?" Beria said. "You do understand, don't you, that we have two problems, the elimination of Sarkov being the easier. We have to protect the Englishman. He must be secure, at all costs, now more than ever. Sarkov can reveal his name, his position in Checka, what he has done for us, what he is going to do. No, he must not be compromised."

"It's an added reason for stopping the traitor."

"If Sarkov exposes him, we lose our most significant source of information, a major loss. Do you know that the Englishman uncovered an insurrection in Germany in

1942? If the group had succeeded they would have assassinated Hitler and turned the Allies, along with Germany, on us. It was a time when England and the US were not yet sure against whom they should fight. It was a major crisis, but the Englishman not only uncovered the plot, but planned the response. The whole group, I think there were a hundred and fifty, were eliminated with a brilliant tactic. No, an agent of such resources must be preserved. Every effort must be taken to stop Sarkov and keep our man in place."

"I see."

"I hope you do because I am putting you in charge of this," Beria said. "You make the decisions, you have full authority, call in the military if you want, the consular people, anyone."

"Fine."

"I will advise you," Beria said. "But it will be your responsibility. Understand?"

Beria handed Merkulov a series of papers and pointed to the lines where Merkulov was to sign. Merkulov looked at the papers, looked at Beria's eyes, picked up the papers without signing and turned toward the code room.

2

Bakov had just begun receiving the message when Merkulov entered his cubicle. Even though Merkulov was his superior, Bakov resented the intrusion. This was his domain. He drew his lamp closer to the transmitter, and huddled, like a scholar studying a manuscript, over the incoming numbers. As chief clerk he had responsibility for all code work in Moscow Center. He oversaw the breaking and reading of enemy codes, as well as the protection of his own. It was secret work, even Merkulov did not know the working of the code.

Bakov accepted credit for the integrity of the Russian system. Cryptanalysis had reached a high point during Bakov's tenure. He had merged the straddling checkerboard with the one-time key, and increased the efficiency of the system by giving the frequently used letters a single digit, so that less time was spent sending and receiving wires.

But it was the "closing" for which he was most proud. It was a stroke of genius. Because of the "closing" Center could take virgin messages from the Rote Kapelle, the Sorge ring in Japan, and the Lucy network in Switzerland without fear of interception. Bakov had proof that the "closing" had withstood the scrutiny of the Germans and the Japanese, although he had suspicions that the English specialists at Bletchley were near to breaking it.

Merkulov flipped the switch for the overhead lights. "Why is it so dark in here?"

"I work with just this one light," Bakov answered. "It helps me concentrate."

Merkulov turned the overhead light off. "We are anxious. Should I come back?"

"No, stay," Bakov said. "It's not long. The last of the numbers are coming in now. Would you like to see the system? How it works?"

"Will it delay anything?"

"No," Bakov said. "I'll decode the message and you watch."

Merkulov leaned over the other man's shoulder, a little too close. Bakov shrugged and Merkulov pulled back.

"These numbers indicate the row, the column, and the page of the *Almanac*," Bakov said. "They have to be 'opened' before they can be read."

"That's what you invented, wasn't it?" Merkulov asked. "The opening."

Bakov nodded. He was fond of saying to those who asked what he did for a living, "I open and close the code." He pointed to the page, "We divide Kislytsin's numbers into sets of five, like this, and separate the fourth set from the right, and the fourth set from the left." He wrote those numbers: 77695 and under those, 67214 on a separate sheet, and then added them together. "Nothing is carried beyond ten in the addition," he said. "Nine and three are not twelve, but two."

"I see," Merkulov said. The resulting figure was 34809.

"Now, we subtract the result from the first five numbers." He wrote the numbers: 92332. "The result is this: 18563."

"This is the indicator," he said, opening the *Almanac*. "The last two numbers designate the page." The numbers on page sixty three of the *Almanac* were the population figures, given in hundreds of thousands, of the major cities in Central Europe. Bakov ran his finger across the page to column five and counted down to row eighteen. He held his finger at that place and copied the forty-five digits which made up that row. Under those forty-five digits he copied the digits Kislytsin had transmitted and subtracted the difference between the two sets. "This is what we call 'the checkerboard plain,'" he said. "Nearly every code system in the world does this. The rest is quite simple." It was simple, as simple as Legrand's deciphering Kidd's message in Poe's "The Gold Bug."

"I devised a guarantee to our system," Bakov said. "The London station uses two key words." He wrote as he talked. "On top he writes LONDON. That's one. Over here he writes this." In capital letters, Bakov wrote ASINTOR. "All English codes use this word because it contains the most frequently used letters in English. Since they are the most used, we assign single figures to them. I'll show you."

"It's not clear to me," Merkulov said. "Single figures. Why? Which ones have double figures?"

"The letters A S I N T O R are used three times as often as any other letters in English. Let me show you."

On a clear sheet Bakov wrote

L O N D O N

A B C E F G

H I J K M P

Q R S T U V

W X Y Z. /

"I'll assign numbers to each of these letters," Bakov said, his pencil touching the space under the letter A. "We will go down the column, vertically, not across, and we look for the letters in ASINTOR." He leaned forward and wrote. "A is the first and we assign zero. O is next, here at the top, and we assign it 'one'; I is there, 'two' and R 'three' and T 'four', S 'five', E 'six' and T 'seven.'"

"What about the other letters?"

"They get double figures," Bakov said. "I'm coming to that." It was clear that he loved to explain his work.

"What's that at the end?"

"A slash," he answered. "It indicates a switch from letters to numbers in the message. We assign the number, ninety-nine, to a slash. Here it is in the checkerboard. We know from the slash that those last three figures, 815, will stay as they are. They're probably the month and a day, August fifteenth."

"I see."

"The less frequently used numbers receive numbers from eighty to ninety-nine, in the same vertical sequence. Look here. L gets 80. We skip A. H is 81. Q 82, W 83 and so on." He wrote numbers under each of the remaining letters. When he was through, he placed the sheet next to the checkerboard and decoded the first line of the Kharmalov "red."

It read as follows:

5 0 3 90 1 98 93 94 5 7 84 6 5 7 0 97 97 6 89 84 88 99 88 11 55 99 99 S A R K O V M U S T B E S T O P P E D B Y / 8 1 5 / /

"I see," Merkulov repeated. "There are so many variables, no one could read this."

"Except the one who knows the variables. If the sender and the receiver know, it's quite easy. If you don't know the changes, how would you ever break into this?"

"That's the object, isn't it? To send so that no one but the receiver can read it."

"Yes, that's the essential element," Merkulov said, "but would you hurry. The minister is waiting." When he saw that the other was hurt, he continued, "You've done brilliantly," Merkulov said as if he were praising an artist. He was standing in the door with the complete message in his hand. "I have an idea," he said. "Come with me. I want you to meet Comrade Beria. I would like that, yes. I have an idea. Yes, come with me. I believe we can use your talent on a problem we are having. Yes, I believe you might be just the man."

3

Beria pressed his fists into his coat pockets as he paced in front of his office. Small, scholarly looking, and partially bald, his flattened down hair accentuated his cultivated, academic, look. To further emphasize the look, he wore a pince-nez and a bright colored vest under his dark coat. When his hands were not in his pockets, he moved them away from his body when speaking.

He saw Merkulov and Bakov coming before they saw him, so he scurried into his office and stood behind the desk. It was a narrow office, spare, with no rugs and only three pieces of furniture: an uncomfortable sofa against the far wall, a desk, and a wardrobe. The Krotkov portrait of Stalin hung on a wall hidden from everyone except anyone on Beria's side of the desk. The photograph, a profile, looked posed, like a death mask, although it had been sufficiently retouched to show some color. The wardrobe was closed, but it hinted that Beria slept in his office.

There were three phones on his desk. They were famous. It was rumored about that the dark phone was a direct line to Stalin, the white a line to top government officials, and the green an open line to any part of Russia, from Murmansk to Vladivostock.

The vents in the room were not working and the windows were battened down. When Bakov walked in the office, he sniffed the air which, like in a vault, smelled close and unhealthy.

Beria stood behind the desk, sufficiently far away that he would not have to greet Bakov with anything but a nod.

"Commissar," Merkulov said. "This is Comrade Bakov."

Beria bowed slightly. "Did your wife have the baby?" He asked.

"Yes, she did," Bakov answered. "She had complications, but she is doing fine. Thank you."

"You like the apartment?" Beria asked. "Near Smolensky, isn't it?"

"Yes, Kormantsky Lane. It's roomy enough and it's only twenty minutes from here," Bakov answered. "My wife used to talk about an automobile, but now she's occupied with the child."

"An automobile is not impossible," Beria said, making a note. "I don't see you, but I see your work. I want to congratulate you. We were saying the other day how much we trust the signals."

"He showed me the system," Merkulov said. "I don't see how anyone could break the code. The real numbers are so cleverly hidden."

"Thank you," Bakov said. "We are fairly certain no one has broken it. By definition Codes are riddles and riddles are solvable, so we have to keep inventing new elements for the puzzle." He placed the Kharlimov message on Beria's desk. "This came at ten twenty." He looked behind at the oversized clock. It said ten fifty.

"It's twenty minutes fast," Beria said. He released his pince-nez and held the message close to his face, moving his head as he read. "Well, you've seen Kharlimov's urgency." After Bakov nodded, Beria asked, "Do you know Comrade Sarkov?"

"I met him twice," Bakov said. After a brief silence he continued, "He came through here when he was working in the first directorate. I remember he was interested in the *omega* machine. He was very quick to understand what we do."

"You didn't show him any decoded messages, did you?" Merkulov asked.

"I didn't go through the system as I did with you, no," Bakov said. "He was interested in how we relay messages to Room Ten."

"Did you say that you showed this Comrade how you decode?" Beria asked, nodding at Merkulov.

Bakov looked at Merkulov.

"I asked him to," Merkulov said.

"Do you think that was wise?" Beria asked.

"I left out an important section," Bakov said.

"I wasn't talking to you," Beria said. "It is a principle in this building that we do not interfere with other peoples' work. If we retain responsibility for what we do, we do not have time to disturb other people. And we don't have to worry later."

"I'm interested in every detail," Merkulov said. "And I want to know how every person does his work. It just happened that I had the opportunity"

"I understand your enthusiasm, and I commend it," Beria said. "I wasn't criticizing as much as pointing out the principle: do your own work and let others do theirs. Then the consequences do not get out of control."

"I agree."

"When was the second time you saw Sarkov?" Beria asked Bakov.

"I had dinner with him and his wife and a half dozen other people. It was last year, I think in February."

"After the ballet?"

"Yes, that's right," Bakov said. "I sat next to his wife. He was on her other side so I didn't say much to him. I remember the wife very well."

"Beautiful?"

"Yes, but smart," Bakov answered. "She knew more about what was going on at the German front than some generals. She talked too freely. I remember she laughed about Zharkulov being drunk and not being able to maneuver troops. No one else laughed except the husband. He adores her."

Merkulov looked at Beria and then asked Bakov, "Would you know Sarkov, if you saw him?"

"I suppose I would, yes," he said. "Unless he has changed: grew a moustache or put on a disguise."

"But you would recognize him, if you saw him on the street?"

"I did see him on the street, as a matter of fact," Bakov said. "He was coming out of the Metro one Sunday morning. If I remember, he was on his way to GUM and had gotten off at the wrong station and was walking the wrong way. I have an idea he does that often."

"Let's hope so," Beria said. "You said you had only seen him twice?"

"To talk to," Bakov answered. "That time I pointed him in the right direction."

"Let me ask you a theoretical question," Merkulov said. "Suppose you were in charge of this operation. What would you do?"

"I have no idea," Bakov said. "I don't know what's at your disposal. Just as the Commissar says, I work in a box and I try to avoid what happens in other boxes."

"I know, but just suppose it was your responsibility to handle this urgency."

"I would try to eliminate him as quickly as possible."

"Let me tell you what I have done," Merkulov said, looking at Beria. Beria was scowling in anticipation that Merkulov would speak too candidly.

"First I sent the brigade from Switzerland. Do you know them?"

"I've seen their names on the lists from Lucy, that's all."

"They're experts at swift assassination, but we don't trust them," Beria said. "They've never been successful in doing their job quickly. They've made serious blunders."

"Then the people from the embassy in Istanbul are searching for Sarkov," Merkulov said, "but the Turkish police are watching them."

"Do we have other contacts in Istanbul?" Bakov asked. "I remember there were two assassins hired by Radchenko, one came from Ankara and the other from Istanbul. I have their names," Bakov said. "It seems to me a native would be the best for locating Sarkov."

"Good idea," Merkulov said. "Get the names."

"The embassy has alerted those people already," Beria said.

"Do we have anyone in the Turk police?" Bakov asked.

"I worked with a man from Zeitum," Merkulov said. "But he hated Russians."

"So, what is left?" Bakov asked. "You sent the brigade, there are embassy people about, some hired killers, whom we don't know. What else?" He looked down at his feet.

"I've been thinking," Merkulov said. "One man might be more effective than an army." He looked at Beria. "If he were intelligent, that man could find Sarkov in one day."

"He must be professional," Bakov said, beginning to suspect Merkulov's intentions. "He would have to know Istanbul, where to look for the man, to whom he would talk. He would need a week to prepare and he would need to be trained in special methods."

"You could search him out, couldn't you? Like code breaking?"

"I couldn't find him if he were in this building," Bakov said. "I don't know Istanbul, the language. I've never been in the field," he said. "If I were on my own out there, I wouldn't know where to look. I'd be lost myself." He was talking quickly. "Even if I stumbled on him, what would I do?"

"Here's what you do," Merkulov said. He moved to the large part of the room and began to walk back and forth. "You see him in Eminonu Square and you tip your hat. He may recognize you. He's trying to remember where he saw you. Then he remembers. He runs," Merkulov said. "But where does he go? You have the advantage. You know him. You are not afraid. He is. You have people around you. Call the Brigade They're at your disposal. There are other people, at the embassy. Whatever. Silence him yourself and we will honor you," Merkulov said. Then he continued, "I know about the shooting at Kama. Death is not a new thing to you."

"The circumstances were..."

"The circumstances were base," Merkulov interrupted. "I know what was involved. But this is patriotism: you are killing a traitor," Merkulov said. "Don't confuse what I say. Find him, just find him. The rest, the elimination, is not your problem."

Bakov stood without speaking.

"The brigade might finish him while you are traveling. They might have found him already," Beria said. "You come back, and we congratulate you."

"Where would I begin?"

"I would say, 'with Sarkov's wife,'"Beria said. "Wouldn't you?" He looked at Merkulov.

"If she's still there," Merkulov said. "There are two children. Perhaps the Brigade has found her and she has told them all she knows. Perhaps the affair is over. You go down and report to the embassy. Deliver this message." He leaned over Beria's desk and wrote on a clear sheet.

"There's a man in Istanbul named Yuki Ekmal," Beria said. "He's adjutant to the intelligence chief. But he's a very dangerous man, probably the most dangerous I have ever known," Beria said. "He would cut your throat for a price, and he will never tell the truth, never. Unless you pay him."

"Where would I find him?" Bakov asked.

"He used to drink tea every evening at Markiz. Go there and ask for him."

"What should I ask him?"

"Don't tell him too much," Beria said. "Ask him if he has heard of Sarkov and where he would find him. He'll know, because you will have enough money." He moved to the desk to write. "How much will he need?" He asked Merkulov.

Merkulov wrote a figure.

"That much?"

"Is it worth it, if we find Sarkov?" Merkulov asked. "If he doesn't need it, he returns it. Where's the risk?"

"You sign the voucher," Beria said, and Merkulov signed. Bakov picked up the voucher and studied the figure. "When do I leave?"

"Within the hour," Merkulov said. "I'll call your wife. The transit papers will be ready. Here is the dossier on Sarkov. Here's a book of his poetry. It might help you decode the man," Merkulov said.

"Don't all poets have codes?" Beria asked. "Aren't they synedochists?" He was smiling. "If you studied his poetry, wouldn't you be able to tell a great deal about the man, even where he was likely to hide?"

"I have no idea," Bakov said, shaking his head.

"One last thing," Beria said. "We are not motivated by rewards, but I want to share a secret with you." He opened the middle drawer and brought out a tray of medals. He held them up, one at a time. "This one is the Marshall of the Union. Here, five orders of Lenin, this one the Order of Suvdrov, first class. Two orders of the Red Banner here. Aren't they beautiful? Seven medals of the USSR and this, my favorite, the Red Star." He extracted the Red Star from it's bed and held it up high. It was a distinctive medal, infrequently awarded, although Stalin had pinned one on his chef, as a reward for an exquisite shashlik.

"I treasure this," Beria said, caressing the medal. "Then you shall have one of these," he said, "If you do your work well."

PART IV

LONDON

1

At nine forty-five the next morning, the eleventh of August, Philip Sloan stepped from the lift onto the fifth floor of MI5 headquarters. The lights over "C's" door were conspicuous in that none was lit. One of them was nearly always on, even late at night after "C" had left. Like the north star, "C's" light had become a standard of permanence in an otherwise transient craft.

Sloan had spent the night at the Park Lane hotel. He indulged himself in the luxury not only because the hotel was only five blocks from headquarters, but also because he had come to the conclusion that he would live less than five more days in England should Sarkov succeed in defecting. He might as well indulge himself in a better hotel. In spite of the luxury, Sloan rose early and arrived at his office just after six thirty, when he began the preparations for the Sarkov dossier. Much of the work was routine, but he still suffered from a residue of yesterday's anxiety. He had difficulty concentrating on the details of the flight, the FO papers, the letters of introduction, and the final items on Sarkov himself.

The records office, in the basement, opened at nine. Sloan was waiting at five to nine. In the days when the building was a residence, the basement had been a wine cellar and the bays were still there, only now they were shielded by a steel door and an inner grid. Instead of wine racks, there were rows of files and further in, agent "bibles": code names, covers, code words, pads, safe houses, drops, and the local contacts—filed under countries. Wilkinson, the guardian of records, sauntered in at nine exactly, unlocked the grates, and sat on his stool, without acknowledging Sloan. Wilkinson was a slight, balding man, water eyed, with spectacles. He had the sallow complexion of a librarian, his flesh as yellow as old paper. Sloan asked him for the NKVD albums which were kept on the top shelf in the strong room. Wilkinson went behind the steel door and returned with the two albums. On each page was a photo of a secret agent; in small print the details on each.

Sloan signed the register and turned toward the lift. He remembered that he would need two passports, so he walked back. The passports were not completely blank. Each had stamps from Calais, Madrid, and Cairo, but they had no photographs, no names, no dates. Sloan would enter the names and his secretary would stamp the dates and enter the photographs.

Although he had commandeered a military plane the day before, Sloan had a note to order air tickets through a commercial carrier. In critical situations it was wise to duplicate means of transport. He stopped at Finance, on the first level, drew money, and signed the voucher "Director's Vote" so that there would be no notation on the purpose of the flight.

"C" had ordered secrecy. It was the one section of the order which was to Sloan's advantage.

He was able to retain his composure and complete the preparations, even if they ran counter to his interests, because he was a professional deceiver. Others dabble in deception: actors, gamblers, churchgoers who assent to one creed and follow another. Not so Sloan. His was not a double life. Not only was deception his creed, it was his vocation.

As a professional deceiver he had many advantages. For one, he had already achieved his purpose: he was a paid officer in the NKVD. That he appeared to be a successful functionary of MI5, a loyal subject of the Crown, a dutiful housemate and father of children, meant little to him, so little that he did them well. In MI5 he worked proficiently, his staff admired him, he succeeded, because the daily routine was not an end, but a means to an end, an end he had already achieved. He would reveal all to his Russian superiors. He was the true poseur: he pretended to be what he was not. He was calm, full of aplomb, confident. It was a wonder that his mother recognized him.

Yes, the first days of deceit exact an enormous amount of energy, but time and habit make deception easy. At the beginning there could be no hint of treachery, even in drunkenness. The impulse to talk had to be checked, the tongue lashed, the will made subservient. With time he practiced lying, even when it was not expedient. Lying became habitual, then natural. Once the habit became natural, it was easy. He discovered that the practical liar need not be wary. Sloan's associates trusted him as much as the Olympians trusted Philoctetes.

He shifted his briefcase from his right hand to his left in order to examine his watch. Just as he was switching, the lift stopped and Carolyn stepped into the corridor.

Sloan was conscious that Carolyn suspected him so he was afraid that Carolyn was about to uncover him, most likely in "C's" presence. Sloan had learned to discipline his panic, must do. He walked leisurely, as he did now, up-and-down, even when his instincts told him to run, as they did now. He kept silent, when he ached to ask what Carolyn knew. He smiled, sadly. But he could not disguise the pain which, like an ulcer, tore at the lining of his stomach.

Being so sensitive, Sloan had a warning in his chemistry about Carolyn, a signal, which detected the slightest imbalance in Carolyn's attitude. Like a couple grown old together, Carolyn and Sloan intuited each others' responses. That Carolyn knew Sloan's secret there was no doubt. The question was, when would he reveal it.

Carolyn walked past Sloan without speaking, put his hand to the outside of his coat pocket, turned abruptly as if he had forgotten something, and then turned back as if relieved that he had found it. It was his tobacco. Carolyn pulled it out from the recesses of this pocket as if it were a lost treasure.

"C's" light was still unlit. Carolyn leaned against the wall, struck a match to his pipe and puffed strongly, as a detective might who had solved a case. Sloan felt that something had gone terribly wrong. He looked down and for the second time in twenty four hours, he saw his hands shaking. He needed relief, even if it were only to speak.

"Has he come in?" Sloan asked.

"The light's off on Friday mornings, always. He talks to the PM every Friday and meets with Petrie just before noon. He rarely schedules anything. Sometimes he talks with Churchill, er, Attlee for an hour or more. Didn't you know?"

Sloan did not know, but he did not answer the question either. Instead he asked, "Is Brigadier Thomas coming?"

"No, he isn't," Carolyn said. "There's been a shift, a new development. That's why I'm here."

A red splotch appeared on Sloan's face, and a smaller one at his hair line, but there was nothing he could do to hide them.

Like a romantic vision from across the bay, "C's" green light flared on.

The two men were shoulder to shoulder at the door when Carolyn said, "'C's' mother was lady-in-waiting to Queen Mary. I think she was related to Churchill's cousin, but I don't know how close." He pointed to the door with his thumb. "His mother was Roman. That explains his morbidity," he said without smiling. He lit his pipe again. Carolyn did not belong to the class, but he studied their breeding and their habits.

They were face to face. "I had heard that Churchill liked him because he kept the cost down," Sloan said.

"That, too." Carolyn said, holding Sloan's elbow as he put his head close to the door and knocked, quietly, with a knuckle.

Sloan did not hear "C's" answer, but Carolyn did. He opened the door.

"C" was standing at the window looking down on Green Park. He was whispering to himself. He turned slightly when the two came in, but did not stop whispering.

Then he said out loud, "Attlee told me that Eisenhower wants a war court against the Nazis. He asked me what I thought of war crimes."

"What do you think?" Carolyn asked. "I say 'get on with it.'"

"I asked him what he thought," "C" said. He sat down.

Carolyn and Sloan sat at each end of the desk. "C" preferred to moderate, his question to the Prime Minister proving that.

Sloan could see him clearly. It was a dim day. "C" looked a little pink on the cheek, Sloan thought. Not flush, but florid, as if he had just come in from the wind. Then Sloan saw the talc underneath the ear and he realized that "C" had not been talking to Attlee, but had been shaving.

"What does he think about war criminals?"

"He says the Americans are too impulsive. If we wait two years, the Germans will be our allies."

"That's difficult to imagine."

"So is General Marshall's plan hard to imagine. So is peace." He pulled the Sarkov folder from the top drawer.

"C" talks like Anatoli, Sloan thought. They are both cautious, often personal, idealistic, and afterward cynical, as if it were the final wisdom.

"Here is all we have on Comrade Sarkov," Carolyn said.

"Who will you send in Thomas' place?"

"I haven't decided," "C" said. "I want you to stay and watch the shop. I have to leave tomorrow, myself. I want someone responsible here while I'm gone."

"If I were head, I would recommend me for Istanbul," Carolyn said.

"I know," "C" said. "But you can't be two places at once, and I want you here."

"I think it's a mistake," Carolyn said. He was silent then, the silence running to sullenness. Sloan felt remote from the scene, like an accused who has been instantly exonerated and the true villain exposed. He felt as though the worst was over and that he could manage the rest.

"I won't keep you," "C" said. "But you will be coming back in half an hour. I want to brief Davies."

"C" looked at his pad and Carolyn left without saying another word. His pipe lay on the desk.

"I'm sorry for the awkwardness," "C" said. "It can't be helped. I wish everyone was as ready to take orders as you are."

"Thank you," Sloan said.

"The Prime Minister talked about the honor, the OBE." He had forgotten that they had talked about the medal the day before.

Sloan nodded that he did know.

"Congratulations," "C" said, offering his hand. "It's for your work in Spain. I think we all appreciate the patching up you have done. Now you're receiving the recognition."

"It wasn't difficult," Sloan said. "Class was never the reason for the dissatisfaction, although my contacts with the 'Indians' helped. Once the two sides agreed to separate responsibilities, the rest was easy." Sloan said repeating the exercise of the day before.

"Will it be so easy in the new section?" "C" asked. "I understand you transferred some agents to Eastern Germany. Is that right?"

"One or two of them operated against Hitler, so they know the territory, have contacts there. I've added two men in Krakow and three in Prague," he said. "We're recruiting people now for the topological survey of the Turkish border."

"I've seen the requests," "C" said. "It will be a major undertaking, beginning in Bulgaria, am I right?"

"Yes," Sloan said. "I am making plans to go there myself. Just to start up, mind you. The border is sixteen hundred miles long."

"I want you to go out there tomorrow," "C" said. "To take care of this Sarkov business. Will you do it?"

"What became of Thomas?"

"Have you ever heard of 'acrophobia'?"

"What?"

"Fear of flying," "C" explained. "He won't fly. He wouldn't board an airplane if the kingdom depended on it. I'm assuming that you will go, that the material is in the right hands. Am I correct?"

"I have a meeting with Section Six," Sloan said. "Except for that, my schedule's clear."

"C" nodded. "You'll need letters drafted and the usual faculties. At most that will take two hours. What else do you need?"

"I suppose letters of protocol," Sloan responded. "I know Reed. The ambassador worked with my father in the Punjab. I wonder what he thinks of all this fuss?"

"Not much, I'm afraid," "C" said. "He will be an obstacle if you're not careful. That's why I want you to go and not Carolyn. Peterson is cut from the same cloth I am. He wants the services to be honorable and the work done with decorum. He knows you, your father. He will welcome you. That's fine. Try not to put him off his form, will you?"

"Who else?"

"Talk to Reed. He is the contact. You know that. He is your key man. He'll establish contact with Sarkov the day you arrive."

"Should Reed hear what I have to say?"

"I wouldn't. I think you had better keep this as 'hush-hush' as you can. Don't let anyone know why you are there."

"Should I fly out with Sarkov?"

"That's not necessary," "C" said. "Reed has provided for that. He has the airplane. Skardon will meet Sarkov in Nicosia. By the way, did you contact Skardon?"

"Yes," Sloan answered. "What about the wife?"

"Whose?"

"Sarkov's?"

"I haven't an idea," "C" said. "Why do you ask that?"

Sloan did not answer. He had to take time and sort out what was being said. What had Anatoli said about the wife and what had been stated in the brief from Istanbul?

Certainly he had talked with Anatoli about the wife being brought out to Greece, but did "C" have knowledge of that?

"She had a thrombosis last year," he said. He read from the file. "You write here that she is the principal reason for Sarkov's defection."

"For medical treatment."

"Specifically for a doctor, Paul White, in Boston."

"I'm glad you brought her up, now that I think of it," "C" said. "I'll make mention of her in my letter to Peterson."

"I've uncovered other complications," Sloan said. "Sarkov's brother was involved in the Trotsky debacle in Mexico. That's another reason for him to leave. The whole family must be suspect."

"That may all be true, but I want to tell you why Sarkov is so important. Behind all our effort is Stalin's interest in the Dardanelles, and the Bosporus. He would like nothing better than a port, a warm port, which would be an access to the Mediterranean. In other words, he wants Istanbul. Its very clear that he wants it. He has never been in a better position to occupy the city than right now. Inonu knows it. He is frightened. He has made desperate calls to the West for help. As you can see, the situation is explosive. Sarkov could do the Russians incalculable harm if he causes trouble."

"How will the Russians respond? To this Sarkov affair? Would you say?"

"What can they do? He's hiding. There's little they can do."

"Where is he?"

"He wouldn't tell Reed. He may be in Turkey, he may not. You needn't worry about that. Your job is to bring him in by next Thursday and help with the embarrassment."

"C" walked to the window. He continued, "It's not like the old days, when things were simple: intercepting cables, tidbits of information, paying informants, sleuthing pictures of airplanes. How easy it was for Paul Duke in Russia. Dangerous maybe, but simple. Even Sidney Reilly in the Persian oil fields for Her Majesty had an easy time compared to today. My service was the old honorable one, the service of Sir Richard Hennecy. Never was there an idea of humiliating the other side. It seems that in every operation, what we must do is make the other fellow a laughing stock. We're trying to get the world to laugh at Beria so that his power is diminished. Ultimately, that's your object in Istanbul. You may even meet one of Beria's henchmen."

"How would I meet him?"

"You're after the same man. You to take him in, him to take him out. We intercepted a message an hour ago. An agent left Moscow early this morning. His name is Bakov. It's like Sarkov, isn't it? He left alone, but he must be good. All we know about him is that he's a cipher clerk. That's all we know, although he must know how to hunt, otherwise Beria would never have sent him, now would he?"

2

Unlike the day before when they stood, Carolyn and Davies sat in "C's" office. The meeting began that way, but Carolyn would not remain sitting, especially after he was agitated, which was inevitable in this company. He would sit while "C" spelled out the details of Sarkov's transfer from Istanbul to Cyprus, but since he was not a participator in the events, and thought he should be, then he would stand, move about, and grumble. But at the beginning of the meeting he sat, and while "C" talked, he turned the pages of Wickham's edition of Horace's *Odes*," a little book, which, like his tobacco, he carried with him.

"What's that book?" Davies asked.

"Quintus Horatius Flaccus," Carolyn answered.

"I prefer Ovid myself," Davies said. "What about you?" Davies asked "C".

"I'd like to finish this report, if you don't mind."

"We both know all we need to know, Leslie. Why go on so?"

"Because I will be in Canada for two weeks and I want you to know the facts, in case there's a crisis."

"Don't be so serious," Davies reprimanded. "The war's over."

"I like Houseman too," Carolyn said, "although he has no taste for the natural virtues, like patriotism."

"He lives in a more complicated time than Horace. It was easy to be a patriot in Rome."

"Why all this talk of poetry?" "C" asked.

"Sarkov is a poet."

"He is? Have you found something written by him?" "C" asked.

It was the question Carolyn was waiting to be asked. He loved to teach. "I couldn't find either of his two volumes, but I found some poems in an anthology. I had one translated." He handed a sheet with Sarkov's poem to "C" and slid another sheet next to Davies' elbow. "It suffers in translation, but it's all right," Carolyn said. "It's about conventions and how they cloud the truth. I would think it would be subversive to communism. I'll ask him when I see him."

"Well," "C" said, "he'll be on our side soon. I've sent Sloan to fetch him."

Carolyn jumped up from his seat, and his color rose. He looked questioningly at "C."

"He's the logical man," "C" said. "He was next." He was about to say more, but stopped in order that Carolyn could break in. But Carolyn did not speak. "He will have ease with the embassy people," "C" continued. "He's studied the file, and he has my mind in the negotiations."

"And he's prudent," Davies said.

Carolyn looked from Davies to "C" and wondered if the conspiracy extended to "C" himself. It wasn't treachery; it was sedition: a binding together of university men in order to protect one another, even if one was a traitor. Carolyn had all but exposed Sloan, but the others would not allow the exposition. So treachery was allowed to flourish. Like a virulent virus, it was spreading throughout the service.

Susceptibility began with the lie that university men were different, better, that they were beyond the lesser

vices, like treason. The virus gestated behind oak doors
where facts were rationalized, where matters "among their
own" were discussed. The plague spread from under the
doors to the whole service. It would effect the whole country, Carolyn believed, if not checked.

"I want to state for the record that I believe Sloan to
be a traitor."

"I've been doing some tracing myself," Davies said,
looking straight ahead out the window. "In *Debrett.* This
man is absolutely first class. Born in India, in Ambala,
where his father did enviable service. He was brought to
middle East after that." Davies opened a folder and spoke
from notes. "Then he came home. Westminster, like his
father, and Cambridge. Second in history, secretary to
Canning, president of JCR, the Gladstone scholarship, confidant of Keynes. Kings, not Trinity, although an Apostle
friend of Dobbs, the don. Magazine, *The Review.* After that
a brilliant career in Spain and maker of peace with the military, for which, as you both know, he will receive the
OBE." He coughed and turned his attention to the lozenge.
His argument was meant to overwhelm.

"C" looked at Carolyn, whose lips were set with
intransigence. "Nobility," he said between his teeth, "is a
precondition for treachery." He hesitated, but then continued, "Brutus was a nobleman. He flourished in respectable
society, but he was a scoundrel. Dante places him in the
lowest level of hell, his head in the Devil's mouth and feet
kicking a few feet off his native soil."

"You have no proof that Sloan is anything but what he
appears to be, a first class man," Davies said.

"I will have proof," Carolyn said. "I will. I haven't
caught him *in delictis*, but this isn't a court of law either.
What I do have persuades me, and it should persuade you,

that he is not to be trusted." Carolyn was deliberate and restrained, as pleader might who in the last desperate moments, has lost his case. "Did you know that he is in constant contact with Zharmalov's aide?"

"I shouldn't worry about that," Davies said. "I've known the General for years. Brilliant at chess."

"Last I knew, he was the enemy."

"Isn't that a little strong," Davies asked. "Sloan has friends in the Russian embassy, and he has some minor idiosyncrasies in his politics. We all have. His father criticizes the government and said some complimentary things about Mister Hitler." He waved his hand. "Injudicious is the worst you can make of it. But the family has been saying injudicious things since 1066. Then it was against the French. They were the enemy in those days."

"Does treason exist in your scale of values?" Carolyn asked.

"Surely, but your values need tempering, that's all," Davies said. "Because a man associates with men who were our allies until a month ago does not make him a spy."

"I did not say he was a spy. I did not say he was a double agent. He is a traitor, pure and simple." Carolyn leaned forward, coldly enraged. "His purpose is *rebellare*: to disrupt the common good of England and provoke a state of war in which he has sided with the enemy. That's what I am saying. This fellow is not a wag or a fool like his father. This man is a traitor to the Crown, and I am going to prove it."

"Haven't we all been less loyal at one time in our life?"

"If you have, you must answer for it," Carolyn said. "Nothing is more worthy of my loyalty than the Crown.

What has his loyalty? Mother Russia for God's sakes! We should all have a kind of shrug for this sort of person."

"Leslie," Davies said. "Calm him, will you? We don't need this sort of disruption, now do we?" He hoisted himself out of his chair. "I'm going to Trump's for a shave," he said. "I hope you take some composure from Flaccus," he said, patting Carolyn's shoulder.

"I hope they cut your throat," Carolyn said as the door closed.

"What was that?" "C" asked.

"I said, 'he seems so remote.'"

"He does, doesn't he?"

"Remote from reality," Carolyn said. "I'm having misgivings about a lot of people here. Some of them treat deceit with indifference and others seek it out," he said. "They seem to prefer deceit to truth."

"I'm afraid you're not going to explain," Carolyn said, "Why you are sending Sloan to Istanbul."

"No," "C" answered. "I am going to explain. But you'll have to wait till lunch. Can you trust me till then?"

"Lunch at your club?" Carolyn said, and when "C" nodded, Carolyn folded his hands as if it were an answer to a prayer.

"Trust is more difficult than faith, isn't it?" "C" asked.

"Trust is the first step of faith, and the most difficult. It demands a sacrifice."

"That's what I'm asking you to do, sacrifice."

"I have no earthly idea what you are doing, or why you are doing it. It must be spectacular."

"It is," "C" said.

"Why can't you tell me now?"

"Because there is one more piece of information that I need and I won't have it till noon."

"So you have a 'pocket secret' until lunch?"

"One o'clock," "C" said. "But I will tell you this. I am adding insult to trust."

"I don't understand."

"I am going to test your trust and your courage."

"What on earth do you want me to do?"

"I want you to drive Sloan to the airport in Uxbridge early tomorrow morning, three o'clock. Will you do it?"

"And assassinate him on the way."

"No, just drive him to the plane."

"You'll have plenty to talk about, especially after our lunch."

"I'd like to talk to him about treachery. It's a little man's game," Carolyn said. "But I doubt that its possible to convert a small man who cheats on a grand scale."

3

Carolyn stood at the bar of the Carlton club. He knew he out of place because he wanted to put his foot on the brass rail, which was purely decorative, and it would be out of form to put one's foot on it. Still, he wanted to.

Nor was he dressed for the Carlton. The man standing next to him looked like a cabinet minister: thin and bent, his nose sharp and red at the end, nearly dripping, he looked like a caricature by Gill for *Money and Morals*. He wore a high collar, gold watch and chain, striped trousers—rented from Moss'—a bowler poised on the bar, and a new umbrella hanging from the support. He balanced a whiskey and soda in his right hand, and in his left a dispatch case with royal insignia showing. Carolyn dared not talk for fear he might speak a different language.

Carolyn was out of place, and he knew it. He tried to appear occupied. He looked to his left and to his right. No one was watching so he boldly raised his right foot and placed it on the brass rail.

On most days he took his lunch at his desk on the third floor of 54 Broadway. Usually he ate a deviled ham sandwich and pickle, and finished in less than fifteen minutes. If he hadn't been invited to "C's" club, at this moment he would be reading the Fleet reports at his desk.

At five after one "C" came into the bar and, after a brief cordiality, walked Carolyn into the dining room.

When they were comfortably seated and "C" ordered parsley soup, whiting roast veal, and cabinet pudding, for both, "C" said, "Before we talk about Sarkov, let me tell you a story. Do you mind?"

Carolyn nodded.

"Two years ago, on July 16, 1943, one of our best men was killed in Gibraltar. The investigation revealed that the man, his name was Sikorski, had been killed on orders from Churchill. All hush, hush. What do you make of it, so far?"

"You haven't told me much, but it looks like Sikorski was double dealing and Churchill put a stop to it."

"That would be the logical assumption, and that is what we thought at the time."

"Did Cumming ever tell you anything else?"

"No, he never mentioned it, I'm afraid."

"Did he tell you Churchill's reasons?"

"That's the difference between him and me. He never spoke to Churchill. He couldn't have."

"Why? One of his men is exterminated and he doesn't do anything about it? It doesn't make sense."

"I called Churchill just before he left office and asked him. He never heard of Sikorski. Imagine how shocked I was! One of our researchers was working on a related matter and unearthed this Sikorski business. He had questions, so I called Churchill. When he told me he had never heard of Sikorski, I started an inquiry. Here is what I found."

"C" held up a sheaf of legal-sized sheets. The writing was in a large, clear hand. "Sikorski became suspicious of another agent in the Iberian Section, suspicious that the man was working for the Russians. So he kept a file. What he had was only a hearsay, mind you, but one notation goes back to 1936 when the two were working in Spain during the war. The suspect was stopped and interrogated by a civil guard in Corduba. The guard swears that the man was a communist because he tried to swallow a sheet of rice paper on which was written a codified message, in Russian."

"It was Sloan, wasn't it? Are you telling me that Sloan murdered Sikorski because he was on to him? Sloan was arrested in Corduba in 1936."

"Yes," "C" said. "But Sikorski's notes fell into the wrong hands. In 1944 Sloan was put in charge of the Iberian Section. He must have found snippets of Sikorski's files and had the man eliminated, using Churchill as authority. Imagine!"

"Brazen. And now you are sending him to Istanbul."

"Why not?" "C" said. "He's the logical man."

"I was thinking on my way here, 'McKenzie does not want Sarkov to live. I have to wonder why?'"

"I'm telling you quite a lot today," "C" said. "But this is the most important. In June Bletchley broke the Russian code. Does that change things?"

"I knew they were close."

"Its an enormous achievement, more important than Ultra. The Russians came up with a 'closing' which stumped us, but we broke it. Turner up there did it. He knows and I know and now, you know. But no one else must, do you understand?"

"If I can keep a secret for two days, I can keep it for ever. Father Martindale of Farm Street church taught me that."

"All right," "C" said. "Beria knows as much about our operation as we do his," "C" pointed to the ceiling. "I'm convinced he thinks his cipher is fool-proof. They are so sure of their apparatus that they send in English. I have all the Russian wires, every last one of them." He leaned forward and snapped his fingers. "If Sarkov comes over, they change the system."

"You're sure?" Carolyn asked. "You think Sarkov might know their method?"

"No, I am not sure," "C" said, "most likely he doesn't know, but I can't risk it."

"So you send Sloan the traitor who doesn't want Sarkov to come either."

"Surely," "C" said. "Sloan delays, postpones, makes excuses why he can't meet Sarkov, and Sarkov drifts back and is taken by his own people. It has to be this way."

"Then there's another factor: the Russians think we trust Sloan."

"Yes."

"When he returns from Istanbul we go through the usual investigation why he failed, and then let him stay in place. Is that right?"

"What harm can he do if we watch him?" "C" asked. "At most he transfers only the information we allow."

"He might concoct other atrocities, like this Sikorski business."

"Not with you watching him, he won't. You might even hint that you know what he's about, although that would not be wise just now. Sometime in the future you might slap his wrist and let him know we are on to him."

"I don't like it," Carolyn said. "He has too many advantages, freedom to come and go, access to files, things he overhears. And we will have to be on our "uppers" as I am in this club."

"No," "C" said. "I think we have the advantage."

"How so?"

"I had this happen once before," "C" said. "I found that a traitor in the shop is like a man who is committing adultery with your wife. He's always trying to please you. He has to keep his secret. Sloan would no more refuse an order from me than he would confess his treachery. He hasn't missed a day of work in three years, and his routine work is flawless. I wish we had more like him."

"I can't believe you're saying that," Carolyn said.

"I know," "C" said. "You'd like to strike him. But think, think of the advantages of keeping him on." Then he said, "Aren't you going to eat your soup? It's best when it burns the tongue."

"I'll wait for the main course," Carolyn said. "I don't eat much at midday."

"Suit yourself," "C" said, "but it is delicious." A spoonful was stopped halfway to his lips. "Now you. What advantage do you see in bringing Sarkov in?"

"Information."

"What kind of information?" "C" asked, and then answered his own question. "The most important information is those three names. We already know Sloan's name tops the list. Whatever else Sarkov knows, we already know: number plates, keys to locks, names of agents we already know, incidental information, all of which is worth nothing compared to our breaking their code. They mustn't suspect we know."

"This morning you mentioned 'embarrassment' and how the Russians hate it."

"We have a probing, if inaccurate, press," "C" said. "There is no such thing in Russia. If Sarkov defected, it would appear on page 3 of the *Daily Mail*, not at all in the *Washington Post*. *The Cumhuriyet* in Istanbul might mention it. But not *Pravda* or *The Red Star* or *Izvestia*. Where would the embarrassment be, if the Russian press didn't cover it?"

"So 'embarrassment' is not an element?"

"Not for the Russians," "C" answered. "It would be for us, if Sloan was exposed. Think of the publicity if he is arrested and put on trial?" He sat back and pressed his fingers together, as if praying. "That a traitor could rank so high! Think of the disclosures we would have to make? *En camera.* If Sloan was convicted, which is unlikely, every facet of the firm would be scrutinized in the press, every man in the field, all the processes of recruitment, even the nature of the service itself would come under question. All this, outside the man's trial. No, I can't afford it. We have to let Sloan dangle in place."

"Or eliminate him."

"Yes, you mentioned that," "C" said. "I find the idea intriguing. But I don't think its time for that. It will come, no doubt, but I don't think it has yet."

"Why not?"

"Because it's too messy," "C" answered. "I don't have to tell you. The family questions, doctor's certificates, questions from other people in the firm, leaks, especially at the inquest, all that."

"C" sat back, the veal being served. "I'd rather watch what happens in Turkey."

"Sarkov sinking?"

"I'm not certain that Sarkov will die," "C" said. "He is a smart man and the Turks are wild people. No one knows what will happen. But consider this: The Russians catch up with Comrade Sarkov before next Thursday. What do they do with him?"

"Eliminate him, quietly. They don't have to be cautious with a traitor."

"Think again," "C" said. "That would be true if it were Moscow, or even here, but not in Istanbul. A Russian cannot murder in Istanbul and expect to get away with it."

"What are you saying? Extradite him back to Moscow?"

"It won't work," "C" said. "They will try to put him under wrappers and whisk him out of Turkey, quietly."

"How?"

"On an airplane, of course," "C" said. "How else?"

"You learned that from their wires, didn't you?"

"See the advantage of breaking their code?" "C" asked. "Yesterday Beria ordered a military aircraft, a PS-84, sent to Yesikoy next Friday morning. It is to be on the ground for exactly two hours. Can you imagine the risk he is taking, sending a military plane to a hostile airport, when he has over a million troops less than a hundred miles from the border? Do you want to talk about explosive?"

"I'm sure Russian planes land in Turkey all the time."

"You're wrong," "C" said. "Do you think the Turks would stand for that?"

Carolyn looked at his meal.

"Please Charles, eat some, will you?"

Carolyn reluctantly cut a section of the veal.

"Kazya Karan Bekit has let it be known that the Turks will fight if the Russians come. Kazya is not an impulsive man. It was a stern warning. The Russians have already put their man in as governor of Azerbaijan. At this very moment Stalin is negotiating for the nine districts in northern Turkey which he insists belong to Georgia. How much will it take before the Turks act?"

"I don't see what this has to do with Sloan and Sarkov?"

"With all this confusion, I am hoping that the Russian bear makes mud on a street in Istanbul." He laughed at the picture of it, his belly shaking. Then he became suddenly stern. "The Russians want Istanbul," he said. "Like all glacier beasts, the bear loves warm water. They make no pretense. Molotov proposed usurping Istanbul in 1940. It didn't work. But the Turks stayed neutral during the war, if you call siding with the Germans neutrality, and the Russians treat them like the defeated.

"Comes the division of spoils after Potsdam, and what do we have? The Russians are in a better position to swallow up the city than ever before. Last week Vinogradoff presented the Allies with the particulars in their revision of the Russia-Turk treaty." "C" held up his fingers to count.

"First, they want a rectification of the frontier. That means that the Russians want Kars and Ardahan back. Isn't that what they mean by 'rectification'? Second, they want military bases in the Dardanelles. And third, they are demanding a Turkish government which is friendly toward them because Turkey will come under their zone."

"I'm bewildered by all this," Carolyn said. "I know the Russians want a port to the Mediterranean, but I am confused by the rest. What does politics have to do with Sloan and Sarkov?"

"You're right, it is confusing," "C" said. "But what interests us is not so confusing. Sarkov is hiding, his wife secure. I am wagering that he knows he is only a pawn in this game, that he may have to be sacrificed for some larger outcome. He's smart, we know that. He does his work, which is to stay hidden until Thursday, when he surfaces at our embassy. What I am thinking is that in those short days the Russians will cause enough turmoil in Istanbul to provoke an incident, an international incident. It is like them to do such a thing."

"Yes, it could happen. Anything could happen. What are we doing to make it happen?"

"We don't have to do a thing," "C" said. "Aren't we in an enviable position? In all the calculus of possibilities, we can only win. All we have to do is sit back and watch."

"I hope you don't mind my saying that I am skeptical," Carolyn said.

"Look," "C" said. "Beria is the loser in almost every scenario. More can go wrong for him than can go right. He's involved up to his neck. He sends those fools from Switzerland. He orders a plane to land on enemy soil. He sends a special agent." He stopped eating his broccoli, a strand protruding from his mouth, and said, "Curious. He sends a cipher clerk to assassinate Sarkov. We have nothing on the man, nothing. I think it is what it appears to be, a wild attempt. Beria must be distraught. It was a desperate move."

"Desperate?"

"Beria will be the big loser if anything blows up. He may," "C" said as he winked, "loose his life."

4

The further north they drove, the worse the rain. In a thousand years Englishmen will have evolved gills, Carolyn thought, and will swim under Shepherd's Bush. The town was not flooded yet, but it was pock-marked by German bombs. The home of Napier Machine Works, a manufacturer of tank and airplane parts, it was a prime target of German bombs.

Sloan drove and Carolyn slumped in the passenger seat. They sloshed along the A3 out of Shepherd's Bush into Ealing, passed the Ministry of Pensions on the left, and then up Hanger Lane. Had it been light and clear, they would have seen Harrow on the left, but it was raining and three in the morning, and they saw wipers and the reflection of headlamps on the road.

"Have you ever heard the old saw: 'one goes to heaven by way of Uxbridge?'" Carolyn whispered.

"It is beautiful country here."

"It's the rain," Carolyn said. And then, "You had relatives at Harrow."

"Yes, my uncle, and my maternal grandfather taught here."

"And your father's cousin, Halcourt, still does."

"Yes, of course. Halcourt."

They crossed over the Grand Junction Canal, which was brimming, and into Woods End. Night lights illuminated the Red Lion Inn, Hayes End.

"This is where Charles the first stopped on his way to meet the Scot army," Carolyn said.

"He had a devil of a time, didn't he? But he was a great man."

"But not a great king," Carolyn said.

Sloan was anxious to avoid any provocation, so he did not respond. He needn't have worried. Carolyn continued, "He had a touch of quality, but only a touch. No patience with thought, only feeling. He detested dogma of any kind. But you have to give him this: he knew beauty and treasured it. At one time he had Reubens on the payroll and, at the same time, he was buying Rembrandt prints. He was the consummate aesthete, but he had no business ruling the kingdom."

They passed Denham where the highway joins Western Avenue in the direction of Ruislip.

As if in distraction, Carolyn began to mumble about a teacher at Stonyhurst. He talked as if he were repeating a memory lesson, only every now and then he turned to see if Sloan was paying attention. He repeated words and phrases, slightly rearranged, as if every detail had to be expressed, and heard, like a formula or a rite.

Sloan had prepared himself to talk about Sarkov, or MI5, even Carolyn's suspicions. When Carolyn began his story, Sloan became unnerved, but as it went on, he become more attentive. From beginning to end, he wondered about the reason for the story.

"It's easy to endow a teacher with romantic qualities," Carolyn began, "but the truth is, D'Arcy was uncommon. He had an obsession with 'primary sources.' He could never write a book because he could never start. Each detail had to be explained. It was the same with his lectures. He would trace sources, always going back.

I remember the lecture on the Armada. He hardly begun when he leapt from the Armada to Philip the Second of Spain. 'But,' he insisted, 'how could we ever know Philip without understanding his father, Charles the Fifth.' Of course it was not possible to understand Charles the Fifth without studying the Holy Roman Empire, of which Charles was the emperor. And so on. He traced the Holy Roman Empire to Charlemagne, and back to the Twelve Tablets of Roman Law. He hadn't said five sentences about the Armada which occurred in the sixteenth century, because he never got past the second century BC."

Carolyn was so absorbed with his own lesson that he did not notice that Sloan had stopped. Sloan interrupted, "I can't remember," he said. "Is the airport ahead or to the left?"

"To the left," Carolyn answered. "The airport is in Ruislip, even though people in London refer to it as Uxbridge." Carolyn was not deterred by the interruption. He continued, and the mumbling became a whisper. "Like great men before him, D'Arcy was an enigma. He ate little, but had a Falstaffian girth. No one ever saw him read a book, but he corresponded with Einstein, and composed the crossword for the *Times*. He had no bed in his room, nor was there a grey streak in his massive head of black hair.

"He was not accessible, hadn't many friends. He liked books better than people. At first meeting he might correct your grammar, distinguish a statement, or criticize your fingernails. He investigated people, just like the Armada. He made no judgment until the facts were in. When he knew you, it was his to be candid and yours to be careful." Carolyn laughed. Despite his wonder, Sloan was intrigued. "He traced a boy the way he traced a fact of history. As a result he was always able to find an excuse." It was evident from his tears that Carolyn was moved by the remembrance. "He was a genius at mercy," he said. "But he was a victim of the old Socratic illusion: that sin is ignorance and knowledge virtue. If you knew what was right, you would do it. The theory works in schools and detective stories, but not in life.

"What influenced me the most, directed the course of my life—was his analysis of the Oedipus' story." Carolyn looked at Sloan for the second time. Sloan had stopped the automobile because they were at the gates of the airport. There were no guards and he did not know which way to turn, but he dared not interrupt again. "I'm sure you know the outline of the story, although the myth developed over time. In its bare bones King Laius left his son, Oedipus, on a mountainside to die, but the baby survived, and years later confronted his father on a road. Of course the two did not recognize each other. They fought and Oedipus killed his father. A plague fell on the city as a result of the regicide, but Oedipus solved the riddle, became the king, and married the queen, who, of course, was his mother.

"D'Arcy was intrigued by the character sources of Oedipus' crimes. He taught us to look back at the father's behavior and find the answer. The father's name was Laius, and he had committed a despicable crime. He had abducted the son of Pelops and violated the boy. Pederasty was not the crime. What was so bad was Laius' inclination toward violence, what the Greeks called *hubris*. This tendency, the impulse which showed itself in his pederasty brought him and his family down.

"D'Arcy made his point and I never forgot it. 'The seeds of the son's destruction were sown in the violent instincts of the father.' D'Arcy had the mind of the Greeks. They believed that character is fate, that tragedy is present from birth. It was Laius' violence which led to his son's patricide and incest, just as the night follows the sunset. And the strange thing is that Laius knew it. He knew years before that he must not cohabit with his wife. That if he did, she would have a son who would murder him. Still he could not control himself. The impulse was so strong that he did it, damned the consequences."

"It was inevitable," Sloan said.

"But not necessary," Carolyn answered. "Even the son had warnings. An oracle told him, when he was a young man, 'Know thyself.' If he had the presence of mind to look back, to search the sources, his character sources, his tendency, the violence he inherited, he might have acted differently.

"As it was, he reaped what his father had sown. Too bad. But the lesson is there. Discern and learn, or reap the rotten fruit."

"Intriguing," Sloan said. He turned, expecting more. His eyes were wide, either from fascination or from fear, it was not possible to tell. "Is there anything else?"

"You have all the information you need," Carolyn said.

"I meant on Sarkov."

"I don't know his sources, only some incidental biography. It won't help much."

Sloan took the folder Carolyn handed him, stepped out and then bobbed his head back inside the compartment. Carolyn did not look at him, but continued to look straight ahead, and pointed to the right where, in the rain, a plane stood ready.

5

I t was only after he was standing inside the hangar at the Marseilles' airport that Sloan recognized the distinguishing marks of the plane he had flown from Ruislip. He had boarded at 3:30 in the morning, in the rain, had been unable to sleep what with the wheezing wind, the groaning motors, and Carolyn's eerie lesson; he dozed fitfully throughout the flight. Though dazed from lack of sleep, he recognized the plane as an old Anson, a reconnaissance plane. In the Spanish war, the resistance used a plane like this one. It was light, with a wide cabin, although this one was pared down for long-range use.

"Isn't that an Arrow nineteen?" Sloan asked the pilot who was standing in front of him in the enclosure.

"Yes," the pilot answered, still looking out. "We've been using it on these trips, although it was not designed for distance. It's cheap, that's the reason. We have a quarter tank left after eight hundred miles, seven hours of flying. But it is fragile. Hope you weren't uncomfortable?"

Sloan did not answer. Instead he said, "If I remember, we used it for 'looking' in Spain. It was too wobbly, an easy target, so we wound up flying it around the mountains. Does it have guns?"

"No, the mountings are empty," the pilot said. "The whole plane has been pared down for speed, although we will slow up a bit with the second passenger."

"Who's the passenger?"

"You don't know?" the pilot asked. "We were told she was meeting you. Didn't the mate give you the message?"

"Strange," Sloan said quietly.

"She has a German name," the pilot said. "It's in the note. Here he comes now."

The mate walked into the enclosure, his hand raised, the message held high like a victory signal. He was young, Nordic looking, with yellow hair. As Sloan read the mate stood too close, like a messenger awaiting a tip. Finally Sloan looked up and the mate retreated.

"Everything all right?" The pilot asked.

"Yes. She used to be my wife."

"Will she be traveling all the way to Turkey?"

"I expect so," Sloan answered. "I don't know what her plans are. I'll be glad to see her."

"I hope you're not in a hurry."

"Weather?"

"I've never flown the Mediterranean in August without a storm," the pilot said. "Which is all right, except there is only one plane from Tunis to Cairo."

"I don't mind," Sloan said. "As long as you log the delays. I'm expected in Istanbul Wednesday."

"You're with the FO, aren't you?"

It was close enough, so Sloan nodded.

"They're dreaming again," the pilot said. "They think airplanes are as regular as the rails."

The Anson motors turned over and the plane bounced unsteadily.

Sloan looked down at the cable and wondered if Litzi was bringing bad news. If Sarkov had been taken in by the British, Sloan would have to change his course toward Moscow.

Up to now he had acted precisely and accurately. He would not change a word he had said in the last two days, but he could not control circumstances.

He had the impulse to talk the matter through, in case he had missed an obvious error. He needed to talk, not just the complications of the Sarkov affair, but also the tenuousness of his work. It was a dangerous impulse—to talk—but he found relief in knowing that he could express his fears to Litzi.

"You needn't worry," the pilot said. "We'll wait for the lady."

"I wasn't thinking of her," Sloan said. "I'm worried about you. For some reason you don't want to go."

The pilot lit another cigarette from the stub of the previous one. "Was it that obvious?" He said and then hung his head like a boy caught cheating. The guilty looked spoiled his mien. Men in uniform should not loose their bearing. "I'm in trouble. Girl friend. Have you ever done that?"

"A wife in England?"

"Leicester. With two kiddoes," the pilot said. "This one wants marriage. Well, her brothers do."

"Can you delay?"

"Trouble is, I've told some things that weren't true."

"About your wife?"

"That, but that's not the worst," he said. He took two steps as if he wanted to pace, but there wasn't room. "I'll have to stop coming here, although I like her better."

"I know."

The pilot looked directly at Sloan for the first time. "I don't mean in bed," he said slowly, "but to talk to. She's smart, and good."

Sloan waited for the revelation.

"She's carrying my baby."

"You do have a problem," Sloan said. "What are your plans?"

"I have no idea," the pilot said. "I'm as despondent as can be. I can't stay with Lucia and I can't stand to be around my family."

"Do these people know anything about home?"

The pilot shook his head.

"It sounds like you better go back to England and stay there."

The mate was outside, standing near the plane beckoning them. The pilot opened the door for Sloan to exit first. "I haven't talked to anyone about this," he said almost in Sloan's ear. "Thanks for listening."

The few minutes of attention were an unexpected gift, like a monogrammed money clip that the pilot had seen in a Burlington shop window. His eyes sparkled as they walked. He opened the hatch for Sloan and shouted above the noise of the motors, "Yes, that's what I'll do. You are right."

Sloan tapped the pilot on the shoulder as he stepped across the wide gangway into the body of the plane. He had hoped that Litzi might be inside the cabin. She wasn't. He moved to the rear and arranged two cushions against the bulkhead, then sat near the window and looked out at nothing but the mist.

6

"Here they come," the pilot shouted, his voice resounding off the cabin's walls as if in a wind chamber.

Sloan tried to stand but could not keep his balance so he sat. He strained his neck to see through the wet window as a Citroen edged close to the wing. It parked for ninety seconds before there was any movement. She is getting her instructions, Sloan thought. Only someone who did not know her would give her instructions; her instincts for espionage were intuitive, and she never followed directions.

"It's her, all right," Sloan shouted. The door on the opposite side opened, but still Litzi did not appear. Then she alighted, and Sloan thought he recognized her kerchief, but immediately the head ducked back insides if for one last kiss. Finally she stood straight, slammed the door with finality, moved back, and the sleek automobile drove off. She waved as one would to a departing lover.

She has changed since their days together, Sloan thought. Her hair was spread out and her face was fuller than he remembered. She no longer had the ascetic look of a rebel. She seemed more maternal. Perhaps the children had tempered her impudence. She walked to the hatch opening, and waited for someone to greet her. Sloan stood, kept his balance awkwardly, made his way to the portal, jumped down, and moved toward her, a little too quickly for a husband, and too slowly for a lover.

"Hello, Phillipe," she said, making a childish wave, then extracting a kerchief from her pocket and tying it around her neck, as if to fence off her face and prevent a kiss. "We had a cable from Merkulov, telling us to meet you."

"I'm surprised, but happy," he said.

"It must be serious," Litzi said. "They don't usually send, as you know. Merkulov is cautious, but the cable was quite firm."

"I need to talk with you more than at Bar Basque," he said. "It's all confusion."

"Three years and five months, it's been," she said. "What's so urgent?"

"They didn't tell you?"

"Only some names—Istanbul—and the 'red.'"

"I thought you might be bringing bad news."

"Tell me."

"An agent from the first directorate defected through Istanbul. He's has my name. Did Moscow give you any information on him?"

"No, but I saw a list," she answered. "Is the name Sarkov?"

"Yes," Sloan answered. "Do you know him?"

"No," she said. "Just the name. Moscow thinks they can take him before we arrive."

"How much more do you know? Is he hiding?"

"Yes," she answered. "What do you think he will do?"

They were seated in the back of the plane. "Anatoli thought he would continue working, which is foolish, I can see now," Sloan said. "I'm angry at Line F. They ought to check these weak people. Do I have to worry about all the failures inside? I don't have enough to think about."

"We'll always have malcontents," Litzi said. "Everybody from Redl to Plotkin. We're all vulnerable from the inside, even families."

"How are the children?" Sloan asked, taking the bait.

"Jessica's breathing hasn't improved, but she's doing much better in school," Litzi said. "Andrea's the same: no trouble. I'm pleased with her." She looked at Sloan. "How do you intend to find him?"

"He'll come to me," Sloan said. "We'll meet at the embassy on Thursday. He thinks he'll be brought in, but we'll have another reception for him."

"Don't forget," Litzi said, "slipping through is a Russian pastime. And don't count on the brigade. The young ones are foolish and the old don't care."

The pilot turned in his seat and raised his arm, a signal that he was about to taxi. The two passengers were quiet while he revved the motors, maneuvered the plane onto the runway, and ascended.

Sloan flew more than the ordinary man, more even than the ordinary civil servant, but he was still afraid on take-off, when the wings tipped and the vents directed the air and there were sudden shifts in altitude. He watched the pilot flick on the operation's switch, heard him talk to the tower—all of which indicated safety—but Sloan did not feel safe.

Then there was the nausea which did not come right away, but as the plane banked, the retch began in the belly, rocked back and forth like a child on a swing, and then settled, only to be compounded by the pressure in the forehead. He breathed in and held his breath. It helped. Litzi leaned back and closed her eyes, another way of neutralizing the queasiness.

When the plane had settled, Litzi asked, "Should I keep this on?" She huddled in her coat.

"It will be cold in a few minutes," Sloan answered. "Do you have hose?"

"Should I put them on over these?"

"Do."

She leaned down and unzipped her valise, searched for her stockings, and then sat upright. "Center is so cautious, especially with penetrators," she said. "I never hear about you. But someone at a party said that you had moved up in Six. Is that true?"

"First assistant, in January," he said. "It was a coup really."

"What about that fellow who was watching you? Is he still there?"

"Carolyn," Sloan said. "A bird dog. Worse than ever."

"Is Percy out?"

"I rerouted some cables from Germany, delayed them down the line. Later I had them pop up in Percy's office. When McKenzie saw the original dates he blamed Percy for the delay. That was that. Was I working to get Percy out when you were in London?"

"Nikitin was after you to squeeze him," Litzi said. "He was right, wasn't he? Percy could be dangerous to us?"

"It wasn't difficult to prick McKenzie's suspicions. They're all a bit neurotic, always looking for disloyalty. I showed McKenzie a letter Percy had written to Lindsay-Hogg, about his being disillusioned with the service. That was the second blow." He stopped to relive the plot, then continued, "I was happy enough just to step over Percy in the Iberian section when another fortunate thing happened. Do you remember Ralph Deakin? Well, he asked me to come back to the *Times*. I showed his letter to McKenzie, who forwarded the letter to Roberts at the FO. McKenzie showed me the letter Roberts wrote to Deakin. He couldn't let me go, he said, because of 'my exceptional ability.' Six weeks to the day they promoted me from Ryder street to Broadway. I've been there ever since."

"What happened to Percy?"

"He shifted sideways, kept his rank. If he stayed, he would have exposed me. I still have to worry about Carolyn. I'm certain he's aware of what I am doing."

"Have a draught of this," she ordered. "You look pale." She handed Sloan a vial.

"I am a little sick," Sloan said, and drank.

"You're free of one crisis and another pops up."

"He drove me to the airport," Sloan said. "Told me this story from Greek mythology. I haven't the slightest idea what he was talking about. God, he is a strange bird." He folded his arms. "Oh well, I shan't worry about him today."

"He is a very clever fellow, from what I know about him."

"He hasn't said a word to me," Sloan said. "But I know he is tracking me. What do you remember about Vienna? I know we were not careful. I was trying to think whether I signed anything after we were recruited." The two of them thought for a few moments. "He knows about you, about the meetings at Gerard Street. He knows about the children and he knows what you are doing. It's damned unsettling."

"We've been through worse," Litzi answered. "Remember Peter?"

"How is Peter? Do you ever hear from him?"

"Poor Peter," she said.

"Why 'poor'?"

"He always chose the wrong side," she said, "something like you. He couldn't admit it, even when the *Schutzbund* collapsed. He had more talent for leadership than anyone in our group, knew Marx, but he kept fighting after the war was over. And then gave up politics completely," she said as an afterthought, "just like that, as if to prove that it was all an exercise in personality all along."

"What do you mean? Chose the wrong side?"

"I don't mean the wrong side, but you idolize the wrong people, especially when they're far away."

"Like who?"

"Marx, for one," she said. "Your father, for another."

"I'm proud of that," he said.

"Have you ever regretted your commitment?" She asked.

The question caught him unawares, although he should have been familiar with Litzi's candor.

On the outside Sloan had that chilling certainty of a true believer. He was one of the converted. Like all converts, he championed the ideal, fed it, nourished it, and denied its blemishes.

Did Litzi suspect that there might be regrets, in time, to his pledge, like one might regret a marriage contract: it was 'made in youth, ill conceived, rash?' Not so in Sloan's case. He never once regretted his attachment to communism.

It began with his revulsion for the English system. When he was on the other side, he did everything possible to further its cause and destroy the English cause. When his information resulted in the deaths of English nationals he reasoned that he was an officer in an army and those people were the casualties of war. Now and again he recognized a name among the dead, and felt a twinge of guilt, but never regret. "No, I have never regretted. Never."

The pilot raised himself from his seat and made his way, awkwardly aft. Close to Sloan's face he shouted, "Electrical storms over Malta," He continued shouting even though they were less than two feet from each other. "We are being diverted to Tunis."

"Tunis?" Litzi asked.

"There's a plane from Tunis to Cairo and onto Istanbul," Sloan explained.

"It's a little 'out of the way,' isn't it?" Litzi asked.

"Made to order," Sloan responded. "Chances are Sarkov will be dead before we arrive. Wouldn't that be good news?"

7

"He's beginning his descent," Sloan said. "I can see the shore."

"What's all that swirling? Is it sand?"

"Yes," Sloan answered. "It could be dangerous. We'll have to stay above it, come in from the south."

"I don't like the wobbling."

"You have to expect that," Sloan reassured. "This plane is not stable. We had one in Spain."

"You and I haven't made plans for Istanbul," she said. "There's all day tomorrow," Sloan answered. "We can talk on Shepherd's patio."

She turned toward him. "You are having regrets, aren't you?"

"No," he said. "Not about what we're doing, but I am afraid of being caught. Wouldn't you?"

"We've talked and talked and talked about this."

"I know, but it was always speculation," he answered. "Yesterday I felt the fear. McKenzie was quite serious. If I were exposed, I hate to think what he might do. Even murder."

"Phillipe!" she said. "Tell me, exactly, what did he say?"

"I told you," he said. "He said that Sarkov was bringing these names and that Carolyn was vetting me. Didn't he know I would make the connection?"

"What makes you think he saw one?"

"We talked about them together."

"Then why did he send you? He must trust you?"

"I don't know," Sloan answered. "But I am almost certain he believes my name's on Sarkov's list."

"Even if he did, is that so bad? If the worst happened, you would live the rest of your life in Russia, as a hero," she said. "Isn't that what you want?" She reached down to straighten her stocking. "I think McKenzie might suspect something. He's always suspicious, but he doesn't have anything to go on. In which case you continue to function, being so helpful." She looked at him. "We admire what you do, all of us."

"I would like to continue for a while," he said, "but not with the pressure."

"I like the story you tell about Corduba."

"Oh, the onion paper?"

"Are we talking about the same thing? Swallowing the code? And the captain making you throw up?"

"Stuck his finger down my throat," Sloan said. "Then he fiddled in my vomit," he said pointing his finger and circling it, "until he found the onion paper. Then washed it off. I thought he could make it out. He tried to make me believe he had. Maybe he did. All I could do was keep my head and insist. Did I ever tell you what the General did?"

"I don't remember," she said. "Tell me."

"When he questioned me, I told him the paper was a letter from my father. He believed me. Can you imagine? I think he believed me because the captain was so irrational."

"Well, that's the lesson," Litzi said. "It's true here, isn't it? Keep your head. You'll come through all right."

"When I talk with you, my worries seem less."

"You've always needed someone," Litzi said. "I suppose that's why Moscow sent me."

"Like a religionist needs a priest?" Sloan asked. "I suppose I do in a way. Nikitin used to say that he could never tell about me, because I never show emotion, 'like a man with a secret vice,' he would say. My only secret is my allegiance to the future."

"But you're so alone."

"It's strange," he said. "But the secret makes my life easier. Last week I was reading records from Scrubs. They weren't important. I was just browsing. Until Anatoli asked me about them. I repeated figures and dates like I had spent hours memorizing them."

"We're circling for the second time," she said. "Do you think there will be trouble?"

"No," Sloan said. "He's estimating the wind. He may make one more pass."

"What will happen in Istanbul?"

"This rerouting helps," he said. "We'll be delayed one more day. One day for the Brigade and one day for Sarkov. The British? Nothing."

"What if we arrive on time, tomorrow?"

"That's all right," he said. "The closer Sarkov comes, the more dangerous, for him.

"Is there any chance he might know you're the contact?"

"No," Sloan said. "No one knows I'm coming, not even Reed."

"Would you recognize Sarkov?"

"He worked in England," Sloan said. "He may have come to Benedict Street, must have. I don't remember him."

"What a fright if he ever knew it was you they sent."

"He won't," Sloan said. "The whole thing will be over in less than a day."

"Did he stay in Istanbul? Do you imagine?"

"Where else?" Sloan asked, and then answered his own question. "Bulgaria? Ankara? He has to be back tomorrow, wherever he went. No, he didn't go far."

"Suppose he covers himself with letters. I would."

"What kind of letters?"

"Letters of information," she answered. "He writes down everything, everything he knows, gives them to his wife and tells her to mail them if she doesn't hear from him in a week."

"His wife is in Athens," Sloan said. "She's being taken care of."

"If not his wife, someone he knows, someone we don't know. He does the same thing?"

"Are you trying to upset me?"

"I'm trying to imagine what I would do if I were he," she said. She lowered her head.

"No," Sloan said. "I know you're right. Go ahead."

After his approval, she continued, "Suppose the British are hiding him?"

"They aren't."

"Let's imagine that they do," she said. "He demands it. They put him in a 'safe house' until Thursday, and someone from the embassy insists on going along with you for the interrogation."

"Can't happen," he said. "No one in the embassy has the authority to protect him. Diplomacy is their first order of business. Do you understand how important 'procedure' is in embassies? And don't forget, Russia and England are allies. They won't hide him. No, it couldn't happen."

"All right, the English don't take him in. He runs."

"Fine. Let him run," Sloan said. "Ultimately the Brigade catches him, don't they?"

"Yes, ultimately."

"The odds are against him. He's relying on London to help. Imagine! He won't make it. He can't go back. He can't stay where he is. What can he do?"

"You're right, he hasn't a chance."

The pilot was making his final approach. Almost immediately after the wheels touched ground, the pilot turned, smiled, and held up his thumb in the victory salute. "The vickers," he shouted, "came through like dear old Mother England."

8

Cairo's Shepherd's hotel was international not only in estimation, but in veneration. Enemies met there for peace, even in wartime. When the Germans were advancing on Egypt, their officers took respite from the desert at Shepherd's, even though the Union Jack flew over its cupola. Before El Alamein, Rommell sent ahead for reservations. Italian soldiers at the circular bar used to tell the story of Il Duce ordering a white stallion to be brought over from North Africa so he could ride triumphantly past Shepherd's, just as Kitchener had ridden his donkey years before.

When the war with Germany ended in May, the management freshened the beds with Irish linen, dusted off the crested china for the English guests, and refrigerated the beer for the Americans. Through it all, Joe Scanlon stayed on as barman. Like the Nile, Joe was permanent—through the swirl of nationalities.

"You don't take gin and lime juice," Joe said to Sloan, "but you were born in India. I remember. You like the 'Suffering Bastard.'"

"Good memory," Sloan said. "I had my last SB in forty one."

"I don't remember the lady."

"I've never been here before."

"Welcome to the source of civilization."

"I'll have the same thing."

When the barman had left, Litzi asked, "Do we eat here?"

"They'll bring it: Khartoum duck. It's the house specialty."

Sloan became aware of feeling free of his troubles. Like all visitors to foreign countries, he felt the change, a good change, as if, at last, he had disassociated himself. He had even changed his clothes from government formal to desert tunic. With distance, and his change of clothes, his attitude changed. He refused to think beyond the duck.

But then, there was Litzi, and he had to.

"Excuse me," he said. "I have to call."

"On the telephone? Who are you calling?"

"I'll only be a minute," he said without answering her question.

He did not want to leave her alone, but he had to. He wanted to find out what time the plane left in the morning, but he did not want to tell her that was his errand. She would not like what he had planned: she was not to accompany him to Istanbul.

There were two phones on the wall in the foyer. He looked back and she was in the same position. He looked up the number of the airfield, dialed, and waited for an answer. After ten rings he assumed that the airport was closed, so he hung up, walked to the desk and asked the houseman if he knew the plane schedules. The houseman told him that there was one flight North, that it left at nine, that a plane in Crete made the connection for Istanbul, and that Sloan could expect to be in Turkey before nightfall.

He sat in one of the cane chairs in the vestibule and marshaled his arguments, anticipating Litzi's rebuttal.

He could not risk traveling with her any further. It was too flagrant. There would be records of her when Carolyn made the investigation. Furthermore, she would be a distraction if there was a crisis. There was also the possibility that the embassy might find out she was accompanying him. There was no good reason for her to go further. She had done her work: encourage him and allay his apprehensions. He would convince her to stay in Cairo, enjoy the city, and wait for his return on Saturday, when they could celebrate his success. He knew that she would object, but he was determined. He stood and walked, resolutely, onto the porch.

She had left the couch. Where was she?

He had that sinking feeling of abandonment. He walked back inside to the bar, around the tables, quickly through the pantry, into the foyer, back to the porch. He looked this way and that, anxiously, feeling alone, like a child searching for his parents. He remembered how his father had left him, without a word, and how abandonment consumed his attention. Even when Litzi came up to him from the side and touched his arm in that tender way she had, the ancient feeling did not leave.

She said something about her dress, but it was lost on him.

"There's one plane, in the morning."

"I know, nine o'clock."

"How do you know?"

"I asked before we left the airfield, while you were rounding up the bags," she said. "We're fortunate, or unfortunate, I don't know which. They'll wait for our plane in Crete. We'll make Istanbul before dinner."

"I have to talk to you."

"I know. You want me to stay behind."

"How did you know?"

"You've been tense all evening. Something's on your mind. It had to be me. You don't want me in Istanbul?"

"I do," he said. "But I have to be careful. Someone from the embassy will meet the plane. How do I explain?"

"I'll take a taxi."

"I wasn't thinking of that. I was thinking he might wonder what we're doing together."

"How will he see us?" She asked. "You get off and meet him, and I'll stay on until you leave. How will he know we're together?"

"I'm wondering if we're not tempting fate to travel together. Maybe you could come on Thursday."

"Thursday?"

"Yes."

"And miss the show?" she asked. "When everything is settled? I get there and turn back. You won't need me Thursday, but you may need me tomorrow. There may be a crisis and you'll want me there. I can be your messenger," she pleaded. "What will Merkulov think when I tell him you sent me home before the matter was resolved?"

"It isn't that," Sloan said. "I wish we were there now. You could help so much. And I do want to be with you. It isn't that."

"It's the meeting at the airport, isn't it?"

"I suppose it is."

"I'll stay on the plane until you leave the field."

"No," Sloan said. "We'll go through the normal channels. You take a taxi and we'll meet at the hotel. I don't want you staying behind on the plane. That would certainly cause talk."

When they had settled in and the duck was brought, he nibbled. Litzi ate voraciously. She commented on the sugared potatoes and the wine. Sloan excused himself again, went to the desk for cigarettes, even though he had a near-ly full pack in his jacket pocket. He watched the Arabs in the central room and wished he could ask them to take him with them through the desert. Again Litzi came up behind him and touched his sleeve. "Just dawdling a moment," he said and followed her back to the couch.

He was sitting in the same position twenty minutes later when the waiter came to collect the plates. The waiter hesitated to take the full plate from in front of Sloan, but Sloan waved him on. Litzi, meanwhile, was humming to herself, pleased at the meal and at herself. Sloan felt as though he had lost his freedom, as if freedom depended on his getting his way.

He would be better off alone.

Part V

Istanbul

1

Their plane landed at Istanbul's Yesilkoy airport at five thirty on the afternoon of August thirteenth.

From his limousine John Reed watched the three passengers alight. The first was a woman and the second a Turk businessman. The woman hesitated, not knowing which way to go, let the Turk walk ahead, and followed him toward a one story building off to the side.

Finally Sloan stepped out onto the stairway like an actor making an entrance. He brushed back his hair with his left hand, walked around the wing to the cockpit window where he shouted goodbye to the pilot. He was wearing an old fashioned, cutaway, collar, and a flowing, Byronesque, cravat. He did not walk, he sauntered, holding out his valise like an actor attracting attention. Reed did not move from his seat behind the wheel. He did not speak until Sloan was standing by the window. "I remembered," Reed said. "Thomas doesn't fly. I wondered who they'd send."

"I have arrived to escort Comrade Sarkov to the West," Sloan said. There was no other civility.

"He'll be in my office day after tomorrow," Reed said. "We have a lot of work to do. Why the delay?"

"The pouch took a long time, five days," Sloan answered. "We're at half staff, holidays and all. The FO gave us fits on procedure. Then our plane was rerouted through Tunis. That took another day. Still we're here in plenty of time." It sounded rehearsed.

Two Turks in baggy pants and collarless shirts ambled out of a shed near the largest hangar. One pointed toward the limousine and the other squinted, showed his teeth, filed down from biting Ottoman coins and olive pits. The two shuffled toward the limousine. They had flat feet, slopping shoulders, and vaulted moustaches. Except for the guns in their belts, they could have been mistaken for a comedy team. They were isolates, men who distrust anyone not Anatolian or who do not give off a hircine smell.

"This is Turkey's answer to immigration," Reed said. "Get in. They won't understand diplomatic immunity. They'll take your passport. Get in. I'll send for the bags."

"Put this in the boot, will you, old man?" Sloan asked. He held out his valise. Reed stepped out of the limousine, ran to the rear, opened the trunk, secured the valise, and the rest of Sloan's bags, and was back in the driver's seat before Sloan had closed his door. The two Turks were within fifty feet when Reed shifted the limousine into gear.

When they passed the gates and dropped into the dusty road, Sloan said, "McKenzie is hesitant about Sarkov. I don't know why. He took his time studying the information, making the assessment. It could be that Sarkov is asking too much. Whatever. He did agree to the whole arrangement." He had to be sure Reed heard every reason for the delay. Reed's recollections would be invaluable in the investigation that was sure to follow. "He doubted the worth of the information: some of it we already have. What tipped the balance was the possibility of embarrassing the Russians."

"The ones I know aren't capable of shame," Reed said. "It's the Turks we have to worry about. Do you realize how close we came to trouble back there?"

"I put myself in your hands."

"Then tell me about the woman on the plane."

"Why ask me?"

"She wasn't with the Turk. She had to be with you." Reed said. "She'll be detained if she doesn't have the right papers."

"She can take care of herself," Sloan said. "She's a friend of mine."

"Is she staying with you?"

"I told her to book a suite at the Park."

"Does that mean you're staying there?"

Sloan nodded.

"It's a mistake," Reed said. "You should room with us."

"Why?"

"Because Peterson expects it," Reed said. "Do you think it wise to bring a woman into this? It weakens your position, which is already weak."

"Why weak?"

"Peterson doesn't like espionage, never has. He doesn't like the Turks doing it, and they invented it."

"McKenzie warned me. I'll be careful."

"Maybe it's a good thing, you staying in the city," Reed said. "Here's what you should do." Reed looked at Sloan. "He's spending tomorrow on the Marmora, but you mustn't go. He'll ask you, but don't. It will give him too much time to think about Sarkov. If you're there, you'll remind him. He won't let it happen if he has his way, so we mustn't give him an opportunity to think about it. Just go through the protocol this afternoon. Show him your papers, talk about the new plays and the scandals in Whitehall, the divorces; drop Sarkov's name in the middle somewhere, as if you did this sort of thing once a month. Whatever you do, tone it down. He goes into despair at the thought of any public outrage. We mustn't make too much of Sarkov or he will scuttle the whole thing."

Sloan nodded in agreement.

"Your most valuable time will be tomorrow evening. He's set up a bridge game. You do play bridge?" Reed did not wait for an answer. "The Russian ambassador will be the third."

"Who else?"

"I don't know, but I do know you'll play in the card room of the Park. You won't have far to go."

"Fine," Sloan said. "What's the drill on Sarkov?"

"He's to come to the south portico on Saturday at ten in the morning," Reed said. "He left a phone number for emergencies. We can call anytime you want. We checked. The number belongs to a dentist in Bayezit. If I use my name, the girl calls Sarkov and he calls me. It's an old routine."

"I may want to talk with him tomorrow. What else?"

"The Brigade is out, in force."

"You mean the *otdyel*?" Sloan asked. "How can you be sure they haven't taken him?"

"They hadn't at eleven this morning," Reed said. "He called my service to let me know he was ready for Saturday. What did 'research' uncover on him? All I know is that he is Vice Consul here and a big man in NKVD."

"He's a catch," Sloan answered. "Belongs to the aristocracy. Unlike Britain, the Russian intellectual leans toward Special Branch. I'll wager Sarkov wears suede."

"Not much ideology there," Reed said.

"There's a place for taste in Marxism," Sloan retorted.

"I suppose you're right," Reed said. "What else did you find out?"

"He had rich parents," Sloan said, opening the folder and scanning the first page of Sarkov's dossier. "The best education. Studied at the Institute of Human Relations, something like our London school, very important for advancement. In '36 he was recommended for Department Ten, after a very few weeks in Kimsmol, and that began his career." Sloan turned a page and reached into his inside pocket for his reading glasses. When they were settled on his nose, he turned back to the first page. "Did I tell you he was born into aristocracy? His grandfather fought with Checka during the revolution, but retreated from the Party. When he was an old man they decorated him, after the battle of Moscow in '41."

"He liked to fight, but didn't like politics," Reed said.

"Listen to this," Sloan continued. "The General's wife was raised in Ankara. She loathed Russians. Is that a hint why the grandson is fleeing Russia?" He lifted both hands from the page. "A hint."

"Next generation," he said as he flipped to page two. "Both father and uncle work at the Ministry of Foreign Affairs, uncle in archives, father a courier. Foreign Affairs are more respectable than our FO. I would imagine these people will be arrested before long, no matter what happens. So will the aunt. She is a psychiatrist at Serbsky. Her clients are mainly party people."

"The family inclines toward government."

"This fellow grew up like Attlee: the best friends, selected social activity, schooled at home for most of his life, all kinds of indulgences. I'll wager he's used to eating paskha, blini, and caviar. Or, at least, sturgeon in jelly."

"Why the devil is he leaving?"

"We don't know," Sloan answered. "Usually it's the attractions of the West."

"He's had better than we can provide, looks like."

"How did he appear to you?"

"Distraught. He made the mistake of thinking our people were all spies."

"He doesn't make too many mistakes," Sloan said. "The word for him is 'cautious,' and 'clever.' He's had some fragile times, but none of his making. His section made a mess of the Trotsky assassination. His brother was in that, but this man didn't have much to do with it. Merkulov advanced him in '43. His first assignment was the Ignace Reuss assassination in Lusanne, which he handled quite well."

"He worked for Merkulov?"

Sloan nodded. "He did. Except for the isolation these fellows enjoy, we should assume that Comrade Sarkov knows nearly everything about Moscow Center, and their workings."

"Why was McKenzie slow in responding?"

Sloan continued as if he didn't hear the question. "He must know the full Canadian operation, which is about to explode." Then Sloan answered Reed's question. "I'm never sure why McKenzie does anything. You know him and his 'pocket' secrets. You said Sarkov was unnerved."

"To distraction. He had no plan. For an intelligent man, he seemed like a child. He didn't know what to do next. He had no where to go after he left our building."

"Didn't he go back to work?"

Reed said. "He couldn't. They were on to him. We tried to follow him after he left, but our man lost him. When we finally located his dacha, everyone was gone."

"Yes, I know," Sloan said. "You flew the wife out to Athens."

The word 'Athens' tolled like a bell in Reed's head. The blood drained from his face. He said, weakly, "No, the Turks took care of that."

"How did the Turks get involved?"

"One of their top operatives owed me a favor."

"He flew her out?"

"Yes."

"Find out where she is staying in Athens, will you? And if she's moved, find out where she's gone. I need to know."

Reed had to call on a reserve of discipline, not only because of the enormity of Sloan's slip, but also because he was impatient to call Colonel Tor.

"Why don't you take this left hand turn and come in from the rear?" Sloan asked. "You've been here before?"

"Oh, many times," Sloan answered.

"Don't let me forget my valise. I have handbills from the West End and a letter from Peterson's brother."

"I'll have the rest of your bags brought up."

"Do."

When they had stopped under the *porte cochere*, Reed disembarked slowly. He waited until Kemal had extricated the valise and Sloan had passed through the front door. Then he quickly walked to the side door which led to the porter's lodge where there was a phone. He prayed silently as the private line buzzed. After four rings the line was picked up and the familiar voice said, "Tor here!"

2

If John Reed had his way, he would have ridden in his limousine to the Burnt Column, but Colonel Tor insisted that he leave the limousine behind, and ride to their meeting in a dolmus.

When the dolmus passed Asker Muzesi, the Janissry band was playing, the musicians in long, flowing robes, some with tall hats, some in turbans. The original purpose of the band was to lead the victorious Turk army into a foreign city, preferably Russian. The intimidating tone remained: the flutes shrieked, the drums boomed, and the men swung around to face each other, like antagonists.

Reed stepped off the crowded conveyance, and skipped up the twenty three stairs to the Burnt Column, the sound blaring so, he could not hear the traffic. He moved quickly not only because Tor disliked tardiness, for whatever reason, but also because the noise agitated him. He was hoping that he would see Tor right away and persuade him to leave the area. Like a vision, Tor appeared from behind the column. As the Colonel walked toward Reed, the pigeons at the base of the column rustled and one, a white dove, flew out and up.

"I see you've changed your tie," Tor shouted. "I should have cleaned it." Then he looked up. "Isn't this a perfect place?"

"Last time it was the smell. Today it's the noise."

"You don't like music?"

"I can't hear you," Reed said. "Could we move over there?"

When they were settled in place between the cracks in the wall where the noise was less, Tor looked up at the obelisk. "The Ottomans believed that the column would topple if they ever lost a war to the Europeans."

"Misplaced faith," Reed said.

"Was it?" Tor asked. "When did the Europeans conquer us? That stone is a shrine to our unconquerable spirit."

"There are too many monuments in this city."

"They support our faith. You ought to have more faith, my unbelieving friend," Tor said. "It's good for your health." He opened his eyes and held up his arms, like a priest at a ritual. "Do you know what is buried here?" He asked. "Noah's hatchet, Moses' rock, a loaf from Christ's feeding, nails from the Cross, the palladium of Troy, something for every believer."

"I'm not sure what I believe," Reed said. "I can't think with all this racket."

"That's your problem: no faith," Tor said. "I believe everything. They could claim that Jesus and Mohammed were brothers, and I'd believe it. Does that surprise you? I caught belief like other people catch typhus. It affected me all over. If they told me God was walking the earth I'd go and find him. I can't get enough of it." His eyes were sparkling. "I pray to Kali, the black mother. She helped me become a man. I love the Virgin. She keeps me chaste so I can think. I pray to Juanyin, the goddess of mercy. God knows, I need mercy," Tor said. "Do you want to know something? A believer can recognize another believer. It's in the eyes. That is why I may bring your Russian friend on a pilgrimage here."

"You've seen him?"

"No," Tor said. "But I've been reading his poetry. He's a god seeker. I like that. I wish you were, my friend. It prolongs your life."

"Will it prolong Sarkov's life?"

"It will if he stops jumping around like a bean in hot oil," Tor said. "Didn't you tell him to stay in one place?"

"I didn't tell him anything," Reed answered. "He's an intelligent man."

"You should have given him better protection. He took a room at the Raman, across from Lizay. The next day he moved up the hill, to be near Yuri Rejans. He had a porter carry his bags and there I was, like a tourist, following him. At this very moment he is riding along Divan Uolu like a rich Greek in a white suit. He sticks out like an Englishman in a mosque."

"He's been safe until today."

"But now we have the Brigade," Tor said. "We counted six. How many from the Russian embassy are looking for him? We don't know. They will capture him tonight or tomorrow early, unless we do something." He waited for Reed's response, but Reed only looked at his knuckles, said nothing. "They talked to the Iskinder. They know his habits. It's only a matter of time. They are watching Yeni's. He'll go there tonight and they will take him."

"But you know all this."

"I watch, but how does that help? To watch." Tor asked. "Understand my position. If the Brigade picks him up, that is diplomatic business. Have they done anything illegal? Am I to detain Russian nationals with diplomatic passports? It's none of my business what they do to one of their own. Worse, it would be foolish of me. If we cannot persuade Sarkov to hide, he will be taken tonight." As an afterthought, he added, "The man is too trusting, too open, too reckless. He couldn't hide if he wanted to. How did he survive as a spy?" Again Tor waited for a response. He was not sure Reed had heard so he moved closer. "I'm waiting. What do you want me to do?"

"I'm not sure," Reed said. "I thought he was safe, for now."

"You know he isn't safe," Tor said. "You knew he wasn't safe from the beginning. Even now, two days before he's to come in, you're not concerned about him. I ask myself, 'why not?' I ask myself, 'why did Reed call me five minutes after the contact arrives?' I ask myself, 'why is it that the English don't care whether the Russian lives or dies?'"

Reed still did not answer. Tor shouted, "What am I to think?" His voice turned soft. "Here is what I think. I believe the problem has to do with the man at the airport. In the worst possible case,—if he had brought instructions that the Russian was to be abandoned,—you would not have called me." He held up his hand to stop Reed from interrupting. "Something worse happened. You call me immediately after you talk with him." He held up his hand to stop Reed again. "Please," he said, "let me play." He was giving Reed a lesson in espionage. Like all good teachers he was acting out the lesson. "If McKenzie wanted the Russian to die, you would not have telephoned. You would have let nature take its course, let the cutthroats slaughter him. But you did not do that. You called me. I ask myself 'why'? Because you are not sure. You're still not sure. That is worse than unbelief: uncertainty. It's impossible to be neutral, isn't it? When everyone takes sides. So you come to me looking for advice. Which side do I take? Why must you take sides? I have to guess. Let me ask you this."

Reed nodded.

"Can you hear me?" Tor asked. "What's wrong with the man from London? Is he spoiled?"

"Yes."

"Something he said made you think he's rotten?"

"Yes," Reed said. "On the way in from the airport."

"What was it?"

"I set a trap," Reed said. "And he fell into it."

"You're learning. You're learning."

"I knew the Russians were listening to our messages so I sent a false message. I told them that Sarkov's wife was brought to Athens."

"She never went near Athens."

"I told you, it was false information."

"Why did you do that?"

"I was trying to catch a rat in our radio room. But I caught a mole."

"So your friend mentions Athens and you wonder where he heard that?"

"Yes."

"He heard it from McKenzie," Tor said. "Didn't McKenzie read your wire, the one with the false information?"

"He had to know it wasn't true," Reed said. "In the pouch I spelled out the whole plan: that you were making the arrangements, that the stop was Cyprus."

"So he wonders why you said one thing in the pouch and another across the wire," Tor said. "Still he mentions it to this man, his confidant."

"No," Reed said. "He wouldn't. I know him. Would you?"

"Do you have reason to believe that McKenzie suspects this man?"

"It's all speculation," Reed said.

"Yes, it is," Tor said. "It's like the information. There has to be more. What else is troubling you?"

"This man, tonight, brought a woman with him," Reed said. "Why on earth would he do that?"

"You're correct," Tor said. "Something is not right." He turned his back to Reed, looked up at the column, and then looked at Reed. "Let's assume he's a traitor. Now we come to Comrade Sarkov," Tor said. "You want to keep him alive. Otherwise you would have let our man here do his dirty work. Sarkov dies," he spat, "another Russian slides into oblivion, and we wave 'goodbye.' But no. You want him to go on living."

"I've been trying to imagine what McKenzie wants."

"He wants the Russians to think that he has not uncovered your man. That's why he sent him. And he is willing to sacrifice Sarkov to maintain the lie."

"What are we going to do?"

"I like the Russian. I like his wife. I've been reading his poetry. We won't let him die, if we can help. Is that what you want?"

"Yes."

"What are the factors in this? The Brigade, the Russian embassy, the traitor—if he is one—who does not know that we know. We have all the advantages."

"I don't see it. What are you planning?"

"I don't know yet. An incident of some kind," Tor said, his eyes expanding, his mouth beaming, his arms out. "Poof. Comrade Sarkov is the trigger. The Brigade is the charge; I will set it off," he said, "And the German press will be the spectators. They will tell the world."

"What will that do?"

"What will it do?" He said. "It will shock the people who can protect my dear city. Mister Attlee, Mister Truman.

They will read about the explosion and they will sit down and talk with Comrade Stalin and they will say, 'Maybe someday you may have Istanbul, but not now. It's too dangerous.'"

3

Sloan was bewildered. He had expected the foyer of the Park to be on the roof as it had been on his three previous trips to Istanbul, but the management had moved the registration desk, the *kebabci*, and the old stick chairs from the top floor to the first floor. The rabble of the city wandered into the foyer just to escape the heat. Two porters stood, one inside the door, the other outside, exchanging cigarettes and melon seeds: an event which would never have happened in the old days when the foyer was above, sixty feet from Argas Pasha Caddesi. Sloan watched an unescorted woman reading a novel translated from the French, and behind her, two businessmen drinking Kanyak. One of the men directed a castaway paper around the parquet floor with his foot.

Sloan was upset that the management would allow this to happen. He expected to be sequestered at the Park, isolated from the citizenry, as well as from diplomatic people. As it was, anyone could drift in, even ride the lifts. Not so in the old days when the foyer was on the top floor and the lifts were guarded and hidden.

"Why did they move the lobby?" Sloan asked the horseman.

"When the Germans left," the man answered, "we had too many empty rooms, even in August, so Zecki opened the hotel to travelers."

"Kurds, you mean."

"All citizens may stand under the fan," the man said with a touch of nationalism. "We know who they are." The houseman's name was Fuad. Sloan remembered him. The man's licit work was *Kahya*, houseman, but his real work was selling stolen gems.

Turks buy and sell more jewels than the French; Istanbul rivals Beirut and Amsterdam in marketing stolen jewels. Fuad was a small dealer, but his cover as houseman in an international hotel gave him an opportunity to be more successful than he deserved.

"I bought a ruby from you. Do you remember?" Sloan asked.

"Your face I remember," Fuad whispered, "but not your name. Are you staying with us?"

"My wife and I are booked."

"What name?"

Sloan did not answer. He did not know whether Litzi had married and signed her new name, her family name, or his name. "May I see the register?" The houseman turned the bulky book around so that Sloan could study the list. He did not recognize Litzi's hand writing.

"Is your name Sloan?"

"Yes."

"The lady said you would be coming. It's room five twenty-seven," Fuad said. "There was a telephone call, a Russian. He called about an hour ago, asking for you."

Was it possible that Sarkov had called? Who else would it be? The Russian embassy would never call, make such a blunder, except under dire circumstances. It was disturbing news.

"What did the caller say, exactly?"

"He asked if you were staying here, nothing else. He wanted to talk with you."

"Did he give his name? Where was he calling from? Do you keep records?"

"He was a Russian," Fuad said. "He spoke English, and there was noise behind him, like street noise. He didn't talk long. After I told him you were not here, and asked his name, he hung up. Like that."

"Anything else?"

"What else? I haven't anything."

"How do your calls come in?"

"From Central," he answered. "I'll ask if they have a record."

"Do they listen?"

"Sometimes. What do you want to know?"

Sloan fumbled with his pocketbook, extracted a five pound note, and handed it to Fuad. He was unaccustomed to buying information, did not know the procedure, and performed it awkwardly. "I'd like to know who called," Sloan said. "Failing that, I'd like to know where the call came from."

Fuad was unresponsive. "You should not offer payment for service before," he said. "It is a great offense in Turkey."

"Yes," Sloan said. "But I am desperate to know." He fumbled returning the money to his pocket.

Fuad snapped his fingers and a porter took Sloan's valise.

"I'll bring the information," Fuad said.

Sloan answered. "As soon as you can. I'll be waiting."

On the fifth floor, the porter walked ahead and stopped at Room five twenty-seven, handed Sloan a key, but Sloan was unable to work the maneuver, and the porter had to do it. Sloan followed him inside, found the *Do Not Disturb* sign and hung it on the outside doorknob. He had the presence to tip the porter and tell him he was expecting a message from Fuad.

Sloan had never stayed on the top floor of the Park. The windows were as large as any he had ever seen. There was less than a foot of space between the top of the windows and the ceiling, the rest of the wall-space was glass. He walked across the room and looked down at the street. Barefoot porters, as active as a relay of ants, scrambled back and forth. Two women, wearing black, squatted against the wall at the corner. Further down Sloan could see the shanties with their peeling stucco, faded paint, and grey gutters. Further, he could see the shine of the straits. He closed the curtain and turned back to the room hoping that he might find some hint of what would happen in the next few minutes in the features of the room, just as one might hope to uncover a hint of a person's past in the incidentals of their study.

The bed, overly large, bulged here and there from the broken springs; the wicker chair was unfit for sitting; the desk decorative, not for writing. There was a large mirror attached to each of the two doors, one of which was a masque, the other opened to the lav.

Sloan stopped to look at his image to see if his face might hold some hint of his apprehension, but all he saw was his past: mouth hardened by lies, eyes sullen and receding, hair graying.

The management bowed to Western habits and installed a toilet in the lav, but the seat was too low and there was no water. He walked back into the bedroom and opened the drawer of the desk. Three pieces of letter paper were piled in the right corner, the emboss of the Park taking up a third of the sheet. In the other corner was a large sheet with phone numbers: police, travel bureau, customs, clothing store, services Sloan would not use. There was no phone in the room. He bent down and pulled out three dusty books which were half hidden under the desk. One was the *Koran*, the second a book of Turkish tales, and the third a copy of the *Iliad*, on one side of the leaf, Greek, and on the other side, the English translation. He wondered why a book about a national defeat would be in the room, but when he saw the opening page, he knew. It was published by a firm on Bow street in London. The binding was broken and the book opened to a section where Dolon, the Trojan, was sent to spy on the Greeks. His mission was to discover whether the Greeks had decided to return home after losing a skirmish. Odysseus, the Greek admiral, captured Dolon and turned him. Dolon was the first double agent. Odysseus's sent him back to the Trojan camp with the warning: "It would not be in your interest to misinform us." Sloan knew the section applied to him, but in his anxiety he could not see how.

He put the book down and walked to the window. Below the street was clear: no women squatting and no porters. From behind a wall a man appeared. He stopped before walking into the street, something a Turk would not do. There were other indications that the man was a foreigner, even though Sloan could not see his face. He wore a white, Western suit, double breasted and buttoned from the left, and he wore a wide brimmed fedora, possibly Italian. Once in the street, the man walked resolutely, as if on a mission. In front of the hotel he stopped and looked up at Sloan's window. The Englishman stepped back, as if struck, although there was little chance that the man could recognize him from such a distance. The man below disappeared into the hotel.

Was he the one who called? Was he from the Russian embassy? What information was he bringing? Was it Sarkov?

Sloan walked quickly to the door, out to the lift, but then thought better of going to the foyer. He went back to the room, sat down, and waited for the houseman. In less than five minutes, Fuad knocked.

"He's downstairs," Fuad said. "The Russian."

"I saw him come in. Is it the man who called?"

"I don't know. I don't think it is."

"Who did he ask for? Did he ask for me?"

"No," Fuad said. "He came in soon after your wife."

"My wife? Where is she?"

"In the cafe," Fuad said. "If you want to speak with him, I warn you to do it now. He will not stay."

Sloan hurried past the houseman but, instead of riding the lift, he ran down the stairs. It was quicker and he needed the activity. On the first platform down, he stepped over a porter who had stopped to smoke. On the next, he had to make his way through a family, two children and their father, sitting and eating fasoulia beans. He opened the door to the foyer, but there was no one. The two shopkeepers had left and the rug bearers had returned to the heat. Sloan walked to the door, then outside, and peered down Necati Bey Avenue. Then he walked quickly to the cafe, which was adjacent to the foyer. It was too early for the bar. An attendant was sweeping up. Neither the Russian, nor Litzi, was to be seen.

"Looking for me, Mister Sloan," Sarkov asked. He was sitting on a white bench beside a pillar.

"I was certain it was you."

"How did you know?"

"The phone call?"

"What phone call?" Sarkov asked. He grasped the arm of the bench and raised himself.

"Didn't you call?"

"No." He was standing and he began to shift his feet, listing toward the front door.

"Don't go. It wasn't anything—a phone call from someone. He didn't leave his name. I thought it might be you."

"Why would I call?"

"How did you know I was here?"

"I didn't, until this minute," Sarkov said. "I saw a woman in the Pasaj. She frightened me. Oh, I have been frightened all week, but she gave me a chill. I knew she was dangerous. I was trying to remember where I had seen her before. She was wearing a German dress,—the belt and the ruffles. But it wasn't Germany. I couldn't remember, until now."

"London."

"Yes, at your house."

"Benedict Street."

"August, 1938. You were back from Spain. Two friends from the London station brought me. You were drunk and harsh with her. I could never forget. She left."

"She went away for good."

"She came back?"

"No, she moved to Germany."

"They sent her here, to be with you?"

Sloan nodded.

"So she came here with you, to help find me." He shuffled his feet and began to edge backward. "But all of that has changed."

"What?"

"Your plans, and mine."

"They shouldn't, you know," Sloan said. "You could go back. I have assurances that there will be no objections if you return. I guarantee it."

"You must be terribly frightened to talk such nonsense," Sarkov said. He stood straight, like a soldier at attention.

"We will give you anything you want."

"What foolish talk!" Sarkov said quietly. "But what else do you have? You must persuade me. Otherwise all is lost. Isn't it?"

Sloan tried to smile.

"We are worn out, you and me," Sarkov said. "Like old travelers. You're tired because you are exposed; me, because I have lost my way. We should go home and rest, you to Moscow and me to my wife. Isn't that the way it's going to end?"

"I can help."

Sarkov leaned forward. "I am going to expose you, whether I live or die. I will see to it that they know."

"What advantage is there in that?"

"Have you forgotten that I read every transmit you sent? Penciled vouchers? I know everything about you. Does McKenzie know the money you've stolen? I have the records. Does he know about the Abwehr cables? Gibraltar? If he isn't interested, I know Savage in Whitehall will be. Your work is finished. They know. And when you return to work, what will be waiting for you? Does Six have their own *voennaya* how do you say? Hired killers? Do they have them?"

"Why talk like that?"

"What were your plans for me?" Sarkov pointed a thumb at his chest. "However you managed it—to come here—I salute you." He did salute, two fingers to the forehead. "I must be cautious with such a clever man. You know my work: the desk. I am no match for a penetrator. My advantage is that I don't care." He took two steps. "Now I must go. I am in a bad place."

"Wait. Where will you go?"

"Would I tell you, even if I knew? Why not? I thought about Edirne and the south, but the *odtyel* will look there. I thought I might hide in Bulgaria with some friends, but sooner or later they will show up there. It is only time and they will come." He took two more steps. "Now I must go."

"Why don't you accept Reed's offer? He's at Trotsky's dock right now. Go there."

"Let me ask you, where will you go?"

"I'm going back to London, no matter," Sloan said. "Why don't you do that? Go back. It's reasonable."

"You must think I am a child." He moved closer to Sloan. "You would go back to England, knowing that I have exposed you?"

"You have been truthful with me," Sloan said. "I'll tell you. I can cover my activities. The climate allows it."

"But the murders, and the double dealing with the Germans, and the stealing. Are they going to overlook that?"

Sloan was silent for a moment and then said, "You know they won't allow a public trial."

"No, I don't know that. I don't believe you," Sarkov said. "What you ought to do is shoot me right here, right now. But you're too smart to carry a weapon. Even if you could kill me, my death wouldn't help. The letters are sent."

"Is it worth it, the running?"

"I know how the Brigade works," Sarkov said. "I can survive for a few years. I know what to look for. I can see my enemy. Can you see yours? It will be frightening, not knowing your enemy."

"I have no enemies."

"You have none because everyone is your enemy. We're in the wrong work for friends. Is this woman your friend? She would let you die without a thought if she believed it would advance the cause. Believe me, I know. Even if you return to England, you will never know who is aware of your treachery."

"You think you will survive?"

"It's strange you should ask that," Sarkov said. "You should be asking yourself whether you will survive. I can run. Can you? I can stay close to friends who hold the same views. Can you? I can live freely in the West with my wife and children. Can you?"

"We all have something to fear," Sloan said. "I've been living with fear since Spain. It's a little like back trouble. One gets used to it."

"Yes, but you've never been exposed. You've gotten away with it. All that is changed. No, your best advantage would be to shoot me, if you could. Because when I leave, your pain begins. When will they arrest you? Will the order come from your enemies in Whitehall? What happens after you're arrested? Will you go to prison? Will you have time to escape to Russia? Then there's the question, if you've failed, will Beria take you in? A disgrace? Will they salute you? No one likes a traitor, do they, Mister Sloan. Not even the country you work for. You know Beria as well as I do. What if Moscow refuses to take you? Where will you go? That's a question you have to ask. There are no guarantees from Center. I know that. You're in a poorer position than I. You have no where to go, nowhere. Am I right? Your best move is to act quickly. Since you cannot shoot me here, leave! Go to Moscow while there is time. Good day, Mister Sloan."

"Wait." Sloan took the end of his sleeve, but Sarkov broke loose, disdainfully. He brushed the place where Sloan had grabbed his coat, as if dirt had spilled on it. "My advantage is to leave now."

Sloan walked to the desk so that he could watch Sarkov leave, into the street and around the corner. As he left Sloan's sight, Litzi came into view.

"Who was that?"

"Sarkov. He saw you, recognized you, and followed you here."

"Where did he see me?"

"What difference does it make?" Sloan asked, and walked past her to the door. "What to do? What to do?"

"The Brigade."

"No," he said. "Go to the Russian embassy and tell Kiktev that Sarkov came here."

"Isn't that dangerous?"

"Nothing is dangerous, any more," Sloan said. "Tell Kiktev to come as quickly as possible. There is no reason to be secretive. The operation is dissolved."

"He won't come."

"Yes, he will. He'll come. Tell him its critical, for me. Go, and do what you have to do. "

4

One of the Khedives of Egypt built the yacht *Makouk* for cruising on the Nile, which is relatively smooth. The yacht was not fit for any kind of turbulence. It had a flat bottom, a squat funnel, and a spacious promenade. The British impounded the yacht after the First World War and floated it from the Nile to the Bosporus. It was a mistake.

On August 12, two days before, the ship nearly capsized in one of the sudden squalls which are common to the Marmora in August. The disturbance caught the delicate *Makouk* and tilted her so that the crockery smashed in the scullery. One of the knowledgeable sailors shouted, "We have no keel. There's nothing under us," in earshot of Ambassador Peterson. When the squall subsided, Peterson ordered the yacht never to float more than a stone's throw from Trotsky's Principio. This morning, August 14, the yacht was lashed to the moorings at dockside.

"Are you a sailor?" Ambassador Peterson asked Reed. Peterson was slumped in a deck chair in the shadow of the gunwale. When standing, he was tall and willowy; slumped he was elongated and spindly, like a puppet in repose. His knees jutted out from his shorts, and his legs, like a crane's, were unnaturally thin, even emaciated. He did not move any part of his body except his right hand. With that, he made passing gestures toward the water.

"Not much," Reed said. "I did a little punting in school, and an occasional ride on the Thames, but I don't like the water."

"Our family doesn't sail," Peterson said. "I'm like you, I don't care for it. But I do worry that the boat is so little used." He looked out to a series of crafts in the water.

"Why are those caiques so low?" Reed asked.

"A year ago they hauled chrome for the Germans. It was indispensable, used in the tip of rockets. I don't know where they're going,-now-a-days, or what they're doing."

"At least we know it's not chrome." Reed commented.

"We don't know that," Peterson said. "But we do know it's not for the Germans. The destination, we don't know. That's the better question. When you've been dealing with the Turks as long as I have, you never presume a noble intention."

"Could they be selling chrome to Russia?"

"No," Peterson said. "There is one thing certain in this foul place, the Turks hate Russians more than they love their own country."

"It must be a torment that the Russians won the war," Reed said, "and are dictating the peace not only in Europe but here."

"A million troops not a hundred miles."

"Will they occupy?" Reed asked.

"We used to believe that Russia was not expansionist, that she had more than enough territory, but it's all rot. Stalin wants Poland, Germany, even Berlin. And every port he can lay his hand on."

"This one?"

"Possibly. Why do you think the Hamidieh steamed through the other day? To let them know Stalin wants an access to the Mediterranean? What better time than now?"

"Will he get it?"

"Who's to stop him?" Peterson asked. "It would run counter to a thousand years of animosity, but what's that to Stalin? He would never garrison troops here, but control, yes. Attlee and Truman are in a generous mood. Stalin already has Windau and Liban. The next step is Istanbul. It's the best of the lot, and it's warm."

Peterson turned his head slightly and looked across the Marmora to the domes, the minarets, a Turkish cemetery, up the hill to the excavation of Justinian's palace.

"How could the Turks prevent a 'take-over' here?" Reed asked.

"'How' is right," Peterson answered. "What can they possibly do? Are they participating at Potsdam? Except among the defeated? They were as neutral as Dame Nellie. Von Pappen gave the order and Ataturk followed. No, I don't see that the Turks can do anything, except," he lifted himself and his wine-colored afghan, which had been wrapped around his shoulders, fell, haphazardly, onto the deck. "One must never underestimate the Turk and his hatred for the Russian. Hate helps him live longer. He is always devising ways to end the life of some Russian. It keeps him alive, that and the yogurt."

"It is vile, isn't it? I'll never get used to it."

"Do you know what it's made of?"

"Sheep milk, fermented."

"Then inoculated with bacteria," Peterson said. Streptococcus Thermophilus. Up-country it is the staple from infancy to death. There was an old man who ate nothing but yogurt, lived to be a hundred and fifty, but, listen to this, sired two children in the last year of his life."

"He had good neighbors."

"No," Peterson said. "These are clever people. Speaking of clever, have you made the arrangements for Bridge?"

"I need a fourth," Reed said. "I've asked Sloan."

"I knew his father in the Punjab. Wild, but he became the greatest Arabist in the world. Brilliant fellow, but crazy as a hornet. Never shut his mouth that I know of. No wonder his son's in espionage."

"Sir?"

"One had to be devious to get a word in with the father. Nasty fellow, really."

"They say the son plays very well."

"That's all right, as long as he brings a fresh attitude toward Kiktev's 'three no trump.' Kiktev will be there, won't he?"

"I haven't called, but I expect he will."

"He wouldn't miss a chance to eavesdrop. Who's the fourth?"

"I was thinking of Colonel Tor. I saw him yesterday."

"Fine fellow. Yes. Get him," Peterson said. "Perhaps Kiktev will inform him of Stalin's intentions."

"Nice mixture: MI6, second secretariat here, NKVD —and you."

"One bad feature of war, espionage. I remember when it wasn't quite so wicked. We had Halpurn and Burnett in the first war. Gentlemen. I suppose 'finding out' helps, like when they pinched the plans for airplanes, but I despise deceit during peace time."

"Unless it keeps the peace."

"I wouldn't worry, if I were you," Peterson said. "You have a bright future in diplomacy."

He sat back in his chair but was looking beyond Reed to something on the dock. "Who's that?" He asked. "He's been standing there for five minutes. He looks like an Italian wine merchant."

Reed turned in his chair, then jumped to his feet. "That's Sarkov, the Russian we are trying to help."

Three young sailors in braided caps and ropes for belts stood near Sarkov and seemed to be whispering conspiracy.

Reed made his way, too quickly, toward Sarkov. He slipped along the gunwale until he had to hold on. He slid on leather soles. The tilt of the yacht slowed him. Rocking down the gangway, he came to the land, and then ran.

"This is a mistake, coming here, in the open." He said.

"My mistake was approaching you."

"You saw Sloan?"

"Did you know he is our man in London? His was the name I was holding?"

"How did you find out he was in Istanbul?"

"I saw his wife in the street. I followed her. He told me you were here."

"His wife? That's not his wife."

"Whoever she is, she led me to him," Sarkov said. "She works for the GRU in Bremen." He smiled. "They must have sent her to help him find me. But I found them."

"Come on board," Reed said. "We can talk over tea."

"No," Sarkov said. "I won't go with you. I can't trust you. Who was that fool you sent to follow me? Why did you do that?"

"Race sent him," Reed said. "I knew you'd recognize him. I hoped you'd understand."

"Understand? What am I to understand? About you? About McKenzie? Answer me."

When Reed did not answer, Sarkov continued, "How far does the betrayal go? I ask myself, 'who can I trust?' Is there anyone in the West I can trust?"

"Colonel Tor flew your wife out. He will do the same for you, tomorrow" Reed answered. "Come inside. It's dangerous here."

"See those men over there? They have been following me since yesterday. Turks," Sarkov said. "I know the *odtyel* are close, but I don't care. I'm tired."

"Hold on until tomorrow," Reed said. "Your wife and children landed in Nicosia. They left Tuesday."

"Where did they go?"

"I don't know," Reed said. "I don't. Colonel Tor arranged it all."

"I wish I could see them one last time."

"Has he talked with you?"

"I'm troubled that the head of Turkish Intelligence is helping a Russian traitor."

"He is doing it for me," Reed said. "The Queen lent Turkey a great deal of money on little credit."

"Nonsense," Sarkov said. "Do you know your Colonel Tor? Do you know what he did in Urgurp? I found out about him. He slaughtered twenty-five people just to protect his interest. I can't understand why such a man helped Irina."

"He told me it was the Credits."

"Nonsense, utter nonsense," Sarkov said. "We have been taken in like little children."

"He promised that he would bring you out, like your family."

"I can walk myself," Sarkov said. "I'm worried about the future, six months from now, nine months, a year. Then what?"

"But they won't know where to look."

"Do you understand the geometry of exposure? They search, question, search. They question you when you don't care anymore. They ask Tor. There is no question of money, or time, or effort. They plod along until they find out. The object is to locate the man and exterminate him, no matter how long it takes."

"Come below," Reed said. "I'll show you Tor's plan."

"I thought the English would help," Sarkov said turning his head. "If they helped I could move, cover, throw them off for a few years. I had a chance, but no more. Alone?" He opened his arms.

"Money?"

"That, and help in moving when the time came, contact with governments. We had a man, Sudarev, who went to the Americans in Uruguay. They liked his information, moved him to Ceylon, then set him up with the Chinese. He's safe," Sarkov said. "The price was high. McKenzie did not think I was worth it."

"We don't know that."

"You are so simple," Sarkov said. "Don't you know what Sloan's coming here did to my chances?"

"Come inside, please," Reed asked again. "I don't like talking here."

"I don't like it either," Sarkov said. "I'm leaving. Tell your Turk friend to leave me alone. I'll make my way the best I can."

"His real interest is this," Reed said, pointing across the water to the city beyond. "He wants to keep Stalin from occupying."

"What can he possibly do about that?" Sarkov asked. "He's right. Stalin wants a base here, and he will get it, if he hasn't gotten it already. Who is going to stop him? Some minor police official?"

"He thought you might help."

"How? With information? He has all the facts I have. Stalin wants this port."

"It isn't information," Reed said. "He has a plan. He has it worked out, and you are an essential piece."

"Why should I become involved in his foolishness," Sarkov said. "I want to see my wife. I want to live away from all this, have some peace."

"One more day," Reed said. "One more day and one more favor and you will have peace. I assure you. Trust him."

"I think you and I are simple, what do you think? Simple and childish. Our kind don't survive."

"It's time for tea," Reed said. "You haven't eaten today, have you?"

"I don't want your tea, and I don't want your protection."

"Then why did you come?"

"I don't know. I wanted to walk, just walk, and mingle with the crowds."

"Where will you go?"

"Sloan asked me the same question. I'm sure he sent the odytel. But I don't know. I don't have an answer."

"So?"

"I can't go to Rio, and then Patna when they come after me. I have no support. I think this is the end."

"What will you do today?"

"Eat with my friends. I know they're my friends. I shall ask them what I should do, and then I will do it."

"Isn't that a risk?"

"You mean dining openly with my friends. I suppose it is."

"It's clear to me what you should do."

"It was clear to you last week." Sarkov broke off, and broke away.

A steward with a white coat and black tie walked down the gangway. At the foot he asked Reed if they wanted tea. Reed turned to answer the steward and, as he did, Sarkov began walking toward the road.

"Stay," Reed implored.

"No," Sarkov said. "I don't want your tea."

"Servings for the ambassador and myself, "Reed said. When the boy was inside the mess, Reed shouted, "You mustn't take this so seriously, old boy. Sloan doesn't shatter your plans, only change them. Take advantage of Tor's offer. You'll be making a mistake if you don't."

Sarkov stopped and answered, "I spent some time in Malacca. I may go there. Or I may go west of here, and raise sheep."

"Don't do anything you'll regret," Reed said. "Think about the plan. And call me "

Sarkov was thirty feet away, walking backward. Reed raised his voice.

He made no further overtures to keep Sarkov near, as if the business of tea had become more important.

Sarkov felt safer in the open and decided he would stay in the open. He remembered hearing about a Pole who was avoiding the police in Moscow. The trouble was that the man was exceptionally tall and spoke no Russian. The police never found him. He escaped back to Poland. Later the police found out that he had stolen a cassock from a monk and had lived in a church. He never had to speak and he could bend over, in reverence, whenever anyone asked him a question.

Sarkov's walking around Istanbul in the open had led him to Sloan and now to his final contact with Reed. From the road Sarkov looked back. Reed was standing on the first step of the gangway, his right hand raised, either in greeting or farewell, Sarkov could not tell.

5

Ambassador Nicolai Andryov Kiktev shuffled out of his *chaika* limousine, pushing himself to the end of the seat, placing his foot on the cobblestones and, with a strain, lifting himself onto the old entranceway of the Park hotel. The doors of the limousine opened from the middle. "I don't come south of Taksim," Kiktev said to Sloan, who had been waiting for him since eleven that morning, "unless it's necessary. We had a man attacked down that street. I know you have been waiting, but I had my reasons. Did they tell you? We have a Bridge game at nine, upstairs here."

"I've been here ever since morning, waiting," Sloan said.

"Litzi told me you were disturbed," Kiktev responded. "About what, I don't know."

"Sarkov was here," Sloan said. "He's sent letters to my enemies in Whitehall."

"Why should that upset you?" Kiktev said. "We know where he is. We'll secure Sarkov tonight before you and I finish our second game."

"He's written letters?" Sloan asked. "The damage has been done."

"You know those people," Kiktev said. "You can persuade them. And if it comes to that, we have ways of intercepting letters. That's not difficult." He pointed to the hotel.

"This is not the place to talk." He walked in front and the three, Sloan, Litzi, and the chauffeur, followed too closely.

"I've been thinking," Sloan said. "I've come to the conclusion that now is the time for me to go to Moscow."

He was too close to the ambassador and when Kiktev passed through the glass door Sloan had to stop and wait.

Kiktev said without losing a step, "We had Bellamy defect last year. It wasn't successful." He raised his hand in salute to Fuad. "I don't mean you shouldn't go," he said, turning his head. "I'm sure Beria will have questions." He waved his hand again, like an actor about to take a bow. "He will want to know whether the work is finished in London. I don't think it is."

"*If* Sarkov is taken tonight," Litzi asked, coming close to the two. "Nothing has changed."

"Except the letters," Sloan said, "and the British security checking me."

Kiktev stopped abruptly, and the others stumbled into one another, like a comedy team. Sloan said, "I've had a bad week. Control threatened me. He told me they were beginning a trace, and he asked me if there was anything in my past which might interest security."

"They might be suspicious," Kiktev said. "But it's unlikely they'll find anything. Don't forget, you're alone, like a man in the desert. Have you ever been lost in the sand? You don't know which way to turn. After two days you suspect the worst. That's how you are. It's not like being lost in the sea. All you have to worry about is the storms. Listen to your friends. You'll be all right."

"Remember what you said yesterday?" Litzi asked. "Security is always suspicious. Either they're spying on their enemies or they're spying on each other. One thing they can't allow is the simple motive."

"To tell the truth," Sloan said. "I'm not worried about that. I'm worried about the danger."

"Do you mean a trial?" Kiktev asked.

"That, and prison."

"We wouldn't allow it," Kiktev said. "Long before anything like that, we would fly you out, the northern route. They've explained the route, haven't they?"

"Think of the new section?" Litzi asked rhetorically. "Counter-Soviet-Intelligence. What information!"

"If there was a trial," Kiktev asked, "would it be in Parliament or the Old Bailey? Let's assume the worst, that they expose you. That will mean a full review. Imagine what they would have to show? The Harrock's report, Room Forty, Dolphin Square, even the machines at Bletchley. A trial like that might be your most important operation for us, even more important than the German cables."

"Wait. Do you believe McKenzie would allow a trial?"

"I could live with a trial," Sloan answered. "If I was sure it would discredit the Service. But you don't know Control. He might think of something. For sure, he won't allow the matter to fester. I will be like the man caught *in delictis* with his wife. He might wait, but sooner or later he will murder you while you're sleeping."

"Why did he send you here?" Kiktev asked. "On such a sensitive mission, if he is suspicious?"

"It doesn't make sense," Litzi amended. "We have to argue back. This is the most important defection since Plotkin. He sends you rather than White or Barrows. Do you seriously believe that he doesn't trust you?"

"I don't like the way they arranged this room," Kiktev said. "We used to come in from this side. It was private.

They will go back to the old way when the right people stop coming here." He resumed walking toward the lift.

"I felt exposed this morning," Sloan said while they were waiting for the lift. They were standing twenty-five feet from where Sarkov and Sloan had talked at ten this morning. "Naked."

"Why should you be embarrassed?" Kiktev asked. "You're not overweight." The elevator arrived and they stepped inside. Three stood side-by-side in the rear and Sloan faced the door. "Now, If I was naked," Kiktev said, holding his stomach with both hands, "That would be another matter."

The others laughed, but Sloan gritted his teeth. He hated levity when he was serious. He had no patience with Comrades who treated his problem lightly. He wanted them to apply their attention to his crisis, and study the remedies. "I have to live with this problem," he said softly.

"I'm going to tell you about Sarkov," Kiktev said, serious again. "He's been trying to reach an old ballerina who takes her meals at a certain place. She's had a breathing problem and hasn't gone out, but she will tonight, and Sarkov knows that. He will meet her and we will pounce." He snapped his fingers.

The lift stopped, but the door did not open. Sloan kicked the door and it sprung open as if on command.

"We have all the choices," Kiktev said. "He has none."

"This afternoon," Litzi asked. "Will he go to the Americans?"

"If he talks to them, the Americans will consult the English," Kiktev answered. "He deserves our sympathy. He has no future and the past has caught up to him. He can't stay where he is, and he can't go."

"We talked about that," Sloan said. "Only Sarkov made me feel that I was the one who couldn't go back."

"What would you accomplish in Moscow?" Kiktev asked.

"Call in the press," Sloan answered. "Tell them about MI5, the structure, what they're looking at now, the petty fights, all the names. Everything."

"Would that help?" Kiktev asked. "Right now?"

"It wouldn't be interesting," Litzi responded. "Who would print it? *The London_Times*? A disgruntled civil servant washing his laundry in public. The party has never been closer to the Allies. It's not the time. Stalin and Attlee shook hands last week." She hesitated. "We could do something else. We could wait, sit and wait. Why not see what happens after Sarkov is eliminated? What the English do. Stay here for a few days."

"Ultimately I'll have to go back. What about the letters, and Carolyn's investigation?"

"Investigation?" She asked. "We make up better explanations than the truth. Remember Claxton and the death at Bangor?"

"What's happening to you is like Bridge," Kiktev said. "Do you play Bridge?"

"You just asked me to play!"

"Oh yes," Kiktev said. He was shuffling the cards. Three or four fell out, onto the floor. "You came to Istanbul thinking you had a grand slam," he said, picking up the cards, "but you only have a small one. You miscalculated. Your opponent shows you that he has one medium trump, the nine say, or the eight. You're disappointed because you thought you had a seven bid, but you don't. Now you have to be a little careful, review the bidding, watch yourself when the contract reaches five, expect help from your partner." He pointed at Sloan. "And don't forget you're vulnerable."

"That's what I feel the most."

"Do you want *Kanyak*?" Litzi asked Kiktev.

"I'd forgotten. No," Kiktev said. "The vodka." He spoke to the chauffeur. He went back to the limousine.

"It's getting late," Sloan said. "Peterson will be here. What are the plans? The concrete plans?"

"Have we convinced you?" Kiktev asked.

"No."

"Then go to Moscow," Kiktev said. "If that's what you want. It's as easy as that."

"When?"

"Tomorrow."

"Tomorrow?"

"Center won't be as responsive as they would be if you brought a public embarrassment, but you will have your honors: a position in the executive, at least as high as London, time to enjoy your dacha, no more risks. That is what tires you, the risks?"

"Last week it was."

"It all ends tomorrow," Kiktev said. "If that's what you want."

"Tomorrow?"

"Is that too soon?" Kiktev asked. "I have a transport landing at Yesikoy at eight tomorrow morning. It's here to pick up the brigade and a dead Sarkov. There is room for you. It does sound interesting, doesn't it? A traitor and a hero on the same plane."

"Which one is the hero?" Sloan asked.

"I like it," Kiktev said. "The more I think of it, the more I like you and Sarkov on the same plane. You arrive to music and he to a cold grave. Enjoy the Lenin library. I know you like books."

"I'm relieved," Sloan said. "Will she be coming?"

"No, she stays," Kiktev answered, "for a few days, and then she returns to Stockholm."

"Bremen," Litzi corrected.

"Bremen," Kiktev said. "She will travel to Bremen by way of the Orient Express. She likes long trips on trains, don't you?"

"It would take less time if she came with me," Sloan said.

"Time is not the issue," Kiktev said, and looking at Litzi, continued, "Is it, *matushka*?"

"You said the plane would land at eight?"

"Leave the hotel at seven," Kiktev said. "Don't arrive too early. I'll write a note to the pilot, and I'll wire Moscow in the morning."

Sloan looked relieved and Kiktev smiled. "Now that business is over, let's talk about the cards."

"Will we be partners?"

"Why not? Tomorrow everyone will know which side you were on."

"That's true."

"We will be playing for high stakes, very high stakes," Kiktev said. "I am putting up this ring. It's worth a fortune. What do you have?"

"I have the money for the transfer," Sloan answered.

"How much is it?"

"Twenty-eight thousand pounds," Sloan said. "I have twenty with me."

"We will make the stakes high, as high as allowed," Kiktev said. "Because we are going to win," he continued leaning toward Sloan. "We don't have time for anything complicated. Here's what we'll do. I put on finger on the back of the cards, like this, when I have the jack of trumps. Two, if I have the queen, three for the king and four if I have the ace. Over here, I do the same for the suits: one for clubs, like this. Two for diamonds, three for hearts and four if I have spades. It's that simple."

"It's so simple it's inane," Sloan said. "Any child could see through it."

"These are not skilled players. "

"I will not. It's idiotic."

"I don't like to lose," Kiktev said. "I will not lose. I am pushing luck in front of me, to help."

"Luck is at your side. Not in front."

"I don't care, I will win."

"Cheating is not the way to win, certainly not in Istanbul."

6

Sarkov had given more thought to dinner than to danger. He had made up his mind to eat borscht with pirochkys, wait for Kiev, the ballerina, and walk with her to the Guliza on Oliva Ciknazi. When the time came, Kiev balked at walking; she was out of breath, so Sarkov set off by himself.

As he was leaving Yeni Rejans' restaurant by the front door, two men in felt hats stood uneasily, like villains in an old movie, underneath the shaded lights in the entryway and when he had passed, they filed in behind him. As he was stepping onto the pavement, each took an elbow, lifted him off his feet, and guided him the four feet to the black Mercedes parked at the curb. The rear door opened, as if on a spring, and the two, like good professional abductors, pushed Sarkov's head down and, with firm hands on his lower spine, directed him onto the back seat. Sarkov did not resist. He had little interest in crying out, and he detested violence. He was in the wrong craft.

The chauffeur wore a peaked cap and a tan dust coat. In the back seat was a small man huddled in the far corner. The automobile lurched into the street. A second Mercedes, with the two abductors, followed.

The man in the seat beside him said nothing, seemed indifferent. He wore a wide brimmed hat, a shiny black coat, and black leather gloves.

The Mercedes sped up the narrow street, escaping. At the intersection of Mesrutiyet Caddesi, next to the Pantokraton Church, it stopped for traffic. Sarkov looked back and saw that there was not one, but two cars following. When the Mercedes turned down Mesrutiyt Caddesi, the second automobile stalled at the intersection. The third automobile, a Russian ZIS, sounded its horn, but the second automobile did not move. The ZIS was blocked, could not follow.

As the chauffeur shifted into first gear down the steep grade, Sarkov looked over the housetops to the Bosporus. The new fear had not settled in, but he associated terror with this city, a city of no assurances, a city in which death came quickly and without notice. The houses were secret and isolated, the religions extreme, the tongues unknowable, the cultures in conflict.

Two women stood on the corner, one with a veil, the other with a scarf. An old fat man in a western suit wore a fez. The fez was a Greek import, but the Muslims wore it because the Koran forbids praying in a hat with a brim. Arabs, Persians, Negroes, Mullahs, dervishes, passed one another without talking. There was so much suspicion: men who worked in back alleys and men in western clothes passed each other without acknowledgement.

They drove into Sisham Square. Sarkov knew the place. It had little to recommend it. In the middle of the square was an uninspired statute, a little off-center, the usual flowers and grass, and opposite, an unused opera house.

He looked down at the door panel for the latch, but there was none. Nor had the door a release bar, nor even a lever to lower the window. He looked over at his captor, who had not changed position, except to look away. Sarkov thought of punching him in the throat, or knocking the chauffeur on the head with his heel. He did neither; he sat back and closed his eyes.

He had worked in espionage for eighteen years and this was the third time he had been in danger. He was particularly careful, his wife had said, scrupulously so. His associates had joked about his caution. He never stepped up a ladder, walked against the flow of traffic, and had never fired a gun. He had no exciting hobbies. He had not known violent danger until the past few days, but at this moment he feared that he was going to die.

He looked at his captor again. The man in black was fingering his tespich, the beads of which were not the ordinary yellow, but black amber, and the tassel velvet. The man had not moved, except his hand and now his gloved fingers. Sarkov was startled when the man said softly, "I have no wish to frighten you, *kolay gelsin*, but there was no time to explain."

"I am frightened," Sarkov responded, "and angry. What are you doing?"

"Do you know who has been following you, *in Ciknazi, effendi*?"

"No," Sarkov lied.

"It was your *otdyel*," the other said, in Russian.

They drove over the Galata, through a wide square and down Divan Yolu toward the Saraglio. It was the same route the Caliphs had taken for centuries on their Friday hajj to the mosque. When the automobile slowed, Sarkov whispered, "I'll make my way from here." He put his hand on the door panel without levers, and looked at the other man.

"That wouldn't be wise, even if it were possible."

"Do you know that I am vice consul, that this abduction will have serious consequences, even international?"

"My orders are simple: transport you to my superior."

"Are you the police?"

"Yes."

They passed through an archway into a patio, and stopped in the courtyard of the Janissaries. The chauffeur jumped out, ran around the automobile, and opened the back door for the man in black. The two spoke briefly and the man in black made his way to the front window on Sarkov's side.

"We want you to walk through that gate," he said, pointing a gloved finger, "to a hall. Colonel Tor is waiting. Must I summon more men?"

Sarkov shook his head. He wanted to get on with the questioning. The man in black opened the door.

They walked past the dry executioner's fountain, over the flagstones, through the Ortakapi gates. They had to step over broken masonry, cracked marble, and the snarled, twisted, arthritic, roots of an ancient Eucalyptus tree. They passed a patterned, silk, rug hung on the left wall, two large, dingy oil paintings with yellow-brown varnish, and gilt armchairs set randomly. At the end of the hall, they stopped before two heavy metal doors, which led to a smaller hall.

When the door opened, Colonel Tor was posing for him. Had Sarkov expected a sultan, cross-legged, and jeweled? To Sarkov's surprise, it was Tor's eyes which held him. They were the eyes of genius: enlightened, translucent, as if—should one be able to stare long enough—one could see into the silvery brain. The brows, like frames, emphasized the eyes.

Tor slapped his falaka against his riding pants and beamed. He was handsomely dressed in a gold-tabbed, marshal's uniform. But to Sarkov the clothes meant little. As Sarkov walked closer, he could see in Tor's eyes not the glare of authority which he had feared, but the twinkle of amusement. A pose, it was all a pose, a lovely, fanciful pose, the playful seriousness of genius.

The two men stood silently for more than a minute, and then Tor did a curious thing: he offered the Russian infidel the pious sign of welcome. He stretched out his right hand, his fingertips resting on the other man's chest. Even more disturbing to the Muslims present, Tor said to Sarkov, "A karmic destiny hovers over you. You should not worry."

The Colonel stepped back and, like a magician, produced a package of cigarettes. "Will you smoke a Buyurum?" He asked. "It's the best we have." Sarkov took the cigarette and Tor lit it. Tor said, almost in the other man's ear, "I distrust a man who does not smoke. He does not know how to solve grief." It was a reference to one of Sarkov's poems.

"Either that," Sarkov replied, completing the line, "or he takes consolation in the wrong place." The words were like a password, a secret communication.

"Like with a woman?"

"I wrote that, yes."

"Now you know that I have read your poems."

"One, anyway. I'm flattered."

"Don't be. You left out an important idea about tobacco. Isn't it true that a man does not fully enjoy smoking until he understands how deadly it is?"

"I'm sure."

"Why didn't you add that? It's a reasonable conclusion."

Sarkov nodded.

"I want to tell you that your wife and children are safe."

"Yes."

"They are staying at the Metropole in Nicosia, at least till Sunday. Then they will travel South."

"She said she would try to come here."

"I know," Tor said. "But that will not happen."

"Will I see them?"

"It's reasonable, and soon. That's all I can say, right now."

"I'm relieved."

"Can we talk about tobacco?" Tor asked. "We have a fable. I think you should hear it," Tor said. He did not wait for Sarkov's assent. "One day the prophet picked up a dying serpent. The prophet held the snake to his chest until life returned. The snake tried to struggle free, but the prophet held on. The serpent hissed that he must be let go, otherwise he would bite the man, since man is the natural enemy of the snake. 'If you insist,' the prophet said, and he held out his arm to be bitten. The snake bit him. Immediately the prophet sucked out the poison and spat it on the ground. From his spittle grew the tobacco plant which combines the venom of the serpent with the compassion of the prophet."

"Like so much of your religion, the story is full of wisdom."

"You do not seem wise to me," Tor answered, "walking around the city like a free man. Why does your government want you dead?"

"I can manage them," Sarkov said without enthusiasm.

"The otdyel are after you. They caught up to you yesterday. Tonight they were going to shoot you in the street. I know because I arrested one of them, an old drunk. He told us how many there were, their names, what the orders were, why you are so important to them. It used to be that Russian agents were clever. My father told me about them. But no more. These men are crude. I told my man to pick you up. Otherwise you might be hurt, accidentally."

"I know who they are."

"Do you know Serebrinsky?" Tor asked. "He's as poor an agent as I have seen, a product of your revolution. He descends on my beautiful city like an infection, but I am going to throw him off, like a fever, with the tonic of my brain. Do you know him?"

"I know many like him."

"It's not nationalism any more. Now it's philosophy, which is very dangerous. What is good advances the state; what is bad impedes the state. What nonsense! Serebrinsky believes in your murder the way I believe in Aralu. How do you handle such a man? Except by stamping him out."

"I'm doing the best I can."

"It's not enough," Tor answered. "I have been thinking about a safe place for you, just for tonight. I am not asking for your opinion since the matter is settled. I've thought about this. I cannot allow you to spend the night in your khan because they know, and I cannot allow you to wander around the city. I ask your cooperation so that there will be smoothness. Not trouble, but smoothness."

"So, it is decided."

"You are a fortunate man," Tor said. "I know that. We are both fortunate."

"Does that explain why you had thirty people shot in the vilayar of Van?"

"You know about that?" Tor asked. "Do you know the circumstances? Do you know how death comes so sudden in Turkey?"

"And everywhere else."

"Do you know where you are standing?"

"This is the harem of Suleyman, isn't it?"

"Why is it that nonbelievers associate seraglio with the bed? This is a palace. At different times it was a hospital, a school, a barn for a thousand horses. At one time a mint."

"Will I stay here tonight?"

"No."

"Can we have plain talk?" Sarkov asked. "I have to trust you. I have no choice. I have no defenses. "

"I'm going to put you in prison, for tonight," Tor said. "Not to harm you, but to protect you."

"Prison? Why prison?"

"Because it is the safest place."

"What does it matter?" Sarkov asked. "I'm going to spend the night in prison."

"I'd prefer that you see it as protection. The *otdyel* will not bother you."

"If I complained, what would that do?"

"You're between allegiances," Tor said. "I'm helping."

"By putting me in prison."

"You will be let out in the morning," Tor said. "You have my word."

"Back to trust," Sarkov said. "I've had a bad time with trust."

"That was the English," Tor said. "You know you can trust me, what I did for your family. You have an extraordinary wife, and children. They are safe now, and they will be safe."

"I'm too tired not to trust," Sarkov said. "All I want is rest, some sleep. Show the way."

"Have you spent time in jail?"

"Every modern Russian knows prison."

"While you're going there, I will be playing Bridge with your man, Kiktev. Do you have a word for me?"

"Yes," Sarkov said. "If you lose, you should be ashamed."

7

Yuki drove the shortest route to the Park hotel because Colonel Tor was late for his Bridge game. The Mercedes bounced past the Grand Vizer's building on Aledar Caddesi, one block from the long market, turned down a sokak which was little more than a foot wider than the automobile. In daylight Yuki's driving would have been reckless, but not at night. He knew that no one would be walking the paths of the old section of Istanbul. He also knew that motor cars in this part of the city are vulnerable to the bullet and the bomb. Denizens of the old city, Stamboul, learn in infancy what strangers have to be told: sudden violence stalks the old city when the sun sets.

They passed a park in which during daylight hours scribes wrote letters in the Latin alphabet for those people who spoke, and wrote, only Turkish, where children played Seksek and adults backgammon, but where, at night, murders and conspiracies were plotted. At the end of the sokak, the Mercedes stopped abruptly, turned right and nosed down the steep incline to the Galata bridge. The increase in human activity spurred the men to talk.

"What do I do with the Russian?" Yuki asked.

"Keep him where he is until midnight. Then put him in the *ceza_evi.*"

"*Sirkici?*"

"Not the jail. The dungeon. *Sagmalcilar.*"

"What did he do? Kill a Turk?"

"I want to keep him safe."

"It's not a good place. Tonight's the worst."

"It is never good."

"No," Yuki remonstrated. "Remember that thief from Ismir? We poured acid on his feet. He'll scream all night."

"I don't want the Russian to sleep. I want him nervous in the morning. It will help if he hears some torture."

"Will you turn him over to the English?"

"You can be certain that I won't." Tor looked at his lieutenant as much to reassure himself as to answer the question.

"He will not survive."

"His chances are good."

"Will you release him?"

Tor nodded yes and said, "Tell Hilmi I want the Russian in a cell near the screamer. If he sleeps, wake him up. I don't want him to sleep."

"Who will drive him to his rooms?"

"I'll do that. You take care of the other, the cipher clerk. Make sure he's in the khan early."

"Suppose he won't go? I can't make him."

Tor did not react. They were crossing the Galata, but there was little activity. The donkeys and the Plymouths were gone, the kayiks tied up, the fruit sellers home in their spare rooms.

"Did he give a sign that he wouldn't go?"

"No," Yuki said. "But I'm suspicious of a Russian trick."

"What suspicion? What makes you say that?"

"I don't like it," Yuki said. "It doesn't feel right. Why did Moscow send this boy?"

Tor shouted, "To assassinate Sarkov, and that's the only reason."

"He wanders around like a sheep."

"It was a desperate move, that's all," Tor said, still loudly. "They're frightened. They're showing their hand. Why did he approach you, anyway?"

"He asked for me. I saw him at Varakci. Beria gave him my name."

"You know Beria?"

"At Zeitum. He's a scoundrel and a lackey."

"So Beria gave him your name. See how grasping they are? What information did the boy give you?"

"Nothing," Yuki said. "He doesn't know anything. He has a weapon."

"So you told him the street and the room where Sarkov could be found."

"I did. And I told him to be there early."

"Seven."

"He was grateful. What could be better for him? A chance to succeed."

"Why are you worried? He'll go. Don't worry."

"I'm not as confident as you."

"I'm not confident at all," Tor shouted. "Too much can go wrong. Even if the clerk appears, he may surprise Sarkov. If he does, Sarkov will die." Tor held up one finger. "If Sarkov sees the clerk first, and decides to go out the back, we have another problem." He held up the second finger. "Third, the *otdyel* must act impulsively. If they wait, we have many problems." He said the last solemnly. "Some of our people may be killed. That would be nearly the worst."

"Why 'nearly'?"

"Better to die in Turkey than to have to live in Russia. That would be the worst."

"What can we do?"

"Keep them out of sight. Wait for the last possible moment. Have you got that? The last second. Keep Nazim quiet. Calm him until you're ready. The nephew will follow the uncle. Nazim is our best shot, but he can be impulsive. Stay close to him."

"Alexki is giving the prisoners instructions in the pistol."

"Who are they?"

"All bad. Three were to be hanged this week."

"For what?"

"Murder. I've forgotten the charges. One killed a relative, another slaughtered a dozen people in Bodrum."

"Did Alexki explain?"

"No."

"What did he tell them?"

"Nearly the truth: they are to shoot Russians. If they do as they are told, they will be free."

"True."

"What else?"

"Arrange the motor cars in front of the building. Leave a space so the Russians will park in the right place."

Yuki nodded. "I'll do that tonight."

"You're using the Greek Turner's building?"

Yuki nodded.

"The Russians will make easy targets." Tor was quiet for a few moments and then continued, "Sarkov might see them if he comes out the front."

"The distance from our window to that side of the street is forty feet."

"How can Nazim miss? Make sure he doesn't kill the people in front. Most likely Serebrinsky will be driving. He's not to be shot. Nor is the man next to him."

"All the rest?"

"Yes, all the rest. I don't know whether it is four or five. There were five in the car tonight, you said. One or two might have come in. However many there are, shoot them all, except the two in front."

"What about the press?"

"What about them? Keep them out of sight until it's over. No, I'll see to it. We'll detain them near Tepebasi."

"Where will you be?"

"In the souk behind. I won't move after I let Sarkov out. Don't worry about me, except if something goes wrong. I'll be a hundred meters away. Who are the press people?"

"Herr Seiler from *Reuters*. Nemeddin Sadak will send three reporters. One from *Das Volk* and two from *Zeit Neue*."

"Who's taking the pictures?"

"The police photographer, and there will be two from the German press."

"Bring them upstairs with you. Make sure they have the best angle."

"What do you want in the picture?"

The Mercedes stopped. They were in the driveway of the Park. Tor opened the door, but made no move to exit.

"Right after the shooting, move the automobiles, and drag the bodies together. Not on top of each other, but close enough for a photograph. It's a massacre. Get the names. Have everything ready when the press arrives. Help them any way you can, especially the German press. Remember, Sarkov's name is not to be mentioned, even if his body is there. No one knows him. No matter what, he does not exist."

"So much can go wrong."

"I know," Tor said. "Just set it up. I'm going to play Bridge. The Russian ambassador will be my opponent."

"Good fortune."

"It's strange about Luck," Tor said, his foot on the cobblestones. "How much she favors those who prepare for her."

8

"We bid that perfectly," Ambassador Peterson said to his partner, Colonel Tor. Peterson slapped the unshuffled cards on the table next to Ambassador Kiktev, his opponent, whose turn it was to deal. "Do you think we could have made five?" He asked Tor.

"Not with the doubleton over here," Tor said, indicating Sloan.

"God," Peterson said, "that was a brilliant finesse of the diamond queen. Don't you think?" He was asking Sloan. The question was inappropriately directed, since it was Sloan's queen who was finessed. "Do that once more," Peterson said to Tor, "and I'll exempt you from all the Credits."

"The game is simple," Tor said, "when your partner communicates."

Peterson beamed.

Then Peterson studied the numbers. "From six hundred down, to three hundred up. Damned if that isn't playing!" No one demurred. But Kiktev shuffled the cards too long. "Deal the cards, will you?" Peterson demanded. "You're rubbing the numbers off."

"Take your time. We have no worries," Tor said. "Nemesis may roam the world, but she lives in Istanbul."

"That's what the Trojans thought," Kiktev said. "Wasn't Nemesis the mother of Helen?"

"You're confusing her with Leda, who was foster-mother. Nemesis never takes sides."

"But the Turks think she favors them, don't they?" Sloan asked.

"She helps," Tor answered, "because the Turks under-stand her."

"How do you mean?"

"Some people play cards the way they live, Mister Sloan. They accept the cards the way they're dealt, haphaz-ardly, by chance, hoping for luck, now and again lucky, but most of the time not getting the most out of what they hold."

"I don't understand."

"Nemesis comes to those who prepare for her," Tor said. "To those who watch and are ready, who know what to look for."

"What does she want?"

"Who knows what a woman wants? She wants what is right. If you don't do what is right, she punishes. Maybe not now, but sometime. So, do what is right, and reap the con-sequences. That's Nemesis."

"We're vulnerable," Peterson said. "Can you believe that?" He shifted his buttock in the soft chair.

Kiktev dealt the cards. The four men were solemn and serious, like devotees about to engage in a sacred ritual. Kiktev said, "I wonder what Nemesis thinks of Inonu. Isn't he moving too fast?"

"I should say he is," Peterson said.

"The devotion of Ataturk is ancient," Tor said. "He won't accept secularization, but how are we to catch up?"

"Why in the world would you want to' catch up'?" Peterson asked.

"Ninety percent of our people can't read," Tor said. "We have to advance into the twentieth century."

"I like the country the way it is," Peterson said.

"Any civilization that could produce this delicious candy is pretty well advanced," Sloan said.

"*Kuru Yemis*," Tor said. "I'm happy you like them."

"They look like insects," Kiktev said, grimacing. "Whenever I see them I think they carry disease."

"What's your position in the government?" Sloan asked Tor.

"I'm director, security police."

"Secret police," Kiktev corrected.

"You seem young for such responsibilities," Sloan said.

"We're not large," Tor said. "We have few men compared to your country."

"Don't let him fool you," Kiktev said. "He knows everything that goes on."

"I'm afraid that's true," Tor said. "You're in government, aren't you, Mister Sloan?"

"Yes I am. I work in the Home Office," he lied, wanting to provoke no more questions from the Colonel, nor antagonize either ambassador.

"You came on yesterday's plane," Tor said. "Are you visiting our lovely city for business or pleasure?"

"A little of both, I'm afraid," Sloan said. "I came to ease some consular matters which are in transition, but mostly to rest and watch the Marmora at night."

"It is magnificent, isn't it?" Tor asked, rhetorically. "There are many things which change, but if you want antiquity and stability, come to Istanbul."

They had all been dealt their cards, but only Tor did not arrange his cards in suits. He studied the others as they arranged their cards, for a hint of the split. It was only after the others had finished arranging that he memorized his cards, and their position in his hand.

"You arrested one of our men last night," Kiktev declared.

"Yes," Tor said. "He was drunk and causing trouble outside Markiz. One of our citizens said that he did not pay his bill, but he didn't harm anyone, as far as we know. We didn't arrest him, we detained him, until two of your people took him. He needed to sleep. There were others with him. Is there a reason for so many to be visiting Istanbul?"

"They're traveling on diplomatic business."

"The drunken man said he was looking for another Russian, a man who was working at your embassy. This afternoon we called, but there was no response. Is someone missing? We'd like to help, if we can."

"One of our men lost his way, but we're certain we've found him. There's no need for an investigation."

"Just to be of help," Tor said. "Nothing more."

"I notice a number of German nationals. Is there a reason for so many being here?" Sloan asked.

"The Germans have had influence here. But you know that." Peterson answered. "Von Pappen is a charming fellow, really."

"That's true," Kiktev said. "Why is it that the Germans are so much more civilized when they live in classical countries?"

"There was no war here," Tor said.

"There wasn't?" Kiktev asked. "Then why was all that chrome going out? And all those auxiliaries?"

"It's difficult to please everyone," Tor said. He said that to stop the conversation. He was occupied with his strong hand. After the initial hesitation, Tor and Peterson began bidding the Culbertson.

But Kiktev was more interested in the conversation. "Speer said that the Germans could not continue the bombings without the Turkish chrome. Is that true?"

"And we couldn't continue without the British help," Tor said.

"Our help?" Sloan asked.

"He's talking about the airplane parts," Peterson said.

"We gave the Turks equipment for airplanes?"

"It's a little more complicated than that," Peterson said. "They have German planes, but they couldn't replace certain parts, so we transported the remains of planes we shot down over North Africa."

"It is complex," Sloan said.

"The pattern of Turkish intrigue," Kiktev said. "Play the game, but don't take sides."

Tor laughed. "There is peace because no one calls Turkey their enemy." He folded his arms, and announced, "But the cards say strength: six spades."

"Double," Kiktev said quickly, and Sloan scowled. Peterson passed, Sloan muffled a pass, but Tor hesitated. He was studying his hand, considering the redouble, but finally he whispered, "pass."

There was nothing unorthodox in Kiktev's lead, the queen of hearts, which was captured by dummy's king, nor was there anything unorthodox in the subsequent play, until Tor began drawing Clubs. All trumps had been extracted, except dealer's five. Here Tor led the deuce of Clubs. Kiktev hesitated for just a moment and then played the seven. Without hesitating, Tor played the ten from dummy, and Sloan played his five. It was a rash, but brilliant, move. Tor then played a heart back into his hand, from which he played the four of Clubs. Kiktev had to play either his Jack or Ace. He chose the Jack and dummy's queen won the trick.

Tor returned with dummy's three of Clubs. Sloan played the nine, Tor the King, and Kiktev the Ace.

The rest of the play was routine, Kiktev winning his only trick.

When it was clear that Tor would make his contract, and win the game, but before the last card was played, Sloan asked Kiktev, "Didn't you realize what you were telling him when you doubled?" The severe question placed a pall over the company, as when a husband criticizes his wife in public. Kiktev stood and glared at Sloan, his partner. Still glaring, he took off the expensive ring, placed it on the table, made a military 'about-face' and marched out.

"I'm sorry," Sloan said, "but it was a stupid bid. What could he have been thinking?"

"He was expecting you to capture one trick?"

"I had a bust," Sloan said. "At the wrong time."

Tor smiled at Peterson and picked up the ring.

"Is this Nemesis?" Sloan asked.

"Could be," Tor said. "Indeed. Could be."

"I have a question," Peterson said, leaning over and folding the money. "If you were so sure that Kiktev had the Jack and Ace of Clubs, why didn't you 'redouble'?"

"Yes, why didn't you?" Sloan asked.

"Because I had redoubled him," Tor said, "earlier in the evening."

PART VI

August 15

1

"You knew how filthy that prison would be," Sarkov whispered. He was slumped on the back seat of Tor's Mercedes. He shaded his eyes from the rising sun.

"Worse than a sack in the Bosphoros?" Tor asked.

"At least you're dead," Sarkov said. "What did that man do, the one in the next cell?"

"We're trying to find out who was with him in the theft."

"The moaning kept me awake. So I could smell the slop. But it was the mosquitoes. No, the filth. Are there dead?"

"We reverence the dead. We like to be reminded." Tor said.

They were driving up the Galata hill, over a souk that was meant for pack animals, not automobiles. The grill of the Mercedes nosed out from the alley into a small square, and stopped. Sarkov recognized the rear of his khan. He fumbled for the latch, not remembering from the night before that there were no latches.

"He will let you out," Tor said.

When the chauffeur opened the door and Sarkov was standing, he deliberately left the door ajar in a gesture of contempt. Although he was exhausted and his plans extended no further than water on the face and a change of shirt, he wanted to show his bitterness at spending the night in prison.

Tor leaned over and grasped the window to shut the door. As he did, he shouted, "Don't forget the British. They expect you at ten."

"You know I'm not going there," Sarkov said.

"Watch for the *otdyel*."

Even at seven in the morning the square behind Sarkov's khan resembled an Arab souk. There were barefoot porters, hawkers of firewood and charcoal, knife grinders, and mattress stuffers with their bow-like instruments. There were Greek traders, all shouting and rushing out, until they realized that Sarkov was not a customer.

The smell, though malevolent, was not the same as the smell in jail. This one was a combination of excrement, garbage, and rats. A cat lay dead on a pile of decaying melons.

The buildings were stacked up, and all of the same color, "ocher," and the roofs, faded red tile. Each building had an iron fence to discourage thieves, and windows jutting out from the second floor. An old woman sat in one of these windows, opposite Sarkov's khan. Up the alley a man with a horse and a covered wagon was delivering bread. Across, a fat man in an apron, a tripe seller, stood just inside his door, watching. Nearer, against the fences, men sat on the stones, all of them with that look of sad indolence which comes from having no work. They spat often.

Inside his gate, Sarkov hurried through the courtyard and up the back stairs to a hidden door. He quietly opened the door which lead to a narrow corridor behind his rooms. Except for the slant of light which intruded through the space of the opened door, and a small dirty window high up, the corridor was dark.

Added to, and because of, his anxiety and his exhaustion, Sarkov had the prescience of danger. So frightened was he that he took off his shoes. Inside the back room of his flat, he hesitated. He stood still and listened for a full minute. Only after that time did he hear the sigh of rustling papers. He took one more step. From his new position he could see the back of the hat of a man sitting on his ottoman in the next room. The man was wearing not only a dark hat but also a dark coat, much like Sarkov's. He was reading some loose papers. When Sarkov took one more step forward he could see the table on which were a valise and a gun. The valise was his own, and so were the papers, but not the gun. He recognized the weapon from his training. It was a cyanide gun which shot a prussic acid pellet. The intruder had to be Russian, and most likely he had another gun, a TK, disguised as a clip, inside his coat pocket. The prussic acid would not kill, even at ten feet.

Clearly the man expected Sarkov to come through the front door. He had not reconnoitered the back, and as a consequence, had left himself vulnerable.

Sarkov stood still, listening to the children in the souk, and a tailor dressing down his apprentice in a shop nearby.

It was all inevitable. In Moscow a small man with a pince-nez had sent his hunters to track Sarkov down. The consequence of that mission was this person in the next room waiting to shoot, while somewhere in the city the Brigade waited for their chance. Neither emotion nor compassion had any part in the process; only logic. Treachery demanded redress. Any attempt, it seemed to Sarkov, at that moment, to stop the inevitable was as futile as arguing with Mister Death.

But he did contend with the inevitable. He picked up a plate from the table and rushed the remaining four steps into the second room. Before the intruder could rise, or even turn, Sarkov hit him just under the left mastoid bone.

He fell like he was dead. The blow would not kill, but Bakov would be unconscious for ten minutes, and his head would ring for the rest of the day, if he had lived.

Sarkov sat on the ottoman, nausea building from his bowel. His lower organs lifted, sickeningly. He leaned over to retch but nothing came. He tilted his head back, breathed deeply, holding the nausea.

Bakov lay in profile at his feet, one arm reaching out, the other folded under his body, awkwardly, in the simulacrum of flight. One leg pointed forward and the other tucked under, as if his pelvis was broken. Sarkov studied the bluish-white color of Bakov's face and the Rorschach blot of purple the blow had made, until Bakov moved his lips to make saliva and changed his position slightly. When Bakov moved Sarkov saw in his breast pocket the envelope with the money: nothing else in the world has that particular suppleness. Sarkov snatched the envelope and stuffed it into his own trouser pocket.

He stood, put his hand on the wall to steady himself, and staggered back in the kitchen area and the corridor. From the door, he saw the Mercedes. He had no wish to recapture Colonel Tor's ministrations, so he stumbled back into his sitting room, stepped over the still unconscious Bakov, and opened the door to the main hallway.

He stuck his head, like a gibbous moon, into the passageway, which was a paradigm of his fate: narrow, circuitous, and virtually endless. The single light was too high, the linoleum worn, its edges curled so that anyone might trip, the length of the corridor too long, so that no one might see where it led.

He took the few steps past the first door, which was open. A woman was cooking at a make-shift stove and two children were playing in the corner. Just inside the door, the man sat reading the paper.

The Turk carries few belonging: a prayer rug, cooking utensils, a bag, a cradle if there is an infant, and a saddle if there is an animal. The wife wears the family fortune in gold pieces jingling from her wrists. Turks may sleep on the floor throughout the whole of their life.

This Turk gave Sarkov a stern look, as if he had heard the blow next door and wished to show disapproval. He fingered his short, wet, cigarette, and threw it on the floor. Sarkov ducked his head and walked on.

In the next room a man and a woman were arguing behind a closed door, while across an old lady, toothless and haggard, in a formless shift, hauled her night bottle to the common lavatory. She smiled, her mouth gaping. At the end of the corridor there were three steps down, a turn, and twelve steps to the foyer.

In the foyer a young beggar-woman cradled her child on a low bench. Next to her was a thirsty fern, the glass front door, like a shop's, not a hotel's. Across from her was a desk too high to see over. A clerk huddled behind the desk. He was reading a paper, waiting for the phone to ring. No one stirred when Sarkov walked through and opened the door. A bell tinkled. Sarkov cautiously stepped down the last three steps of the enclosed vestibule into the street.

He waited for someone, anyone, to pass, as proof that the street was safe, but no one did. An infant lay in repose on a cushion in the building across the street: signal to him that the street was safe. It was another mistake.

He hadn't taken two steps in the open when, out of the corner of his eye, he saw the lash of gun fire. He heard the whack of the brick, the splash of shattered glass, and the

wail of the beggar-woman. Her moan began low, plaintive
and haunting. The moan became part of the atmosphere,
like the lowing of the lodos, which, according to Turkish
myth, brings madness and death.

Before Sarkov could turn to run the gun exploded
again. He felt his coat split near his thigh. He cried out, not
from pain, but from violation. He was not hit. He jumped
back and twisted sideways into the recessed vestibule.
Another report sounded and the bullet blew a hole in the
masonry near his ear, a segment stinging his cheek, and
more glass shattered behind him. The woman raised her
moan one pitch.

Then there was silence which was not safe. He heard
the ignition, the screeching of tires and the shift into
reverse. The Peugeot crashed in its haste. Bumpers collid-
ed, headlights popped, more glass shattered, and the automobile accelerated.

Sarkov pressed against the wall, maneuvered away
from the street in order to cut down the angle. When the
automobile accelerated, he jumped the three steps, crouched
through the glassless panel of the front door, and ran
through the foyer. The woman, moaning and bobbing cata-
tonically, cradled her child. Sarkov could not tell whether
she or the child had been hit, or whether she was simply
frightened. Halfway up the stairs he thought he heard more
gunfire, although it may have been memory, or backfire.

At the beginning of the corridor he saw the residents'
heads, like cattle on a stanchion, protruding into the hallway. At Sarkov's appearance, they ducked back, as if on
cue, and slammed their doors.

Sarkov ran down the passage to his rooms where
Bakov, on his knees, head bowed, was trying to stand. In his
right hand he held the small gun.

In a flash of grace, Sarkov stepped back and across the threshold of the room opposite his. He reached behind for the door and closed it just so much that he could see, but not be seen.

Three of the Brigade had followed him up the stairs, clamoring in Russian. Sarkov could hear the wailing from the foyer; it sounded like a banshee. Certainly, Sarkov thought, I am cornered. He looked behind, but he was in a room slightly larger than a closet. He strained to look directly above him at the window which had perpendicular bars. There was no way out.

As the Russians reached the top of the stairs, Bakov, gun in hand, stumbled into the corridor. It was most unfortunate for him. He saw the men at the other end and understood the error they were about to make. He shouted, like a man who accidentally falls from a high place, aware of the inevitable, yet, in a futile effort to stay nature's law, shouts and gestures. "Wait," he shouted, "I am Bakov." His mouth opened and his tongue flopped, his eyes walled, he bent forward, extending his right hand, either in defense or greeting, no one would ever know.

The first bullet thudded into his chest, the second shattered his left ileum. The impact of the first bullet lifted him, the second turned him half way around. He slapped against the wall and, dead weight, tumbled to the floor. A muffled, piercing sound, like air from a tube, whistled from his chest. His head twisted, fell, and he expired.

Sarkov could have reached out and touched him. Instead, he recoiled and fell into the corner of the closet.

The three Russians ran up the corridor to Bakov's body and dragged it into Sarkov's room. They stayed in the room less than three minutes, just enough time to roll the body into the Bergama carpet. One Russian tied his end of the rug securely, while the other man could not tie his end. Each took an end of the rug with the body enclosed, while the third man led the way back along the corridor and down the stairs.

The woman continued to wail, but now there were intervals when she breathed in, like a baby, and then screamed again.

When he was sure that the men were gone, Sarkov opened the closet door and looked to his left, down the passageway. It was another mistake. He heard footsteps but, before he could turn to see, he was hit, like Barkov, low on the back of his head. Like Barkov also, he slipped into unconscious.

2

On a first floor window of the building across, a mother had nestled her infant on a cushion between the grill and the sill. When the child was settled, the mother strummed the udi and sang, ululating, words prolonged with broad vowels, quiet sibilants, and modified "u" sounds. A second and a half after the shots rang out, the music stopped and the mother and child disappeared.

Above, the police did not react. When the shooting began, Yuki, the two other policemen, and the photographer, did not stir. From their position in the second floor window of the building next to the mother's, they had a better view of the whole scene. They had orders to wait, although their impulse was to react to the shots.

Their vantage was better than the mother's because their building had three levels, the police being on the second. The first floor was three feet below Sarkov's khan, the gradient on the Galata hill being so acute. But the second floor was only fifteen feet above and forty feet away from the Russian automobile and fifty feet from the front door which now had no glass. There were two cornices projecting over the sidewalk, like boxes in a theater.

Two of the Turk policemen stood in the projecting cornices. They watched Sarkov avoid the gunfire, and they saw the Russians chase him into the building. Behind the two policemen, in a cradle vault between the window and the stairs, Yuki sat and smoked. He did not watch.

Turks either sit or carry. Yuki was too slight, and disinclined, to carry. He liked being Tor's chauffeur. He would hold to the Colonel's order: 'wait for the Russians to spill out from Sarkov's khan into Persambe Pazar Sokage' before shooting.

"Do you think they killed your man?" Nazim, at the right window, the one with the best vantage, asked. He was leaning against the zigzag support. He could be seen from the street.

"It makes no difference," Yuki answered. "Step away from the window." He snuffed out his cigarette in a saucer, exhaled smoke through his nose, and spat, something he did habitually, whether indoors or out.

Nazim opened the breach of his Kalashnikov rifle, looked to see if the folding hinge was in order, shut the bolt, and flicked on the safety. His hand was trembling. He felt inside his coat pocket for the extra cartridges, and then moved his hand over the outside of his pocket. He turned toward Yuki. The two smiled at each other.

The policeman in the next window was Nazim's nephew. He had only recently been elevated to the Second Section. He wanted to make an impression even though he was nervous.

"Don't shoot before I do," Nazim ordered. "Release the safety."

Yuki walked over to the window and looked to the left to see if he could see Tor's Mercedes. He couldn't. "The plan will work," he said. "Alexki didn't send them out. I was afraid he might. Now it will work."

"Why don't you go downstairs and help. We know what to do," Nazim said.

"I want to watch from here," Yuki said absently.

"They're coming," the young policeman shouted, releasing the safety and cocking his pistol at the same time.

"Wait," Yuki ordered. "Wait."

The first Russian backed out of Sarkov's building. He was bent over, pulling, as best he could, the rolled carpet with Bakov inside. The Russian on the other end dropped his end when he stepped from the building into the street. Bakov's hand flopped out and the second Russian stuffed the hand back inside the folds of the rug. The third Russian, a blond, carried nothing but a Mauser. He cursed and pushed the second man the twelve feet from the entrance-way to the automobile. Then he opened the back door of the Peugeot. The first Russian backed in and pulled the body in the rug with him. The two men in the front seat neither moved to help, nor turned to see.

Yuki ran to the staircase and shouted down, "Send them out. Send them out."

The building the Turks occupied was more like a fortress than a house. A Greek turner had fortified it. He believed that the Turks would persecute him for his moderate success so he built a two-foot moat around the front of the building, and outside that, an iron fence. The window shutters were battened and the door made of iron.

In response to Yuki's order, the big door creaked open and three men were pushed into the street. They had these things in common: baggy shalway pants, thick black hair, thirty eight caliber pistols, and capital sentences. They were convicted murderers.

The first prisoner, a young man in collarless shirt and charcoal jacket—the only one of the three with shoes—ran up the street waving his arms and shouting. The second, an old man, huddled in a crouched position on the running-board of the nearest automobile. The third prisoner, no more than an adolescent, walked into the street and fired his pistol at the first Russian, still bent over in the back seat.

The boy did not have the presence of mind to take cover, nor did he see the blond Russian who had taken a position on the other side of the Peugeot. The Russian spread his legs, extended his arms on the roof of the automobile, and grasped the Mauser with both hands. The gun was at eye level. The thumb of his right hand settled on the safety and eased it forward. As he had done many times in practice he lay his first finger along the barrel for direction. He squeezed the trigger as gently as he could knowing there would be a kick but expecting it.

His bullet hit the boy in the upper left chest where a medal might have been worn. The three point sixty-two millimeter slug burst into the boy's chest, tore at the lungs, ripped the muscle and delicate bones of the back, and exploded through the loose shirt, splattering gristle against the building behind.

Alexki opened the iron door a crack and shouted at the old man who was huddled on the running-board. When the old man did not move, Alexki fired two shots at his feet. The old man jumped up and did a curious thing: he stood liturgically straight and deliberately fixed his cloth cap on backward, as if he were about to pray. When his head appeared above the roof of the automobile, the blond Russian shot him like a turkey. The old man's cap fell to the ground as the back of his head disintegrated.

It was only then, after he had shot the second prisoner, that the blond Russian looked up at the window. He saw Nazim's forearm and elbow outstretched, the rifle at the shoulder, the head bent slightly toward the right and the single eye at the sight. He squinted, concentrating on the period of the barrel. Recognition was half a second, after which he moved, but Nazim's bullet slashed threw his neck.

The second Russian hid at the left rear fender. The door was still ajar, but there were two dead bodies in the back seat, Bakov and the first Russian, and now his blond comrade lay gasping on the sidewalk.

The two men in the front seat were frantic, the man on the rider's side doubled over, his head against the dash, while the driver fumbled with the clutch. Though both men were exposed, neither had any reason to fear. They were not targets. The Peugeot jerked forward. As it did, the second Russian pulled his dead comrade from the back seat onto the sidewalk, and he fell over Bakov.

Nazim's nephew was waiting for this. The second Russian was his target. He shot the Russian in the left shoulder and then, when he retrenched, the young policeman shot through the top of the automobile and hit his man again, this time in the lower back. The man fell out of the automobile onto the street.

As the Peugeot made its way from the curb, the blond Russian crawled, like a soldier through barbed wire, on his elbows. His mouth gaped like a fish pulled from the water. He gasped, and the choking could be heard by the policemen forty feet away. Blood pulsed from the wound in his neck.

Nazim shot him a second time in the side below the ribs. The second wound was not as grotesque as the first because blood from the neck splattered on the boy's blond hair and pale face. His dark clothes absorbed the blood from the second wound, but the second bullet pierced his spleen. He reached out for the bumper of the Peugeot. As the automobile moved down the street, the boy held on, tenaciously, for eight or ten feet and then let go, spread eagle. He sprawled, like a peace signal, on the cobblestones.

Silence settled on the scene like a sting after a slap. It was a full two minutes before the iron door opened and three Turk policemen hedged into the street. The first man, a corporal, bent down to examine the old prisoner whose skull was in pieces. Alexki came out and looked up at the window for orders. Yuki made a wide, gathering, gesture. As Alexki walked slowly up the street, Yuki shouted, "Move the autos."

The first two policemen scampered to the automobiles; it was the less nauseous task. However, the second ran over the blond Russian. When the automobiles had been moved, each policeman dragged one body to the center of the street.

"No good," the photographer said, shaping the scene with his hands. "Too close together," he said to Yuki.

"Spread them out," Yuki shouted. "Scatter them."

The policemen dragged the dead by their feet a few paces apart, and then looked up for approval. They were arranging a group photograph.

The photographer was still not satisfied, but Yuki shouted at him, "This is not a wedding. Take the picture."

He sat down, lit a cigarette, and waited for the press.

3

S arkov returned to consciousness with a headache. He opened his mouth wide, in the rictus of a laugh, in order to relieve the pain behind his left ear, but the stretching did not help. His cheek rested against a calf-skinned boot, light brown and hand sewn, his ribs fitted painfully over the drive shaft, his legs cramped in the fetal position against the front seat. He had been stuffed on the rear floor of Tor's Mercedes.

The automobile was speeding along a dirt road not meant for speed. Sarkov felt the bumps as jolts to his ribs and blows to his head. He put his hand on the rug in an effort to rise.

Tor laid his hand on Sarkov's shoulder. "Don't get up. There's nothing to see. We are on the Airyar Road, two kilometers from the airport. In front of us, maybe half a kilometer, an automobile is speeding, kicking up dust. Outside, the country is barren. There is nothing to see. We will be at the airport in five minutes." He patted Sarkov's shoulder. At the same time he ordered the driver to slow down.

"They're shooting at us, but they won't hit," Tor said, as if he was describing a sports event. "About as much chance as a bullet hitting a bullet. Can't be done. But what is the point of offering a target?"

The Mercedes swerved to avoid a peasant on a donkey cart, and then settled back in the tracks. They passed a white, domino hut, out of which a farmer came to sniff the wind, to test the weather. He stared, vacantly, at the two speeding autos.

"From early June through September the farmers work on the other side of the ridge, harvesting rye, wheat, and barley. They're in a hurry, not because of rain, as you might think, but because of locusts. Do you have locusts in your country?"

"I don't know."

"They don't often invade this far down usually; unless there's nothing to eat. This year they're coming."

Random goats nibbled scarce, tussock, grass. Now and again an isolated dwarf shrub and kuru pine shot up, but nothing else. The fierce sun had baked the land into straw colored dust.

Sarkov rested his head against the floor. The pain was no better. He had no notion why he was heading for the airport, but he was too tired to be anxious. Was this another ruse, like persuading him to spend the night in prison?

Tor was humming. Sarkov looked at his watch: eight fifteen. He assumed that Tor was the rescuer. Was that another mistake?

The automobile slowed, shifted down, nearly to a stop, and then zipped along a smooth surface for less than a minute, and then stopped for good. The door was opened from the outside by a boy in the lambskin kepi of a private soldier. He helped Sarkov out.

Before Sarkov could straighten up, Tor had marched fifteen paces ahead. Sarkov had to run, in his stocking feet, to catch up and, as he did, Tor walked between two aluminum hangers. He came to a halt and faced Sarkov, who, breathing deeply, leaned against a rusted gasoline pump.

"Who was that ahead of us?"

"What was left of the *otdyel*," Tor said.

"Were you chasing them?"

"I wanted them to think we were."

"But you were not?"

"No."

"What were you doing?"

"I was trying to persuade them that I was chasing them."

"Why?"

"So they would hurry."

"You want them to escape?"

"Hmm."

"I'm not getting any information. Do you want me to stop?"

"No. No. I want you to ask. Don't you understand? This will be the only time you and I will ever be able to speak about what happened."

They had to stop talking because the Russian plane, a PS-84, a low monoplane, revved its motors noisily, and rumbled onto the runway close to them.

Tor pointed, "See the guns in the nose and there in the turret? No taking chances." He walked a few steps behind a door and beckoned Sarkov.

"Where are they going?" Sarkov asked.

"You should know. First Ismail, then Odessa, Moscow, with a treasure."

"They have the other man and they think it is me."

"That's right. Like Carthaginians, they are sneaking the treasure out in a rug, but it is not a treasure. It is a viper. It will sting them all." He smiled.

"Why didn't you tell me what you were planning?"

"How could I?" Tor said. "You're an intelligent man, but not devious. What I conjured was so full of chance anything could have happened, and almost did. And all of it involved you. If I allowed you to chose, you would never have gone along."

Sarkov rubbed the bump behind his ear. "These hours have been madness."

The Russian plane banked to the right, away from them. "You had a long night and a few minutes of danger, but you are alive. How's your head?"

"Who hit me?"

"I won't incriminate him," Tor said. "Would you have done what I wanted if I asked you?"

"Certainly not."

"Who hit me? The driver?"

"You were unwilling, and yet I needed you. So I couldn't explain. If you and I had talked, you would have scoffed at such nonsense. I couldn't risk it."

"What was your purpose in all this?"

"It was simple," Tor said. He squatted on his haunches, like a pathfinder. Sarkov tried to squat, but he had to rest his back against the wall. Tor picked up a straw and drew lines in the dust. They looked like original settlers. "I had a free hand," Tor said slowly. "Your wife gave me the plan."

Sarkov looked up and beamed.

"It entered into my head when she spoke to me." Tor said. "Everything was at my disposal. I had you. I knew the British had no intention of rescuing you." He picked up a handful of dust and threw it in the wind. "Contemptible."

"How did you know that?"

"I knew about Sloan before you saw him."

"Reed told you."

"The English were concerned with your safety, weren't they?" He asked with irony, but then, in earnest, "Why did McKenzie send Sloan? Do you have an idea?"

Sarkov leaned forward. "Sloan is Russia's most important operator in the West. He is a major in the KGB." He pointed to Tor. "He transfers top secret information: the 'B' division on running agents, the Spanish ring, Camp 0200. Do you know the British have opened a new section —Counter Soviet Intelligence—and Sloan is head? Do you know that he is given instructions, weekly, on how to run his section by General Kharlimov? How could Moscow have it better?"

"Does McKenzie know?"

"If you know, and I know, McKenzie knows. That's the law."

"Why send him then?"

"My guess: to keep Sloan in place. At least McKenzie knows where he is, and what he's doing." He walked toward the one window in the barren hangar and then came back.

"There has to be more," Tor said. "McKenzie would kill him if that's all there is. I would. Would he allow Sloan to be head of this new section? There's too much power, too much damage. No, McKenzie is hiding something. He has a secret, I know it. I can feel it. What could it be? You should know what it is. Help me. Would it be a double in Checka? More information? The planting of an agent? How many men do the British have in Checka, would you say?"

"I'm sure there are many, but how would Sloan's coming to Istanbul advance that? It's speculation. Espionage doesn't work that way, and you know it."

"Would it be possible to break your code?" Tor said and blinked, as if he had been in a dark room and had come into the sun.

"Two years ago, yes. Today, no. We have a new closing which is break-proof."

"You know the British system, the daily pad?"

"We knew what was going out from here, but not the system."

"Could the British break your code?"

"No, it's impossible," Sarkov said. "We use an Almanac which allows changes on a whim." He looked at Tor again, this time he was not sure. "At least Moscow is certain it can't be broken."

"Suppose the British broke your code. What would that mean?"

"We trust it. It would have bad consequences if they were listening and we didn't know .Think of May in Canada, atomic secrets, China, even Mister Sloan."

"It has to be the code. Either that, or McKenzie works for the Russians."

"You have an expansive mind."

"Is that impossible?"

"I would know if he did."

"Not if he worked for the GRU."

"Yes," Sarkov said. "If he was controlled by them I wouldn't know."

"So?"

"The way you talk, anything is possible," Sarkov said. "At this moment it all sounds like speculation, like the codes."

"Is it? Let me tell you what they know. London was aware of that PS-84 landing this morning," Tor said. "What does that tell you? And there's one more fact. Sloan was on that plane."

"I told him to go. It's the only answer for him."

"It may have been an answer yesterday, but not today. It won't go well with him, and you know it. There will be some hard questions. He made some errors which Beria will

not like." Tor stood and walked toward the door. "We don't
have much time. Is there anything else?"

"I'd like to know what happened this morning."

"Two of the Brigade survive. They are on the plane.
Three are dead in the street. Right now, the press are scurrying about; the photographers taking pictures. I staged a
massacre." Tor clapped his hands as if he were applauding.
"Wait. Wait. I wanted Mister Attlee and Mister Truman to
pay attention to my city. I wanted them to know that Turks
and Russians are natural enemies, that this holy place cannot be dishonored by Russian control, must not. How else
could a small policeman who loves his city bring attention
to such important matters except with an explosion which
expands into an international incident? I want the politicians to read about the killing of three Russians and three
Turks and stop, if only for a time, granting Stalin's wish to
occupy this city. That's all."

"I don't see how it will work."

"Six dead in the street. Herr Seiler is a witness. He is
shocked. Paul Rogers from Reuters writing about the scene
and sending the story to Germany. There will be pictures,
big pictures, in tomorrow's papers in Potsdam."

"What will that accomplish?"

"Maybe nothing, maybe something. Perhaps Mister
Truman will hesitate in the negotiations. That's all I want, a
hesitation."

"My part?"

"You said it last night. You were the bait."

"I was almost killed."

"Remember," Tor said, pointing like a teacher, "our
second interest was in keeping you alive." He shrugged.
"We are plain talking, aren't we? We will not see one another again. When they shoot at you in the street, we almost

killed them but the best circumstance happened. My men waited and you were not hurt."

"Where were your men?"

"Across the street, up high."

"They watched while the *otdyel* tried to kill me?"

"Yes."

"Who hit me?" Sarkov rubbed his head again.

"The driver. He would have taken either man. Those were his instructions."

"Either me or the other would do."

"Your chances of surviving were slight."

"If I was killed, it would mean nothing to you?"

"Less than perfect, but acceptable, yes."

"You're no better than the British."

"No, but I don't have their reputation."

"But I survived."

"Just to prove how hopeful I was, I had a plan for your escape. Let me show you."

Tor walked outside and Sarkov followed. In the middle of the runway, Tor turned and faced the door of the second hangar, extracted a cigarette from his chest pocket and offered one to Sarkov.

The day was clear, so clear that Sarkov could see the stone houses of Ambarli, the Ceyhan River, the olive groves beyond, even the outline of Istranca Daglari. The airfield was quiet and the sun reflected off the aluminum, like shining from shook foil, until the glare was too much, and Sarkov turned away. He looked toward the small farmhouses and the nets covering the tobacco.

"We're in the country," he said quietly.

"Don't get romantic," Tor responded. He was waiting for something. "See that stone house," he pointed to the limestone building which looked old and uninhabited. "It was built four years ago and its falling down already. This is earthquake country during the season of Mehlten. The tremors begin in Northern Anatolia and widen through here. Adapazari is the center. The quake that toppled that house devastated the area. Six point five on the Richter."

"Is that plane for me?" Sarkov asked. He heard the wheezing after the ignition.

"Yes."

"Where am I going?"

"I could tell, but I'm not going to. Do you know why? Think about it. If I don't tell, you will trust that I will never tell anyone. Isn't that true?"

"Why are you doing this for me? You have no obligations."

"I've asked myself. Your wife is magnificent. No, it's not that. I think it was the game, the excitement, the defeat of the Russians. Think how wonderfully it worked?" His eyes expanded grandly. "We succeeded. What memories we'll have!"

"And no one to tell it to." Sarkov spat.

"Ah," Tor said. "The secret," Tor said rubbing his hands, "that's the best part."

"The British, will they know?"

"They have what they want, and they have what they deserve. No, they don't care what happened, not interested. You've met Reed. He may wonder, but I won't tell him. After this talk, I will never tell anyone," Tor said. He looked behind. "What else?" He seemed to be asking himself.

The plane taxied out of the hangar and the two men began walking toward it.

"It's not as advanced as the Russian plane, but we didn't have Douglas to build ours," Tor said. "It's the best Nuri

Demirag can provide, and it's good enough to take you on your first leg to freedom."

"Is this the end?"

"Here is a gift," Tor handed Sarkov a knapsack. "You'll find a passport in there, Dramamine for your head," he rummaged through the bag. "Your first stop will be Cyprus, not Crete." He found what he was looking for in the bag. "An order-in-council for citizenship in your new country. Don't lose that. Don't ask the pilot your destination. He doesn't know. Sit up front. The back is drafty. There's money in here, quite a lot of money: twenty thousand pounds I won from Sloan and Kiktev last night. Enough for two years for a family if they're careful."

"I have the other man's money," Sarkov said and reached in his pocket for the resilient envelope.

"His name was Bakov," Tor said. "August fifteenth was not his day."

"But it was mine, wasn't it?"

"It certainly was," Tor said. "One more gift. I won this ring from your ambassador. I have no use for it. Perhaps you will buy a gift for your wife," he said giving Sarkov the ring. "You're not only safe, but rich. Maybe with leisure and some money, the world will have some decent poetry."

The plane was ready.

"Also," Tor said as Sarkov opened the plane's door. "Your wife and children wait."

Sarkov looked with affection at his benefactor.

"I'm grateful," he said.

"Let me tell you a story before you go," Tor said. It was a solemn departure. "Two heroes met at Canakkale. They were enemies, fought on opposite sides. One was the leader of the invading Achaeans and the other a hero of the local people, the Anatolians. The Achaeans were winning, but before the victory the Anatolian hero was whisked off by a Divinity, before he was killed. Do you know the story?"

"I do," Sarkov said. "The god not only helped Aeneas escape, but helped him found a new culture, Rome."

"You know the story, but who was the god?"

"I don't remember."

"It was Poseidon," Tor said, shaking hands. "He was the real hero." He clicked his heels. "If you will accept your part in the fiction," Tor beamed, "I will accept mine."